No ....   Class ....

Author ...JUSTISS

Title ...A Scandalous Proposal...

He saw only her.

A slender figure in lilac, her pale oval face framed by dusky curls above full, petal-pink lips. When she raised enquiring violet eyes to meet his mesmerised gaze, a frisson of pure energy flashed between them, rocking him to his toes and riveting him, speechless, to the spot.

A faint scent of lavender teased his nose. His heartbeat stopped, then stampeded. After-shocks darted to every nerve. "Perfection!" he whispered, his voice unsteady.

As if compelled, Evan walked towards her, only dimly aware of shouldering aside a heavyset matron who appeared to be conversing with the Vision. "Lord Cheverley, Madame Emilie." Seizing her hand, he brought it to his lips.

He felt it again, that...current, passing between them. By the faint pinking of her porcelain cheeks Evan knew she must have felt it as well...

As a child, **Julia Justiss** found her Nancy Drew books inspired her to create stories of her own. She has been writing ever since. After university she served stints as a business journalist for an insurance company and as editor of the American Embassy newsletter in Tunisia. She now teaches French at a school in Texas, where she lives with her naval officer husband, three children and two dogs.

Recent titles by the same author:

THE WEDDING GAMBLE
THE PROPER WIFE
MY LADY'S TRUST
MY LADY'S PLEASURE
MY LADY'S HONOUR

A SCANDALOUS PROPOSAL

Julia Justiss

MILLS & BOON®

First published in Great Britain 2005
Large Print edition 2005
Harlequin Mills & Boon Limited,
Eton House, 18-24 Paradise Road, Richmond, Surrey TW9 1SR

© Janet Justiss 2000

ISBN 0 263 19294 6

Set in Times Roman 13¾ on 15¼ pt.
42-1105-82094

Printed and bound in Great Britain
by Antony Rowe Ltd, Chippenham, Wiltshire

A SCANDALOUS PROPOSAL

Julia Justiss

To critique partners
Theresa Scardina, Louise Harper and
Kathy Cowan, for their exceptional advice
and even more exceptional friendship.

To the published authors of RWA-ETC,
who have given unstinting assistance
and support, particularly RWA Lifetime
Achievement Award winner Roz Alsobrook,
Sheli Nelson (Rachelle Morgan),
Eve Gaddy and the best conference
roomie ever, Lenora Nazworth
(Lenora Worth).

With deepest thanks and gratitude.

Prologue

Emily Spenser crept along the shrub-shadowed edge of the garden at the center of St. James Square. After years of fierce Portuguese sun, the damp morning chill seeped into her bones, and she shivered despite her woolen shawl. Halting at the corner, she pressed herself deeper into the overhang of branches and scrutinized the town house opposite.

Was the knocker off the door? Given the distance and the swirling mist, she couldn't be sure. The windows overlooking the square were certainly shuttered, but as it was barely past dawn, that didn't necessarily indicate the owner was out of town.

Cautiously she retraced her steps, crossed the square behind the shelter of garden, and slipped to the mews beyond. Heart hammering at her ribs, she made herself enter the back gate. Surely at a great house like this, where vendors and suppliers came and went constantly, in her shop girl's apron and mobcap she would attract no special notice.

A soft lull of voices emanated from behind the half-open door of the kitchen wing. Gathering her courage, she hurried across the deserted stable yard, knocked once and entered.

A knot of workers gathered around the glowing hearth, mugs of steaming brew in hand. Picking out an older woman with keys hanging at her waist, Emily dipped a curtsey.

''I've a parcel for his lordship,'' she announced, mimicking the broad accent of the Hampshire peasantry among whom she'd grown up. ''Mistress says as how I was to deliver it personal.''

''Lawks, missy, you've a far piece to walk, then,'' the woman replied with a laugh. ''He ain't in Lunnon now.''

Damping down a rush of relief, Emily made herself utter instead a dismayed squeak. ''But Mistress'll box my ears iff'n I don't get this to 'im. He be back today, ma'am?''

''Not likely. Seein's how he sent half the staff on holiday, tellin' 'em he'd fetch 'em back later, we don't expect 'im anytime soon.''

Emily couldn't believe her luck. ''He be gone that long?'' she asked faintly.

''Aye. Last week, you mighta caught 'im, but he left out suddenlike, and Mr. Daryrumple—that's the butler, lass—told us he'd not be returnin' afore Easter, 'n likely not afore summer.''

Emily hid her excitement behind a woebegone look. ''Mistress'll be that unhappy.''

''Nay, don't fret yourself. She canna expect you to make here what's gone by wishin' it. A reg'lar dragon, is she?'' The woman clucked. ''Have a mug o'tea and rest your bones, then, afore you go back to face 'er.''

''Thank 'ee kindly, ma'am, but I daren't. Mistress'll rap my knuckles iff'n I'm not back by seven.''

Amid sympathetic murmurs from the staff and a general grumble about the unreasonableness of employers, Emily bobbed another curtsey and made her way out.

Once outside the back gate, she tore off her servant's mobcap, threw it in the air and hugged herself fiercely.

He was not in London. She could begin.

Chapter One

"Fetch a bonnet for your mother? My, what a dutiful son!"

Evan Mansfield, Earl of Cheverley, widened the swinging arc of his walking stick just enough to whack the speaker behind his ankle. Over the ensuing yelp, he replied, "Since your own mother had the good sense to expire when you were an infant, you have no idea how to care for a lady."

Grinning as his friend Brent Blakesly shot him a baleful glance, he continued, "Actually, Mama intended to collect the bonnet herself, but I wouldn't hear of it. She's not yet fully recovered from that putrid cold. There's no need for you to come, though. Why not hie on to White's, and order us wine? Charge it to my account." Evan directed a look at Brent's ankle. "'Twill ease the pain."

Brent's frown smoothed. "Feel better already. Mind you hurry. I should hate to drink all *your* wine before you arrive." Tipping his hat, Blakesly set off.

"I'll not be long," Evan called after him. "Madame Emilie's shop is just off Bond Street."

Brent halted in midstep. "Madame Emilie?"

When Evan nodded, his friend strode back. "On second thought, I'll accompany you. Let's be off, shall we?"

Evan raised his eyebrows. "What possible reason could you have for visiting a bonnet shop?"

"Let's just say I might find it...interesting."

As they strolled, Evan pressed him again, but Brent would vouchsafe nothing further, only shaking his head and saying Evan must see for himself.

After a few minutes, they reached the neat shop front. Entering to the tinkle of a warning bell, Evan murmured to Brent, "Shall I now discover what great myster—"

A tall woman in the shop's shadowed interior turned toward them. As Evan's eyes adjusted to the relative darkness, the rest of his sentence dissolved on his lips.

Shapes and colours blurred; the mutter of voices faded to a distant hum. He saw only Her: a slender figure in lilac, her pale oval face framed by dusky curls above full, petal-pink lips. When she raised inquiring violet eyes to meet his mesmerized gaze, a frisson of pure energy flashed between them, rocking him to his toes and riveting him, speechless, to the spot.

A faint scent of lavender teased his nose. His heartbeat stopped, then stampeded.

"Damme, Ev, she's as enchanting as Willoughby claimed!"

At his friend's awed undertone, Evan shook his gaze free. Aftershocks darted to every nerve. "She's perfection," he agreed, his voice unsteady.

"Fortunate sod, to have a perfectly unexceptional reason to speak with her," Brent murmured. "Well, get on with it!" He gave the earl a shove.

In truth, Evan could not have stayed away. As if compelled, he walked toward her, only dimly aware of shouldering aside a heavyset matron who appeared to be conversing with the Vision. "Lord Cheverley, Madame Emilie." Seizing her hand, he brought it to his lips.

He felt it again, that…current, passing between them. By the faint pinking of her porcelain cheeks, Evan knew Madame must have felt it as well.

Amazingly, she gave no other sign, her pansy eyes expressionless now as she fixed a cool gaze upon him. After a moment, she frowned and tugged at her gloved hand, which he continued to retain in rather too tight a grip.

With a mumbled apology, he released it.

"Lord Cheverley?" she repeated in cultured tones. Then her forehead smoothed. "Ah, yes. I received the note from your lady mother, and her bonnet is ready. A moment only, my lord."

With a nod to him, she turned to the stout woman beside her, who was regarding Evan with a frosty air of outrage. "Lady Stanhope, I'm honored the bonnet pleases you, and grateful for your patronage. Now, if you will excuse me?" She made a deep curtsey. With a disdainful sniff in Evan's direction, the client stalked off.

"This way, my lord."

He followed Madame closely toward a small office, his eyes glued on her graceful sway of hip. When she halted inside the door, he nearly ran into her.

She turned to him with a quizzical look, her long, alabaster fingers holding out something. "Is the bonnet acceptable, my lord? Shall I box it?"

The fullness of her moving lips, the tantalizing glimpse of tongue fascinated him. Her subtle lavender scent, stronger now, clouded his brain. A nearly overpowering urge filled him to touch that ivory cheek, to feel those lips yielding under his own. He would pursue her elusive tongue into its warm wet haven, trace his fingers toward that swell of bosom.... His body hardened and moisture broke out on his brow.

"Yes, well. Mama... I'm sure," he murmured from within a suddenly too tight neckcloth, trying to yank his thoughts back to conversational channels. "'Tis fine—exquisite. The, ah, bonnet."

Madame arched a dark eyebrow and studied him. Evan gazed back, thinking he could stare forever into the depths of those wood-violet eyes. No, more like sweet violets, or the pure blue-tinted petals of an unfolding Dutch iris.

Then the tempting lips curved into a half smile, and he realized with a jolt what a perfect idiot he must appear. Before he could try to make a recovery, Madame Emilie handed him a hatbox. "Please convey to Lady Cheverley my gratitude for the great honor of her patronage. Good day, my lord."

She curtseyed, then nudged him toward the door. The touch of her gloved hand seemed to sizzle through the layers of cloth, leaving him once again speechless.

When coherency returned, he found himself standing beside Brent on the street outside the shop. An elaborately painted iron hat with the words *Madame Emilie* swung gently from its bracket above him.

"*Bouleversé,* were you?" Blakesly looked him up and down and chuckled. "Can't recall seeing you so thrown off your stride by a woman since that ballet dancer years ago, when we first came down from Oxford."

Evan shook his head, not sure himself what had just transpired. His hands and feet tingled, as if he'd been in the proximity of lightning. "The dancer couldn't hold a candle."

"No, indeed." Brent gave a wistful sigh. "But come. To recover, I recommend a strong liquid restorative."

Though his feet moved in the direction of St. James, Evan's glance kept straying back to the shop. "What does Willoughby know of her? Tell me!"

"Aye, your lordship!" Brent snapped a mock salute. "But 'tis little enough. She's a fairly recent widow, to judge by the half-mourning she wears."

"Half-mourning?"

"You didn't notice?" Brent laughed. "I expect you were too busy envisioning her *un*dressed. Though I must warn you, based on the bit Willoughby knew, if you've seduction in mind, you're likely to be disappointed. Seems St. Clair discovered her first, and his whole set of bucks started dropping by her shop on the slenderest of pretexts."

"St. Clair?" Evan sniffed derisively.

"Indeed. Knowing St. Clair, the hints were probably none too subtle, but she apparently turned down every invitation to tea or dinner or the theater. In fact, Willoughby says, no one got more from her than civil words about ordering bonnets for their womenfolk. He concluded she must be middle-class and hopelessly virtuous.''

Evan gave him a sharp glance. ''You seem to have listened closely. Rather unusual for you to display so much interest in a woman.''

Brent returned a hard stare. ''And you? Surely you're not considering setting up a new flirt, after just ridding yourself of La Tempestina. Besides, I thought when Richard left to rejoin Wellington you promised to drag Andrea to town. Didn't you two have some sort of…understanding?''

''Nothing formal. You know how shy she's grown since her accident. I just assured her that if she didn't find anyone else to her fancy by the end of the Season, she could always marry me. But—'' he waved a hand dismissively ''—that's a long way off. Have *you* an interest in Madame?''

''I'd hardly have much of a chance.'' Brent twisted his lips into a wry smile. ''If she wouldn't consider St. Clair and all his blunt, she's not likely to grant her favors to an untitled younger son with a modest competence. Now you, on the other hand—'' he made a sweeping gesture ''—might breach the citadel. Rich, handsome, society's darling—''

''Stubble it,'' Evan growled. ''I must find some reason to return—oh, blazes, what a sapskull!'' He halted abruptly.

''What is it?''

''I was supposed to tell her Mama wanted to commission another bonnet, but I was so busy making a cloth-headed cake of myself, I forgot. Nor did I settle the account.'' His irritation dissolved in a grin. ''Well, I'll just have to go back immediately to rectify that. And redeem myself as well. At the moment, she must think me a mutton-headed idiot. I'll meet you at White's.''

He paced off so swiftly, Blakesly had to run to catch up. ''Wait, Ev! The shop's probably closed by now.''

Evan shrugged off his friend's hand. Not even to himself could he explain his irresistible compulsion to see Madame Emilie again, now, immediately. ''She can't have left yet. We've only just departed, and she had other customers. Go on—I'll see you shortly.''

Brent fell behind, chuckling. ''Don't need to tell me when I'm de trop. All right, I'll see you later,'' he called after Evan. ''But don't say I didn't warn you if you encounter nothing more amorous than a bolted shop door!''

Emily Spenser sighed after the figure of her last departing customer. Mrs. Wiggins might be a nouveau riche, name-dropping mushroom, but at least her closeness to her middle-class roots led her to pay her bills on time. Unlike most of the Upper Ten Thousand who frequented her shop.

Emily dropped into the chair behind her small desk and pulled out a bag, inserting Mrs. Wiggins's money. She could hear Francesca bustling about overhead, singing softly in Portuguese as she fixed her mistress's tea. Maybe a warm drink would soothe her jangled nerves.

Not as much as a few dozen more clients with ready cash would, she thought ruefully. She much preferred hard coin to the heated glances of that last titled gentleman. Indeed, she wished fervently that Lady Cheverley herself had collected the purchase. Her ladyship, though of impeccable ton, always paid upon delivery.

He'd surprised her, though, Lady Cheverley's son. Given the still-youthful beauty of the mother, Emily had been expecting a mere stripling. Certainly not the tall, broad-shouldered gentleman who'd seemed to fill her little office, dwarfing her and his surroundings, while his smoky gaze hinted at far-from-juvenile pleasures.

An altogether arresting man, she admitted, assuming one was susceptible to that sort of thing. Which, of course, she was not. Nonetheless, a sudden vision of the fiery sparkle in a pair of dark blue eyes sent a little chill skittering down her spine. One that was but a faint echo of the…she refused to put a name to the sensation that had seized her when he'd first gazed at her, when she'd casually touched his sleeve.

In any event, she should mistrust such looks. What she required was honest payment for her labors, not another dose of the degrading innuendo she'd already endured from others of Lord Cheverley's ilk. Though she'd mastered the art of masking her outrage and gracefully turning such remarks aside, the insult of those veiled offers still rankled.

Resolutely she looked back to the ledger. Neat figures recorded the sums demanded for buckram padding, felt stuff, straw and lace, trims of feathers, silk tassels, satin and cording. When she'd calculated the amount necessary to run her millinery business, she'd not envisioned a clientele of fashionables who seemed more willing to wager their blunt on silver loo and faro than to pay their haberdashers.

Well, she'd simply have to retrench. She'd not survived long bitter months in that Portuguese village watching Andrew die by inches, then a year of painting aristocratic portraits across the length and breadth of Spain, only to succumb to despair a few bare months after returning to England.

Somehow they would earn enough to pay Drew's tutor and save for his eventual tuition at school. Drew, the best and most beautiful reminder of her life with Andrew. The image of her son's face, mischievous light glowing in green eyes so like his papa's, warmed her troubled heart and sent the gray tide of grief and worry receding. A bittersweet backwash of longing followed.

With resignation she quelled it. Having him here with her was impossible, she knew. An aristocrat's son who would one day return to an aristocrat's life could not live over a shop. Reminding herself of that fact each Sunday as she left after a too-brief visit at the genteel home of his tutor, Father Edmund, did little to ease the ache of loss.

Best, she told herself briskly, that she cast off maudlin thoughts and concentrate on her task: ensuring their survival, stockpiling funds and keeping Drew hidden from the threat that would rip from her even those precious few hours with him.

The tinkling of the entry bell interrupted her. Though she'd neglected to bolt the door, 'twas past regular business hours, and she wondered which tardy customer was paying her a visit. Hopefully one with pockets full of sovereigns, she thought as she summoned a welcoming smile.

Before she could exit her office, a burly figure entered. Her smile faded.

"Mr. Harding," she said in a chilly voice. "Your employer requires something? The next rent payment isn't due for a sennight."

"'Afternoon, ma'am." Short, stocky, with hulking shoulders and a barrel chest, Josh Harding ambled toward her. She stepped away from his advance across her cramped office, until he had her backed up against her desk.

His insolent leer as he deliberately looked her up and down made her fingers itch to slap his face. "No, it ain't rent time, but being a business *lady*—" he gave the word scornful emphasis "—ya musta' learnt there's other expenses to keepin' a shop healthy. Like makin' sure ya gets protected from the raff 'n scaff what might try to rob honest folk."

Emily thought of the cash bag on the desk behind her. "Indeed? I was assured 'twas a fine neighborhood. The high rent certainly supports that conclusion. Did your employer dissemble when he assured me 'twas so?"

Mr. Harding grinned, showing a gap between uneven, tobacco-stained teeth. "Even in fine neighborhoods, ya needs protection. My boss means to see ya gets it—for a small fee, a' course. He figures annuder ten pounds a month should do the trick."

"Ten pounds a—!" Emily gasped. "'Tis preposterous! Rather than pay such a price, if protection is truly needed, I shall unearth my late husband's pistol and provide it myself! Thank your employer for his kind offer, but I couldn't possibly afford it.''

''Mayhap ya can't afford to be without.'' Harding stepped to her worktable, reaching out to stroke the satin and velvet of an incomplete hat. She bit back the command that he keep his grimy hands off it.

''Things...happen sometimes, to them what don't get protection,'' he was saying. ''Didya hear about that dress shop over on Fiddler's Way? Burnt to the ground last week. Lost ever'thin, poor wench what owned it. Thought protection come at too dear a price, she did. Deal of a lot cheaper than starting over, though, I 'spect.''

Emily stiffened. ''I believe what you're suggesting is called extortion.''

Mr. Harding shrugged. ''Never much on book learnin'.'' He stared directly into her eyes. ''Best remember that dress shop, little lady.''

Emily pressed her lips together. She could barely meet her expenses now—raising another ten pounds a month would be impossible. Besides, this was clearly illegal. How dare this bully try to intimidate her?

She straightened and turned to Mr. Harding. He lounged against the table, watching her, the trace of a mocking smile on his full lips. She felt anger flush her cheeks.

''Tell your master I cannot avail myself of his—protection. Advise him also that such threats are illegal, and I shall go to the authorities should he persist.''

To her fury, Harding's grin widened. ''Oh, I wouldn't advise ya t'do that, ma'am. Knows a powerful lot a' folk, does Mr. Harrington. How ya think he got to buy up so many lots hereabouts where all the nobs spends their blunt?''

His small eyes beginning to shine, he approached her again. ''Now, ya needn't fret, little lady. For special cases like yourn, old Josh here's got another answer. Be nice to me, an' we can talk about that ten pounds a month.''

Licking his lips, he seized her with one beefy arm. Foul panting breath descended toward her.

Bracing herself against the desk, she thrust him back. ''Take your hands off me, Mr. Harding. Go peddle your threats amongst the streetwalkers of Covent Garden.''

He held on, his look turning ugly. ''Think yerself too good for the likes a' Josh Harding? Fancy one of them fine gentlemen as is always sniffing 'round yer skirts? Well, I been watchin', an' ain't none of 'em stayed 'round to keep ya company. Nor will any, once they cast their peepers on this.'' He showed her the bunched fist of his free hand. ''So ya best be nicer, little lady.''

He yanked her roughly against him and plastered his heavy wet mouth on hers. His tongue probed her firmly closed lips and one hand fumbled at her breast, fingers groping the nipple.

Outraged, she shoved at him with all her might, managing to push him back enough to prepare a stinging slap.

He caught her hand and held her motionless. His eyes gleamed brighter, his breathing quickened and he laughed, the sound low in his throat like a growl. ''Sweetheart, ya don't even know how.'' Before she could think to struggle, with one burly fist he backhanded her across the mouth.

The blow spun her into the desk, smashing her hip against its oaken surface. A hot trickle dripped from her stinging lip. Frightened but furious, she groped with trembling hands for some sort of weapon. Seizing the heavy glass inkwell, she moved it behind her and straightened to face Harding.

Utterly nonchalant, he was walking away. After two steps, he paused to make her an exaggerated bow. "Ya think about them offers. Both of 'em. 'Cause I can promise ya, little lady, yer problems is just beginnin'."

A man strode in, then halted. "Madame Emilie?"

Hand clenched on her weapon, she whirled toward the door. In that first instant she saw not one of Harding's cohorts, but a figure whose fashionable attire proclaimed him a gentleman even as her mind registered the cultured tone of his speech. In the next moment, she recognized Lady Cheverley's son. Relief coursed through her.

"Excuse me, I didn't realize you had a customer," he said, his dubious gaze fixed on Mr. Harding.

Averting the injured side of her face, she released the inkwell and tried to gather her composure. "N-not at all, Lord Cheverley. The man was just leaving."

After subjecting the nobleman to a careful inspection, during which he must have noted his superior height and obvious strength, Harding defiantly curled one hand into a fist. "When I gets ready, little lady. When I gets ready."

Cheverley glanced coldly from Harding's hand to the man's swarthy face. "I believe the lady asked you to depart. Immediately."

For a moment, the two men's gazes locked. Then Harding shrugged, letting his fingers fall open. "Makes no matter. Just remember, when all the fancy toffs be gone, Josh Harding'll be here." He sauntered to the doorway and tipped his hat mockingly. "Ya got my word on it, little lady."

"Was the ruffian disturbing you?" Lord Cheverley walked toward her as the shop door closed behind Harding. Two paces away, he must have caught sight of her bleeding lip, for he stopped short. "That villain struck you? By God, I'll cut him down!" He spun on his heel.

Emily grabbed his sleeve. "Please, my lord, 'tis not your concern. Let him go."

Lord Cheverley paused. Emily could feel the tension in the coiled muscles beneath her fingers. The scent of shaving soap and warm male filled her nostrils. She had a sudden, dizzying perception of the leashed power within the body towering over her, and for an instant she felt almost—safe. Like with Andrew.

Bitter memory flooded her, and her grip on his sleeve slackened. Giving her head a shake, she pushed the surging emotions back and fumbled for some rational comment. "Y-you wished something else? Did the bonnet not suit?"

"You must allow me to pursue him!" Cheverley pulled away from her hand. "I cannot permit the blackguard to get away with such an insult."

"He was only delivering a message—rather crudely, I admit—from his employer. But my trivial affairs cannot concern you. With what can I assist you, my lord?"

"Should I not rather ask you that?"

Emily opened her lips to explain, then closed them. She had carried her own burdens for so long, 'twas vastly tempting to pour out her troubles to this seemingly strong, intelligent and interested stranger. *But he is a stranger,* she reminded herself. *He is not Andrew.*

"Is the man's employer threatening you over some matter of business?"

Emily hesitated. The Earl of Cheverley could have no real interest in her...except, she thought, as she remembered the blatant admiration on his face earlier, of the same sort Harding had so crudely expressed. She pushed the degrading notion aside. Then again, his lordship might well serve as magistrate for his county. Perhaps she might chance requesting legal advice. She looked up to find him smiling.

"Come, after so distressing an encounter, you must sit." Tentatively, he took her arm. With a sigh she let him lead her to the chair.

"Now, please allow me to help." There being no other perch in the tiny office, he indicated a cleared space on the desktop. "May I?"

At his continued solicitude, her scruples collapsed. Nodding acquiescence, she let him seat himself, and briefly recited the facts of her encounter with Mr. Harding.

"I cannot be sure he really spoke for his employer. It could be that he works this game on his own, to augment his income, and Mr. Harrington would be shocked and disapproving should I inform him of it."

"Perhaps." Lord Cheverley frowned thoughtfully. "He'd probably express outrage in any event. But if this Harrington is indeed in collusion, confronting him might bring down immediate harm of the sort you've just suffered. You must not risk that."

"I shall have to risk it. I cannot pay, and I certainly don't wish to—well, I shall have to settle it sometime. Better sooner than later."

"Have you no family, preferably broad of muscle and deep of pocket, to take care of this matter?"

In her rattled state, that simple question shredded the ragged bonds restraining memory. A tide of hurt, betrayal, pain and grief flooded forth. She struggled to stem it, for a moment unable to utter a word. Despite her efforts, one tear escaped. "No one," she managed to whisper.

"Dear lady, you mustn't distress yourself!" Cheverley leaned forward, his forehead puckered in concern. "I shall look into this personally. My solicitor will check out the gentlemen, and I'll have him round up some off-duty runners to keep an eye on your shop. I doubt that ham-fisted coward would dare make a move if he sees able-bodied men on guard."

When she started to protest, he waved her to silence. "No disagreement. We cannot have brigands going about menacing honest citizens. Besides, my mother would insist, for she holds you in the highest regard. As do I."

"But you barely know me."

"Everything I needed to know, I learned the moment I looked into your eyes."

His low voice vibrated with emotion. Uncomfortable under his scrutiny, she turned away. "Don't misunderstand, I don't wish to appear ungrateful, but I..." She flushed. "I simply cannot afford to pay your solicitor, much less hire runners. As Mr. Harding well knows."

Cheverley made a dismissive gesture. "Don't trouble yourself. I shall take care of it."

"Oh, but you don't understand!" Humiliation deepening, she forced herself to add, "I'm afraid the profits of shopkeeping are vastly overrated." She managed a weak smile. "I cannot even predict when I should have sufficient funds to repay you."

He smiled back. He had, she noted despite her distress, a singularly engaging smile that dimpled the skin beside the lean mouth and brought that devilish sparkle to his deep blue eyes. "Ridding the streets of such vermin constitutes something of a civic duty. And, as you doubtless know, I'm a wealthy man. Think no more of it."

"But I could not be under such an obligation—"

"Please." He put one finger to her bleeding lip. "I should consider protecting you a very great honor."

She ought to protest further, but his touch seemed to tangle her already tattered thoughts. As she sat speechless, he slowly traced his gloved finger around the circumference of her swollen lip.

The soft brush of chamois against her stinging skin mesmerized her, sent little ripples of sensation throughout her body. Her startled gaze flew to his.

His finger stopped its tracery. He drew in a sharp breath and met her eyes with a glance so intense she felt herself drawn almost physically closer. The steady pulse of his warm finger quivered against her lip.

When at last he removed his hand, the only thing she could think to stutter was, "Y-you have soiled your glove."

Cheverley looked at the bloodstain on the fawn surface. He raised his finger and kissed the spot. "I shall treasure it. Don't worry, Madame, that villain will trouble you no more. You have *my* word on it."

Evan whistled as he walked back down the street, a bounce in his step. He breathed in deeply, his nostrils still filled with the enchanting scent of lavender, his senses still heightened by the heady euphoria of holding that slender arm, touching those delicate lips.

He'd roust his solicitor from the tea table and ensure the runners were dispatched immediately. The mere thought of that slimy little villain putting his foul hand on Madame Emilie's perfect face sent a blistering rage through him. He would check back personally to make sure guards were posted this very day.

But he shouldn't be too angry at the fellow who had provided him such a perfect opportunity to act the rescuer, he reminded himself as the rage cooled. Surely the divine Madame would look kindly on him for intervening. Be she ever so virtuous, surely she could imagine a way to repay his concern, one that might be immensely gratifying to them both.

Not that he would so much as hint such a thing. Indeed, doing so would relegate him to the same crass category as the unspeakable Mr. Harding. The Earl of

Cheverley normally had only to express interest, and the chosen lady hurried to do his bidding. The impossibly beautiful Madame, however, seemed reluctant to accept even protective assistance from him, despite the real danger in which she stood.

Vividly he recalled that sizzling glance, her smoldering touch. She was aloof, and yet undeniably responsive.

Winning her would not be easy, he recognized, his instincts piqued by the challenge. Once she was won, however, he could imagine no more enjoyable a task than lifting every burden from her slim shoulders and sheltering that exquisite body close.

A discreet little house in Mayfair, perhaps? With furnishings in the first stare of elegance, a loyal staff, gowns, jewels, carriages, whatever she wished. He would move heaven and earth to grant her every whim. He imagined dressing her in amethysts and deep plum satin to match those incredible eyes. Imagined even more vividly undressing her....

Excitement tingled in his veins, and something else tingled lower. Not for months had he felt so alive, so buoyed with anticipation.

He would ensure her safety, of course, whether she smiled on him now or not. But sooner or later, he vowed, she would.

Chapter Two

Emily saw the man immediately after she unbolted the shop door the next morning. As she stared through the fog-wisped air, shocked into immobility, the burly figure lounging in a doorway opposite snapped to attention and gave her a jaunty wave. The bright red waistcoat under his buff frieze jacket proclaimed him a runner, apparently detailed, as Lord Cheverley had promised, to protect her.

Her immediate rush of relief was succeeded by a worry that gnawed at her all morning as she fashioned her bonnets and waited on customers. His lordship was obviously a man of his word. Could he, as he claimed, construe it his public duty to ensure private citizens such as herself were not molested in their homes and businesses? And the wages of the watchman now loitering on the street outside—did she truly, as he insisted, have no need to concern herself over the matter?

Her thoughts went round and round, but always returned to the same point. Despite his lordship's promises, she could not deem it prudent to permit him to fund her protection.

For one thing, the very thought of accepting so great a boon from one entirely unrelated grated against every principle upon which she'd been raised. More ominously, as bitter experience had taught her twice over, rich and influential men like my lord of Cheverley did nothing without calculation. Debts owed would be called in sooner or later, generally when most advantageous to the lender. Worse yet, she thought with more than a touch of annoyance, the earl's immediate, high-handed action—taken without any consultation as to her preferences—had stuck a spoke in the wheel of Josh Harding's game, a curb that villain was unlikely to forgive or forget.

She recalled the strength of the bully's rough hands jerking her close, the stench of his wet tongue assaulting her mouth. An involuntary shiver skittered down her spine. She had few illusions as to what sort of vengeance he would choose if he could get her once more in his power.

Which meant, unless she were prepared to relocate her business—a financial impossibility—she was likely to need protection for some considerable time. Yet more reason to stand alone now, for who could predict how long the quixotic Earl's interest in her welfare would last?

Perhaps it would be possible to have his solicitor maintain the defensive policies already set in motion. She should consult the man immediately. And determine safety's unpalatable price.

That unpleasant conclusion reached, she instructed Francesca to take over the shop, and embarked on the long walk to the offices of his lordship's counselor.

The bored-looking young clerk who answered her knock subjected her to an insolent inspection her glacial manner did nothing to discourage—until she stated that her business concerned the Earl of Cheverley. Instantly the clerk turned respectful, ushering her to a seat and announcing he would immediately inform his master of her presence.

Yet another indication of the Earl's power, she thought uneasily as she leaned back to rest her tired shoulders. The chair on which she sat was luxuriously appointed in leather; heavy damask drapes hung at the windows, and a Turkey carpet graced the floor. The entire establishment reeked of exclusivity and expensive cigars.

Suddenly she was transported in memory to a room very like this, where a lifetime ago a defiant young lady had informed her sire she intended to embark, not on the London Season planned for her, but on a vessel bound for the Peninsula, as the bride of Lieutenant Andrew Waring-Black. When she remained steadfast in the face of her father's adamant disapproval, he alternately mocked, threatened and finally raged he'd see her dead first. *"Where do you think you would find yourself, missy, when that impertinent jackanapes got himself killed? Destitute in some heathenish land, that's where, earning a living upon your back!"*

"Mr. Manners will see you now." The clerk's deferential words startled her out of reverie. Clenching her fingers on her reticule, Emily followed him.

Behind a huge desk sat a thin man with spectacles perched on his narrow nose. Shelves of legal tomes lined the walls; a leather armchair astride another tasteful carpet poised before the desk. A lamp glowed, adding the piquant scent of its flaming oil to the melange of cigar and lemon wood polish. The heavy curtains were drawn, as if the occupant did not wish even the daylight to intrude into his sanctum. The polite but piercing look he fixed on her said he resented her intrusion as well.

"That will be all, Richards," Mr. Manners said. The clerk, who had been staring at her again, hastily bowed himself out. "A chair, Mrs. Spenser?"

Emily sat. This forbidding man did not seem likely to trouble himself over one such as her. More than ever, she sensed the excluding wall that barred all that was weak and womanly from the world of male privilege and power.

An old, familiar resentment revived her flagging spirits. "Mr. Manners, Lord Cheverley consulted you about me. A matter of attempted extortion, you may remember."

"Yes, Mrs. Spenser, I'm fully cognizant of the details. Has there been another...incident?"

"No, sir, the, ah, guard his lordship promised has been dispatched. There have been no further threats. I just wished to inquire as to the normal procedure in such situations."

"There is no 'normal' procedure, ma'am. I don't usually prosecute matters of this sort, but as his lordship refers all his legal business to me, I have of course undertaken a full investigation. You need have no further concern for your safety, I assure you. Now, if you'll excuse me..."

Emily resisted his clear dismissal. "Oh, but I wish—"

"Mrs. Spenser, I am sure his lordship, at his convenience, will acquaint you with any details he deems appropriate. I simply cannot discuss a pending case with other than my client." This time, he rose and indicated the door.

"And if I were your client?" Emily persisted, rising, but refusing to let his obvious annoyance intimidate her.

"I see no need for that. His lordship already retains me, and as I've informed you, everything needful is being done."

"I am sure it is, Mr. Manners. You must not think I doubt your competence, or that I am not grateful for his lordship's intervention. But if this…situation should recur in future? Sadly, there are always rogues only too ready to prey on the honest. As a woman alone, I would wish to be informed of my alternatives."

Mr. Manners tilted his head and tapped at his chin. "'Tis true, ma'am, that despite taking appropriate action now, one cannot rule out the possibility of future difficulties." He looked her up and down. "You are a widow, I understand. You have no near relatives, yours or your late husband's, to see to your protection?"

"If I had, would I be here now?" she replied, an edge of anger in her voice.

To her surprise, the humorless face creased in what might be construed as a smile. "Excuse me, I meant no disrespect. Please, sit back down, Mrs. Spenser. What is it you wish to know?"

Emily felt some of the tension leave her. "How does your office handle such a matter? Should I report any future threats to the authorities? And what…" She faltered. "What fee would you require, were I to retain you?"

"First, I would not have you contact the authorities—not initially. Come to my office first. Most of the magistrates are honest folk, but from time to time a bad apple falls into the basket, as it were. My contacts would ascertain the background and intention of the perpetrators and proceed from there. And my normal fee would be two hundred pounds, plus the expense of hiring runners if I thought the need justified."

Emily tried not to gasp. Lord Cheverley was laying out two hundred pounds, plus expenses, to thwart Mr. Harding? And she had thought another ten pounds a month exorbitant!

She forced herself to rise on shaking legs. "Th-thank you for the information, and for your time, Mr. Manners."

He rose and nodded. "Think nothing of it, Mrs. Spenser." His shrewd eyes scanned her again, and she colored, sure he must have realized how staggering was the sum he'd quoted her, how impossibly far beyond her means.

"Don't distress yourself, ma'am," he said, his tone kind. "Lord Cheverley will pursue this to its conclusion, regardless of time or expense. I have had the privilege of his patronage for many years, and one could not find a more conscientious member of the nobility. You may trust him to do the right thing, Mrs. Spenser. And I doubt you will be troubled again."

His attempted reassurance was nearly as daunting as his fee. She had known pursuing the miscreant would be costly, but had never dreamed the total would be that vast. How could she allow a virtual stranger, be he ever so noble, generous and dutiful, to absorb such an enormous expense on her behalf? But then, how could she ever reimburse him?

Emily sat in her tiny garden, absently eating the nuncheon Francesca had insisted on preparing for her when she returned. She was still pondering the dilemma, and no closer to a solution, when a shadow fell across her teacup.

Lord Cheverley himself stood over her. As her gaze met his, he gave her again that enticing, intimate smile. ''Forgive me for disturbing you. I just wished to ascertain that the runner we sent was satisfactory.''

''Yes, of course. I hardly know how to thank you.''

''There's no need.'' He was looking at her intently, waiting, she realized, for her to offer her hand. When she raised it, he brought it to his lips, lingering over it a fraction longer than was proper.

''I would have called last night to report the guard was in place, but I had several appointments, and 'twas late when I returned to check. I saw no lights, and did not wish to disturb you.''

''You came by last night?'' she echoed in astonishment.

''Of course. I told you I would. I could not have slept, had I not been assured of your safety.''

It had been so long since someone other than Francesca had expressed any concern whatsoever for her well-being that in spite of herself, she was touched. ''You are too kind. Again, I thank you. And you must allow me to defray some of the costs—the runners, perhaps—''

He waved away the suggestion. ''Certainly not. A business as clever and stylish as yours must surely succeed, but hardly needs any additional expenses at its inception. I am fully recompensed by knowing you are safe.''

Again, she felt absurdly touched. ''I do feel safe. Thank you for that.''

His compelling gaze captured hers. ''I would not beteem the winds of heaven/visit thy face too roughly,'' he paraphrased from Hamlet. Gently he touched one finger to the bruised corner of her mouth.

A jolting spark tingled her lip. She stood mesmerized as he slowly removed his hand.

Bemused, she raised her own hand to the spot. *'Tis the bruise that throbs,* she told herself.

''Ev, the runner wishes to speak with you.''

It seemed to take a moment for the newcomer's voice to penetrate. With a grimace, Lord Cheverley stepped back. Waving at him from the garden door, Emily saw, was the man who had accompanied him to her shop the previous day.

His lordship turned on her another dazzling smile. ''I shan't keep you any longer, ma'am. The patrols will be properly maintained, so you may rest easy. If anything occurs to frighten or trouble you, send to me at once. Number 16, Portman Square. Someone there will know where to reach me if I'm from home.''

Once again he raised her hand to his lips. ''I shall call again later.''

"'Twould be an honor, my lord," she managed to murmur.

As Lord Cheverley strode from the garden, his companion ambled toward her. "Brent Blakesly, ma'am," he said with a bow. "You *can* rest easy, you know. Evan is as good as his word. Trust him to guarantee your safety."

"So I've been urged," she murmured, recalling the solicitor's advice. "I only wish he were not doing so at such great expense."

She must have looked troubled, for Blakesly's friendly face sobered. "You mustn't distress yourself, ma'am. Evan is wealthy enough that his kindness places no strains upon his purse." He gave her a deprecating smile. "I suppose, having always had vast sums at his disposal, he never realizes it might be difficult for his friends to easily accept his assistance."

"But I am not a friend," she replied, her voice low. "I have no more claim to his largesse than I have the means to repay it."

"May I speak candidly, Mrs. Spenser?" At her nod, he continued, "Evan has a great dislike for bullies. 'Twas how I first met him, when as a runty lad at Eton he pummeled the two upperclassmen who were tormenting me. Seeing some villain attempting to take advantage of a lady, he would feel compelled to prevent it, even—" he grinned at her "—did he not so greatly admire the lady. But you must not imagine his doing so places you under any...obligation whatever. Indeed, I am certain he would be appalled should you even consider such a thing."

Somehow, his certitude didn't raise her spirits. She followed as he walked out to join Lord Cheverley on the street. No obligation whatsoever, Blakesly assured her. Trust him to do what is right, the solicitor advised.

But what is right? she wondered as, with a wave, the two men started down the street. And why did her dratted lip still tingle?

Hours later, Emily looked up from the tangle of bills on her desk. Dusk had fallen, and she could hear the lamplighters going about their tasks. Through the salesroom window she glimpsed the glow of a lighted cheroot. Another guard on duty, she surmised.

Sighing, she rubbed the tight muscles at the back of her neck and took another sip of her tea, long cold now. She had entered all the invoices into her ledgers, and though several customers had settled their accounts today and Lord Cheverley had brought his mama's payment along with an advance on another order, the debit and credit columns still were nearly equal.

We are just barely surviving, she thought with a sigh. If she did attempt to repay Lord Cheverley, 'twould likely be his great-grandson who signed off the debt. Would he give her that long? Dear God, what was to become of them if he refused?

Immediate reimbursement in coin was impossible, the ledger clearly showed. A woman had but one other asset.

She recalled his heated glances, his lingering hand on her lip. She had seen lust in other men's eyes, during and after her marriage. If she could bring herself to offer, would Cheverley accept that means of canceling her debt?

For an instant, she imagined those hands cherishing her bare skin, that lean mouth at her breast. A deep tremor sent heat rushing through her.

A flush of guilt succeeded it and she felt as if caught out in some unforgivable indiscretion.

Nonsense, 'twas ridiculous. She could not be unfaithful to a dead man.

Oh, but I didn't want him to die, her heart cried back. How many times had she gone down on her knees on the rough stone of the village church, imploring God as Andrew's life drained away breath by ragged, painful breath? Promising to go anywhere, do anything, if only God would spare him?

Well, her prayers had been for naught. At the end, her husband had died in that small dusty village. And if God had not heeded her desperate pleas then, He was hardly likely to concern Himself with Emily Spenser Waring-Black now.

No, if salvation came, she would have to arrange it herself. And while her shop teetered so precariously between success and failure, having, for a time, a rich protector to keep trouble away could only help.

The very idea of it ate at her soul like acid.

She gave a bitter laugh. For years while she scraped together the funds to return and open her shop, she'd managed to avoid the fate so often dealt beautiful but impoverished widows. How ironic that it threatened her now, back in the homeland she'd pined for and imagined a haven.

"Mistress, 'tis darkness you work in," Francesca scolded as she entered. "And your tea, *é frio!* Another pot will I fetch, and light up the lamp. What's to become of us, *querida,* if you lose those bright eyes?"

"What's to become of us anyway?" Emily replied, more than a hint of despair in her tone. "And don't make fresh tea—we can scarce afford what we drink now. I'll make do with this."

The maid sat herself on the desktop and, head tilted like a small brown bird, gazed down at her mistress. "Be of good heart, *querida.* Always, we have worries, but always, you prevail. We shall—how you English say it? Ah, yes, we shall comc into."

Emily had to smile. "Come about, I believe you mean. And I wish I had your optimism. Just now, I am having a difficult time imagining how we shall ever come about."

"Yesterday, that *porco* threatens you, and today, poof—" the maid waved an expressive hand "—he is gone. Other worries, they too will go."

"'Twill take more than a—" Emily stopped abruptly. "What know you of Mr. Harding?"

Francesca shrugged. "I hear things, yes? When I hear that voice, I come. I see what he does. Almost I am running to you, but then, the beautiful one arrives. And saves you."

"Aye," Emily said in a whisper. "But for what?"

The maid raised her eyebrows, as if the answer were all too plain. "He is a great lord, *querida.* He saves you for his honor."

Emily made a scornful noise. "Heaven preserve us from the 'honor' of great lords!" She turned accusing eyes toward her maid. "Or have you forgotten, Francesca?"

"Not all lords threaten like the *padre* of your husband. Also I remember Don Alvero. He would have had you for his lady wife, would you but pledge your troth. But no, we must return to this—" nose wrinkling, she made a sweeping gesture that encompassed the tiny office "—this *England.*"

"Incomprehensible to you, I expect." Emily smiled as she squeezed Francesca's still-outstretched hand. "Dearest friend, to have left your homeland to follow me! I thought we could build a future here, that at last we would be safe." She sighed and put a weary hand to her forehead. "Was it a fool's journey, I wonder?"

"The great lord could keep us safe."

Emily straightened. "In exchange for what?"

When the little maid remained silent, Emily gave another cynical laugh. "Ah yes, his *honor.* Would those troopers who battled the French for your village have released you out of 'honor,' had not my husband's sword insisted? No, the safety your 'great lord' buys us carries a price. He will extract repayment—perhaps not now. Perhaps not soon. But eventually he must...."

The thought that logically followed so dismayed her that she jumped to her feet. "Merciful heavens, 'twould be much worse were he to wait a year—or two or three!"

"Tsh, sit, *querida.*" Gently Francesca pushed Emily back in her chair and moved behind her, beginning to massage her neck. "Perhaps, as he vows, he wants only your safety.'' When Emily made a scornful noise, she shrugged. ''Of a certainty he wants more. But 'tis beautiful he is, *querida*. Would yielding to him be so terrible? And safer to do so now, eh?''

Emily could not deny that truth. Her earlier visit to her father-in-law's town house confirmed that for the moment he was unlikely to discover them, despite the notoriety a liaison with such a wealthy, prominent man might engender. But how long would the man's absence continue?

She knew he would lose no time wresting his grandson from her unworthy care should he find them back in England. And though for Drew to return to his rightful place in society, she must eventually turn him over, she intended to treasure every moment before inescapable duty forced her to give him up.

A man's lust was generally short-lived. If she gratified Lord Cheverley's now, the affair should end long before it could threaten her with exposure. If she delayed, his lordship—and his whims—would keep control of the whole dangerous business.

After years of evading her father-in-law's agents, she'd had more than enough of being at the mercy of a rich man's schemes.

No, far better to take the initiative now. She might never have a more opportune moment to cancel her obligation for good and all.

Francesca had been watching her face. ''Whatever the tall lord wishes, you should grant. He is beautiful, but kind as well. That man outside, who keeps away the filthy pig Harding, he sent him, yes? He will be good to us, mistress. This I know, *here.*'' She tapped on her chest above her heart.

''I suppose in any event I must invite him to dine.'' Emily sent the maid an acid look. ''You can cook him an oh-so-beautiful meal.''

''Ah, *perfeito!* With greatest glee will I serve him, mistress. And you—wear something to show off the eyes, in *violeta.*'' She clapped her hands, looking absurdly pleased. ''He is beautiful and *rich,* no?''

''Francesca...''

''Bah, I will be silent no longer. You are young, *querida.* Too many years you have been without a man. If this great lord, one of your own people, desires you, I say 'tis a gift.''

''Francesca, don't!''

''You know I adored the *comandante,* your husband, may he rest with the blessed saints!'' With a swift gesture she crossed herself. ''But he is dead, mistress, *morto!* You must go on.''

Emily put her hands to her eyes, too tired to stem the tears. The passage of years seemed to have hardly dulled the edge of anguish.

''I know,'' she whispered. ''Do you think I want to linger in a past that holds only pain? I want to go on, truly I do! But how?''

Francesca wisely remained silent. After lighting the lamp, she patted Emily's shoulder and walked out.

Emily drew blank paper from her drawer and stared down at it, soft amber in the pool of lamplight. Ignoring the lump that lodged in her chest, she reached for her pen and scrawled an invitation.

Over dinner she would offer Lord Cheverley her grateful thanks. And then, while he sipped his brandy, she could delicately hint...

Her imagination failed her and a tide of heat flooded her cheeks. Just how did a lady go about "hinting" so brazen and immodest a proposal? One could not just bluntly say, "My lord, you have expended sums on my behalf that I cannot repay. However, if you are interested, I could warm your bed until such time as you consider the debt canceled." No, 'twas impossible!

Merely considering how to word such a proposition made her head ache and tied her stomach in knots.

But mayhap she misjudged him. Perhaps he would prefer cash, however slowly repaid. After all, so rich, handsome and highly titled a gentleman undoubtedly already possessed a mistress, doubtless one more beautiful and skilled than she.

The fire she remembered in his eyes didn't lend much substance to that wistful hope. Since when had powerful gentlemen felt any compulsion to limit themselves to one woman at a time?

She'd worry about that later. With a deep breath, before her nerve failed, she sealed the note and propped it on the desk for Francesca to deliver.

In the tiny kitchen behind her she could hear the trickle of water and clinking of pots as the maid prepared their frugal dinner. Twisting her hands together in her lap, Emily stared sightlessly into the darkened salesroom. She should go in to dine. But at the thought of what she must do if Lord Cheverley refused cash repayment, her normal appetite vanished.

Chapter Three

His hands holding the ends of the untied neckcloth, Evan gazed again at the note propped on his dresser. "Lord Cheverley, I would be most pleased if you would honor me with your presence at dinner this evening at eight of the clock...Mrs. Emily Spenser," he repeated to himself, though he had no need to look at the paper to recall the words.

Closing his eyes as he worked the knots, he could see her again as she'd looked that afternoon in the tiny garden behind her shop: thick, glossy black hair pinned in simple curls atop her head, a plain lavender gown that emphasized her elegant figure, the long fingers as fine as the bone china teacup she held.

In less than an hour he would present himself. A whirlpool of desire, anticipation and excitement spiraled in his gut at the thought. The maid would admit him and Madame would receive him, probably in some upstairs room.

Would she be wearing that proper lavender gown, or a shimmering sweep of satin night rail? At the image, his breath caught, his heart pounded and his fingers clutched at the linen cloth.

Get hold, he told himself, taking a deep, calming breath. *She asked you to dine merely. Probably she just wishes to thank you, quite properly, for your kind intervention.*

Ah, but if she intends more… After all, a *virtuous* middle-class lady didn't ask a man to dine alone with her. And a widow, if discreet, might allow herself liberties forbidden a wife or unmarried girl.

How would he get through dinner without touching her? If she made him no offer, how could he compel himself to leave without taking her?

He looked down at his clenched fists and realized he'd just ruined another neckcloth. With an oath, he pulled off the crumpled linen and tossed it on the heap with the other failures. Already he'd dismissed his valet, insolent lad, who'd laughed after he'd hopelessly wrinkled his fifth attempt. If the fellow hadn't been with him since Oxford, he'd have boxed the man's ears.

Lord, he thought in disgust, Brent was right, he was behaving more like a green sapskull enamored of his first wench than a seasoned man of eight and twenty. He'd enjoyed the favors of a number of women, appreciated their company and paid cheerfully for services rendered. Even with his mistresses, he'd dallied in their beds and forgotten them the moment he'd left. Why should this be different?

With mercurial speed, his irritation faded and he grinned. *Because I* feel *like the greenest sapskull, for the first time truly enamored of a woman.* He'd been distracted and out of sorts ever since her note arrived, consumed by a fierce desire to be with her again. Ah, what a woman!

In just a short while he would see her once more. Somehow, he would restrain himself, concentrate on exerting all the charm a bevy of ladies had previously found irresistible. And then, this very night, she might be his....

If he ever got his bloody neckcloth tied. With a growl, he took another cloth from the stack and set to work.

"Excellent dinner," Lord Cheverley complimented Francesca as she poured his coffee.

"*Obrigado,* my lord."

"Have you set out the port?" Emily asked. At the maid's nod, she continued, "You may go, then. Thank you, Francesca. My lord, if you please?"

With a smile, she indicated a small settee poised beside a woven floral carpet that adjoined the dining area. Lord Cheverley carried his cup and placed it on the side table. She followed him and took the adjacent armchair.

So far, so good, she thought, her nerves on edge but under control. Dinner had been excellent, one of Francesca's best, and conversation had flowed with no awkward pauses.

Over the meal she'd drawn out her noble guest about his family and interests. He'd remained in town through the winter, he informed her, because of his work for the Army Department, something to do with the always-tangled supply routes for Wellington's forces. She learned he was the sole protector of a mother and a younger sister soon to make her come-out, that he had estates in three different counties, that he loved riding and hated peas.

"You've discovered all my secrets," he remarked, taking a sip of the strong brew, "and yet I know almost nothing of you. Your late husband was with Wellington, I understand?"

Careful, her inner voice warned. "Yes. He fought in almost every peninsular battle."

"And you followed the drum?"

"Yes."

"You must have been very young when you married."

That brought a smile. "Indeed. I was but sixteen."

"Sixteen! I'm astonished your family permitted you to marry and hie off to the Peninsula at such a tender age."

Her smile faded. "Neither family approved the match. We eloped. After our scandalous runaway marriage, my father cut me off completely, so I had no choice but to follow the drum. Though never did I regret it, I assure you! I cherished every moment with—" Biting her tongue, she stopped herself before she made any rash disclosures. "More coffee, my lord? Or can I pour you some port?"

"Port, if you please."

She took a glass from the tray and poured the deep cherry liquid. "What sort of work do you do at Horse Guards, my lord? Or are you not permitted to discuss it?"

He smiled when she handed him the glass, as if amused at her diversionary attempt. "I don't discuss it. Though my silence has more to do with avoiding boring you to death than any real need for secrecy.'' He took a sip. ''Did your father never forgive you?''

''No. He's dead now, so it doesn't matter.''

''And your husband's family?''

She suppressed the urge to return a sharp answer. Better to respond pleasantly than reproach his curiosity or attempt to evade, she knew. ''My husband's father was just as autocratic as mine. His plans for his youngest son did not include soldiering in the Peninsula with a child-bride, especially one in disgrace who brought him not a groat of dowry. Even when I contacted him that his son lay d-dying—'' she choked, unable to keep the bitterness from her voice ''—he did not relent. Where he is, and what he is doing now, I neither know nor wish to know.''

She realized she was gripping her cup so tightly the fragile handle was likely to break, and she loosened her hold. A demand that she give up her son had been her father-in-law's only reply to her frantic message, but his Inquisitive Lordship didn't need to know that. The less he knew of her, the less he might divulge in careless gossip at his club.

Cheverley was gazing at her thoughtfully. ''Have you been in London long? I wonder I've not met you before.''

''I returned to England only a few months ago.''

''But—that means you remained abroad for years after your husband's death! How did you manage?''

''When he was wounded I took him to the closest town, a small Portuguese village. He'd taken a ball in the lung and there was no doctor to remove it. He lingered for a time before... Well, I had done some painting, and after...it was over, the local lord, Don Alvero, commissioned me to do a portrait. It pleased him, and he was kind enough to recommend me to other nobles. Eventually I amassed sufficient funds to return to England and open my shop.''

''Alone, unprotected, a new widow in a war-torn country?'' Cheverley shook his head in wonderment. ''Madame, I'm appalled! 'Twas exceeding dangerous, was it not?''

She smiled at the dismay on his face. ''On, no! The villagers were wonderful to us. As the widow of an English hero who died fighting the French invaders, I was everywhere treated with the utmost respect. And I wasn't alone. Francesca has been with me since I arrived as a bride.''

''You are the most courageous woman I've ever met,'' he said flatly, awe and respect in his voice. ''The English lady who stayed behind to nurse her dying husband. I expect you became nearly a legend.''

She shrugged uncomfortably. ''Hardly that.''

''A legend,'' he repeated softly. ''And no wonder. I have trouble myself believing you're real.'' Slowly, as if he couldn't help himself, he reached a hand toward her. ''You are so very beautiful.''

She forced herself not to flinch from the warmth of his gloveless fingers when they touched her cheek. ''Be assured I am quite real,'' she replied somewhat unsteadily. ''And safe, thanks to you.''

She thought for a moment he might kiss her, and swallowing hard, closed her eyes. But he removed his hand, and relieved, she looked back at him.

His fingers were trembling, as if he were holding himself under rigid control. "And so you shall remain. I spoke with Mr. Manners late this afternoon, and he's already amassed quite a dossier on the, ah, enterprising Mr. Harding. Indeed, so full was his account of that gentleman's activities that I'm told the man was moved to book passage on a ship leaving next week for the Americas."

Before she could thank him yet again, he waved her to silence. "His master is under scrutiny as well. Even if Mr. Harrington is indeed involved, I doubt he'd be foolish enough now to find another tool to implement his illegal designs. Though we plan to continue the surveillance another few weeks, to be sure all danger is past, I think you may feel safe in truth."

"I cannot adequately express my thanks for all your efforts. Indeed, your consideration quite overwhelms me! You must allow me to reimburse your expenses. I could not cover them all immediately, of course, but—"

"Out of the question!" He held up both hands, as if warding off the suggestion. "Dear lady, under no circumstances whatsoever could I take your money. Knowing you are safe is reward enough."

He would not take her money. As the full implications of those words sank into consciousness, Emily barely heard the rest. Could she not leave it at that? Oh, how the thought tempted! Mayhap he'd never press for repayment. Mayhap he'd smile, and leave, and 'twould be the end of it.

Mayhap he'd be back next month or next year with a proposition she was in no position to refuse.

No, she mustn't risk it. Conjuring up the image of her son's face, she took a deep breath. Her heartbeat accelerated and she felt light-headed.

You can do this. You will do whatever you must to keep Drew.

Tentatively she put her hand on the Earl's arm. She felt his muscles tense, heard his rush of indrawn breath even as she spoke, her voice near a whisper. "To express my gratitude in any way that pleases you would be my greatest honor."

She looked up into his eyes, praying he understood, that she would not have to utter words any more explicit. Her heart thudded in her chest and a flush of shame and anxiety heated her cheeks.

His eyes searched hers. She forced a smile, though her lips trembled.

He placed his hand over hers and gripped it tightly. "There is no compulsion." His eyes glowing brighter, he made a move with his other arm as if to embrace her, then dropped it back to his side. "I don't wish you to think—"

"I don't. I know you would never force me."

Though he retained her hand, he sat back a little, his eyes dimming as if affronted. "Of course not!" He gave her a twisted smile. "You cannot help but know it is my fondest hope to establish a more...intimate connection, but I would have you do so from desire, not out of—*gratitude.*" He almost spat out the word.

Though the statement nearly choked her, she made herself utter the lie. "'Twould be *my* fondest hope as well."

His body tensed again, his gaze so heated she felt she must go up in flames. "Are you sure?"

Unable to voice another affirmation, she merely nodded.

It was enough. He seized both hands and brought them to his lips, kissing them fervently. "If you truly wish it, you make me the happiest man in England."

So the die was cast. She felt detached, as if observing the scene from a vast distance. What should she do now? She couldn't bear the thought of coolly choosing a date and time for the assignation. No, better it begin tonight, lest she be tempted to renege on the bargain.

Gently she disengaged her fingers. "Let me pour you another port." She was proud that her voice wobbled only a little. "Now, if you'll excuse me a moment?"

Evan watched her as, with a sensuous sway of hip, she disappeared through the doorway across the hall from the little parlor. He moved the glass to his lips with shaking hands, then set it back down.

No, best not drink more of that mind-dulling liquid. He was already too close to losing control. When she'd touched him, it had taken every bit of restraint he could muster to avoid sweeping her into his arms.

But she'd just invited him to do so, hadn't she? Normally he'd know just how to proceed, but now... With his body on fire and every nerve screaming at her closeness, he couldn't be sure he wasn't misinterpreting her response, was only imagining she shared some part of the enormous desire that consumed him.

After all, if her story could be believed, and he had no reason to doubt it, she'd been a virgin bride and a faithful wife. Despite what must have been severe pressure to do otherwise, she seemed to have remained chaste even after her husband's death. Certainly her rejection of the lures cast out by St. Clair and his set confirmed that assessment.

How she must have loved her soldier-husband, to leave what had obviously been a privileged home and follow him to the privations and dangers of war. Evan felt a swift, irrational flare of jealousy.

Well, she'd not rebuffed him. He'd given her every opportunity, reiterated his insistence that she owed him no additional thanks, but when he'd boldly admitted his desire, she'd avowed her own. What could be plainer than that?

He remembered the darting thrill yesterday when he'd touched her lip. He'd felt it in every nerve, and she'd felt it, too—he'd seen the shocked recognition in her eyes immediately after. Perhaps attraction didn't burn in her as fiercely as in him, but she was hardly indifferent.

Mayhap, having been years without a husband and lover, she was as ready as he.

Well, she was unlikely to be that ready, he conceded. But she was drawn to him, he was certain of it, and he could build on that.

He *would* build upon it, court her until she welcomed him with anticipation as fervent as his own. Never, he vowed, had any woman been wooed as persistently, passionately and persuasively as he intended to woo Emily Spenser.

But to do so, he must finish his port and depart before her intoxicating closeness destroyed what little was left of his control. Before he did something rash.

He didn't want this to be rash or hurried. He wanted their time together to be like her—perfection.

The door across the hall opened and Emily emerged. His mouth went dry and the glass slipped from his fingers. Smiling, she walked toward him clad only in a night rail.

'Twas not the flannel garment of a prim, virtuous middle-class matron. Oh no, the most skilled of courtesans would have delighted in how this gown of slithering, shining emerald silk swept from her shoulders over her full breasts to her narrow waist and past rounded hips to whisper about her thighs and calves as she walked. It clung to the taunting outline of pebbled nipples, the round of belly, the tempting fistful of curls at the junction of her thighs.

Beyond speech, he merely stared as she halted before him. Her violet eyes, enormous, caught his dazzled gaze as a drift of delicate scent, lavender and heat and woman, dizzied him.

"My lord?" she said softly.

Any reservations he may have retained crumbled. With trembling hands he drew her down beside him on the settee. His blood pounding in his ears, every sense knife sharp, he gently touched the faint bruise on her lip with one finger, then lowered his mouth over hers.

She tasted sweet, ah so sweet, of coffee and wine and Emily. Mindful of her hurt, he licked her lips gently,

gently sought entry. She opened her mouth, and when her tongue met his, every iota of control dissolved.

With a cry he crushed her to him. Leaning her back against the cushions, he plundered the depths of her mouth, nibbling, sucking, voracious. With fevered impatience, he moved lower, tracing the satin length of collarbone, tasting the pulse at the hollow of her throat, then lower still, forcing the satin bodice beneath her breasts so it thrust them up and out to him, like trophies.

He cupped the warm, heavy rounds, licked their fullness, drew a nipple into his mouth. He thought she gasped when he squeezed the breast to take in yet more of its fullness, then withdrew to lave the sides and nibble the nipple's rigid top.

He couldn't seem to get close enough, kiss deeply enough. She tried to help, truly she did, struggling to pull off his neckcloth and unbutton his shirt as he carried her across the hallway and shouldered open her chamber door. She was fumbling with the buttons at his straining breeches when he laid her on the narrow bed, but impatient, he wrenched the cloth free. When his manhood sprang forth and she touched him, an explosion of heat and need shut down his brain entirely.

How he got her gown off without ripping it to shreds he couldn't remember, but somehow she was lying under him, all warm, glorious naked skin. He managed to restrain himself long enough to tangle his fingers in the thatch of dark curls and part her, to briefly taste her fragrant womanhood. Then he was plunging into her, burying himself as she tilted her hips to take him deeper, and the whole world erupted in a searing fireball of sensation.

He must have passed out, or dozed, for when he came back to himself Evan lay sprawled against the pillows— alone. Sitting up with a start, he saw Emily at the doorway to a small balcony that overlooked the back garden.

Strong emotion washed over him, followed by guilt. So much for courting, for flowers, gifts, sweet words. He'd said nothing at all, then taken her too fast, like a callow youth with his first woman. He recalled the ladies who had sighed with satisfaction after his bedding, swearing him to be the most skillful of lovers, and almost laughed. There'd been no trace tonight of that vaunted technique.

'Twill be better next time, he promised her silently. Next time he would go slowly, slowly. Everything, each touch and taste and stroke, would be for her. Not until she writhed under him, clutching his shoulders and begging for release, would he sheath himself in her, and even then he would hold back until her cries of pleasure freed him to find nirvana again. He recalled the brain-melting, heart-stopping intensity of his response, and had to grin. Well, at least he would *try* to hold back.

Naked, he slipped out of bed and approached her. She must not have heard him, for she stood silent, still facing out to the garden. He halted a step away, savoring her incredible beauty and marveling at its powerful effect.

She'd put the night rail back on. Light from the street-lamp beyond shone in lozenged patterns on its shiny surface. Her lush hair, only a shadowy outline in the gloom, hung forward over her breasts. He bent to kiss her bared nape and suddenly realized what he'd taken to be patterns on the silken gown were, in fact, fold lines.

Peering more closely, he examined the evenly spaced repetition of the rectangular shapes. So sharply creased were the lines, so spicy and deep the clinging odor of lavender, that he was forced to conclude the night rail must have lain folded in tissue wrap for a very long time.

Had she welcomed her soldier back from battle wearing this? When he returned to her wounded, had she tenderly set it away, waiting for the day when he had recovered enough that she might wear it for him once more?

An unexpected and shockingly intense feeling of outrage engulfed Evan at the thought of her with another man. As if laying claim, he placed his hands on her shoulders.

She'd been trembling, even before his touch startled her. She turned her head toward him, and he saw star-spangled droplets clinging to the ends of her long lashes. She was, he realized with horror, weeping.

Remorse swamped him. He pulled her into his arms, grateful that instead of resisting, she rested her head against his chest.

After a moment, she moved away, swiping at her eyes. He stayed her hand and kissed the moist lashes. ''Ah, sweetheart, you truly are a virtuous matron.''

She managed a glimmer of a smile. ''I used to be.''

''You *are*.''

Some fleeting emotion crossed her face. Gently she pushed him back and walked to the bedside table, took a sip of wine from a glass left there.

Keeping her gaze averted from his unclothed body, she turned toward him. ''I'm sorry, that wasn't very good. It's been a long time.''

''You've had the gown since...'' He couldn't complete the thought.

''Yes. Be assured, I've never worn it. After A— After he was wounded, I kept it as a sort of talisman for the time when he would be well. But you cannot wish to hear of it.''

She was right; he didn't want to hear about it. At the same time, he was morbidly curious, and absolutely sick with jealousy.

She poured another glass of wine, spilling a little, and handed it to him. Then she lit a lamp, retrieved his shirt and breeches, and brought them over.

After he'd drained the wine, she held out the shirt. ''Shall I help?'' Her glance grazed his naked form, and she flushed. ''I mean, are you...ready?'' She smiled slightly. ''I'm sorry, I'm not sure what I'm supposed to do.''

No, no, don't let it end like this, his mind screamed. ''Nothing,'' he choked out. ''You don't have to do anything.''

Nonetheless, with another determined smile she assisted him into his shirt. Had she tenderly dressed her husband after loving, when he'd left her to go on duty? As she attempted to do up the buttons, Evan brushed her hand away blindly, stupidly furious.

Idiot, he castigated himself. *Of course she isn't a trollop, though you just treated her like one. Of course she bought this sumptuous, sinful, will-melting gown for her* husband, *the man she all-too-clearly adored—and adores still. He was her husband, dammit! 'Tis only right she loved him.*

He gave the last button a savage twist. "Just don't regret this," he said gruffly. "I couldn't bear that."

Her violet eyes looked up in surprise, their puzzled depths trapping him. Helpless, he could not look away.

"I don't regret it," she said slowly after a moment. Squaring her shoulders, she straightened. "Truly, I don't regret it."

"I wish I could believe that. But you needn't worry, I'm leaving. I don't, as a rule, rape grieving widows."

He reached for his breeches. Her hand caught his, and with the other, she turned his chin so that she could look once more into his eyes.

He tried to jerk away, sure his face mirrored all his roiling emotion and stupid, little-boy hurt. But she held on and gazed up searchingly.

After a long moment, she whispered, "I don't regret it." And kissed him.

She was right—this *was* better, so very much better than before that any thought of leaving expired on the spot.

This time her tongue sought out his, circling and stroking it, teasing him deeper. As she alternately sucked and nibbled at his lips, he groaned and yanked up her gown to knead the soft roundness of her buttocks and mold her torso against his. She pressed herself higher and, still teasing his tongue, rubbed her springy curls against his rapidly hardening shaft.

He lifted her, and she wrapped her legs about his waist and thrust down, taking him inside. One arm about his neck, she brought his mouth to one taut, silk-encased nipple. She moaned as he tongued her, tensing the muscles inside her hot, slick canal about his burgeoning manhood.

Gasping, he wrapped his arms around her and carried her back to the bed. With each step, she rocked her hips to take him deeper. By the time he eased her against the pillows and settled himself over her, he was already throbbing for release.

He managed to hold himself back this time. Driving in as deeply as he could, he stilled and bent to bare her breasts. Slowly he sucked and nipped each nipple in turn while she quivered under him, straining to rock her hips. He rested his weight against her, pinning her motionless while he savored her skin. When her breathing turned to shallow gasps, when a fine sheen dewed her chest, only then did he shift his weight and slowly draw himself out to the very tip, then slowly ease himself back in. She moved her hips urgently, her hands clutching his shoulders. ''Please,'' she whispered, ''please!''

Digging his thumbnails into his hands to slow himself, gradually he increased the rhythm. She lay back, her hair streaming over the pillows, her eyes closed, and arched into him. He bent to suckle again her full, taut nipples, and she cried out, nearly destroying his disintegrating control.

"Evan," he gasped as he drove harder, "call me Evan."

"Evan," she whispered, and then "Oh, Evan!", until finally she sobbed out his name and he let her exquisite, sweet convulsions set off his own.

Afterward, he cradled her close, loving the feel of her sweat-drenched skin against his own. "Emily, sweetheart, don't ever regret this," he murmured as he slid his hands over the slick satin of her hips, her breasts. She cuddled into him and he massaged her shoulders and back, reveling in the sheer sweet pleasure of touching her.

She stretched out, languorous as a cat, one soft leg draped over his. After a few moments, her relaxed, even breathing told him she slept.

Though there was no need, he continued to gently stroke her. He felt a deep satisfaction that, this time, he had undeniably given her pleasure, and a sense of awe at the intensity of the pleasure she gave him.

He ought to wake her, let her dress him, take his leave. He never spent the night with his mistresses; once the loving was finished, he was usually eager to be off.

It seemed in this, too, being with her was different, for he had not the slightest desire to stir from her bed. There was utter contentment in holding her silken body close, watching moonlight play across her face.

She looked peaceful now, and happy. That was how he wanted her to be when she was with him: safe, content and satisfied. 'Twas his last thought before he, too, drifted asleep.

When later he woke, pink dawn painted the sky beyond the balcony. Emily, clad in a dressing gown, sat beside him on the bed.

Seeing him stir, she smiled. "Good morning, my lord. Should you like coffee before you go? Francesca has some ready, as it's almost time for us to be in the shop."

He nearly groaned with frustration. Though 'twas not much later than he sometimes returned from a night's ramble, she was a businesswoman, and must rise early. Her subtle hint warned him 'twas too late for any further dalliance.

She seemed matter-of-fact now, both sadness and contentment gone. "No, I suppose I'd best be going," he replied, still strangely reluctant to leave. Nonetheless, he let her help him into his shirt. As she buttoned it, he bent and pressed his lips against the softness of her neck.

"Oh, Emily," he whispered.

She stilled. Then, somewhat awkwardly, she put her arms around his neck and drew him close.

After he'd dressed, she walked him downstairs, through the office and out to the front door.

"Lock it well," he admonished as she slid the bolt open. "Shall I see you tonight?"

She angled her head to look up at him. "If you wish."

"You know I do. Emily, sweetheart, I can't dissemble about how much I want you." He laughed shortly and ran a hand through his tousled hair. "I expect that's only too painfully obvious.

"It may be foolish," he continued, "but I would wish for you to want me, too. If you do not, I can respect that." He managed a grin. "I cannot like it, but I'll respect it. Unless you truly wish it—'' he forced the words through reluctant lips ''—I'll not return.''

Despite that show of nonchalance, his pulse stampeded and sweat broke out on his forehead as he awaited her response.

She smiled faintly, and he began to breathe again. ''I wish you to return as often as you like, for as long as you like.''

An upsurge of joy brought the grin back to his face. ''Rest assured, I shall thoroughly enjoy coming at every opportunity! But be cautious what you wish for. Were I to visit as oft as I'd like, you'd have me underfoot constantly.''

She merely smiled, and he bent to give her a lingering kiss, which she returned, he thought, with some enthusiasm. ''Until this evening, then.''

Before he could pull away, she stopped him with a touch to his cheek. ''I'd forgotten how beautiful loving can be,'' she said softly. ''Thank you...Evan.''

His spirits soared to the rooftops. ''Call upon me at any time.'' Giving her one last kiss, he forced himself to exist. A few steps down the sidewalk, he turned to look back. She gave him a little wave, closed the door, and he heard the bolt slam home.

'Twas all he could do not to run back and knock.

Chapter Four

Several hours later Emily looked up from her worktable in bemusement. "Put them on the desk, I suppose," she told the urchin with his paper-wrapped parcel of flowers.

"Where, ma'am? There be's a pow'rful lotta posies a'ready."

In truth, the top of her small desk was nearly buried beneath a floral avalanche. The bouquets—some small, some large—had begun arriving early this morning, and the parade continued steadily all day. Francesca had long since run out of vases, and the most recent offerings reclined in an odd miscellany of pots, mugs and bowls.

The numerous bouquets contained only pansies or violets. Deepest purple, pale lavender, near white, the shimmering velvet blooms and their perfume filled the office and spilled out into the salesroom beyond.

Searching for a spare inch, Emily surveyed the assortment with a mingling of amusement and exasperation. Lord Cheverley must have bought up every blossom in the city. They'd be reduced to water and cold mutton for dinner, as there was hardly a kettle or teacup left in the kitchen. She didn't know whether to be touched or annoyed.

The delivery boy still stood, flowers in hand, looking at her expectantly. Sighing, she laid down her scissors. "Just bring them to me."

The boy handed them over, but when she dug in her pocket for a coin, he waved her away. "The toff what sent 'em paid me good, 'n offered me an extry yellow boy if'n I wouldn't try'n fob a tuppence off ya." Tipping his grimy cap, he gave her a gap-toothed grin and ambled out.

Francesca entered from the kitchen behind her and raised her eyebrows. "By the Blessed Virgin, Mistress, your noble lordling must be pleased with you." Eyes twinkling, she leaned over to pat Emily's cheek. "And you, *querida,* look like a woman who has been well loved."

"Enough, Francesca."

"Ah, you grumble, but me, I think it very fine," Francesca replied with unimpaired good humor. "You are tired, no, mistress? Rest, and I will deal with the *clientela.* Then I cook another special dinner."

"Lord Cheverley is not invited for dinner," Emily replied stiffly.

"But he comes tonight, surely as a saint's reward," Francesca said shrewdly. "Go rest yourself, mistress. He must not see your beauty dimmed. Take the *violetas*—" the maid wrapped Emily's hands around the flowers "—and sleep. I left upstairs a vase."

In truth, she was tired. With a sigh, she allowed Francesca to urge her toward the stairs. "All right. But for an hour only."

"*Good,* I will wake you," the maid agreed. "A hungry work, this loving is. Tonight will I prepare a hearty paella."

"If you can find anything to cook it in," Emily muttered as she walked out.

Emily slipped the fragile, fragrant blooms—deep violet with tiny white eyes—into her favorite vase, a delicate piece of blue-and-white Portuguese pottery in a fanciful pattern of birds and animals. Setting it down on the desk that also served as her dressing table, she caught her reflection in the little mirror propped against the wall. Solemn eyes, somewhat shadowed perhaps, stared back at her over a straight, narrow nose and generous lips. *I look no different,* she thought. Should not becoming a Fallen Woman have left some tangible sign?

Steeling herself, she picked the miniature off its easel beside the mirror. In defiance of convention, Andrew had wanted her to paint him relaxing rather than posing formally, and so she had. The neck fastening of his dolman was unhooked, his capless hair tumbled as if in the ocean's breeze. She'd managed to capture the sparkle in his emerald eyes, his high-spirited grin with just the hint of the devil.

Oh, Andrew, what would you think of me now?

The ache went too deep. Replacing the miniature on its stand, she wandered to the balcony. Wan sunlight, a feeble imitation of the fierce peninsular light that had bathed the quarters they'd shared in a score of different villages, cast a mellow glow. She leaned against the railing, gazing down into the garden below.

When she first returned after years under the Peninsula's bright sun and sharp blue skies, she'd found London's mist, fog and smoke impossibly grim. 'Twas as if, she joked to Francesca, the city itself wept at her loss. Then she'd come upon some pots of lavender at a farmer's market and set about turning the abandoned, weed-choked lot behind her shop into a replica of a peninsular garden.

Now, pots of herbs surrounded a sundial fashioned from a broken milestone, an old deacon's bench salvaged from the parish burn pile set invitingly near. Her beloved lavender thrived in the barren, rocky soil around the sundial, its scent, released by the gentle sun, floating up to her.

How the smells of sun-baked earth and herbs brought it back—the sharp-cut scenery of rock and scrub, narrow gullies and steep ravines. The simple, whitewashed dwellings clinging to hillsides and gazing at the distant azure sea. How she'd loved to set up her easel on the wide balcony and work furiously to capture the changing light on those hills, that glimmer of ocean.

She'd painted Andrew, too, of course, and Rob, his rascal of a brother and fellow soldier, and all their comrades. Canvases of men in uniform relaxing on the balcony, dining about her table or playing an impromptu game of cricket on the village square had begun to crowd her baggage, for when the troops were billeted in towns between engagements, the quarters of Lieutenant Waring-

Black and his beautiful bride became a sort of junior officer's mess. Many an evening had they laughed and played at cards, while Boyd or Matthew sang to Francesca's guitar.

Melancholy filled Emily's chest along with breaths of lavender-spiced air. She loved this little garden, a tangible reminder of the happy sunlit days with Andrew. When accounts did not total, or a tradesman bickered, or some well-born lady puffed up with her own consequence belittled her, Emily would somehow find herself sitting on the bench below. She'd run her fingers along the stiff gray wands and inhale the herb's sharp, cleansing scent. Whenever something troubled her.

Like the thought of the tall, well-formed man returning tonight. Her lover.

Her cheeks burned, her body heated and the thought escaped before she could check it: *I'm sorry.*

Don't be an idiot, she told herself crossly. *You've chosen your course. There's nothing to do but go on and make the best of it. Only children and cowards whine and regret.*

She was too honest to deny Cheverley's lovemaking brought her intense—and sorely missed—pleasure. Nor could she deny the idea of receiving his caresses again, soon, sent a spiral of warmth to her very core.

'Twas just her pride that ached, and old memories she should have long since laid to rest. She should view the matter pragmatically, as Francesca suggested.

A businesslike arrangement without long-term or legal complications might suit her very well. And if his lordship's ardor lasted until she managed to build her income to such a level of security that she would never again be forced into this position, it would, as Francesca said, be all to the good.

And just what does that make you? a little voice in her head whispered. She turned away from the garden, trying to shut out the ugly word that burned, unspoken, in her ears.

After leaving Emily in the lightening dawn, Evan sought his bed. Too keyed up to sleep, though, he soon gave up the attempt. From the exasperated look his mama gave him when he left the breakfast chamber two plates of eggs, ham and sausages and three steaming cups of tea later, he must have missed half her conversation.

Deciding in his present fog of abstraction he would likely run his high-perch phaeton into a post or allow the highbred cattle to bolt, he waved away his groom and elected to walk to his Horse Guards office.

But during the stroll, instead of reviewing details of Wellington's supply routes, his mind kept slipping back to the sounds and images of last night. The low velvet timbre of her voice. The curve of her little finger as she held her teacup. Her eyes, sometimes deep plum, sometimes the lighter veined lavender of a woodland flower.

Flowers. He halted, electrified. To the woman beautiful as a perfect, fragrant violet he would send every blossom he could find. Grinning, he hailed a hackney and instructed the jarvey to carry him to the closest florist.

Two hours and a good deal of blunt later, he had dispatched enough blooms, he calculated as he mounted the stairs to his office, to cover her desk and most of the dining table. Mayhap she could even strew some petals on the sheets.

An immediate wave of heat assailed him. No, he dare not start thinking of that. Besides, he wanted this evening to proceed differently. He'd promised himself to court and woo her, then had taken her like a street-corner strumpet. The very thought of it galled him anew. He would have been well-served if she'd kicked him down the stairs afterward and bolted the door.

Instead, she'd wept.

His stomach twisted and his chest tightened. *Ah, sweetheart,* he vowed, *never again will I make you weep.*

With a start he realized he now stood before the door to his office. Gathering his disjointed thoughts, he entered, extracted a supply ledger from the stack on his desk and sat down to review it.

He was gazing out the window, thinking of violets and amethysts rather than account totals, when his door opened and Geoffrey Randall, his college mate and assistant, strolled in.

"'Morning, Ev. Have you reviewed the ledgers yet?"

Evan glanced at the page he'd smoothed open at least half an hour ago, unable to recall a single total. "Not quite," he mumbled.

"When you finish, could you check this report for powder and shot? I've added the columns three times, but the figures don't make sense." Frowning, Randall tapped the paper he held.

Ah, figures. With a private smile Evan called to mind one particular willowy, well-rounded form.

"Something doesn't seem right," Randall was continuing. "I'd appreciate your looking at it. If you would, Ev. Ev?"

His drifting attention recalled, Evan focused on the secretary. "Y-yes. You were saying?"

His assistant eyed him with some concern. "Seem a tad done-up this morning, old friend. Rough night? Surely you didn't lose, for a change?"

A sudden vision of Emily in his arms, and he in Emily, warmed him like a candle flame. "'Twas a wonderful night, and I certainly didn't lose."

Raising an eyebrow, Randall laughed. "Ah, that sort of night. Why don't you go get some sleep? You're not doing any good here."

"Thank you most kindly," Evan replied with a grin. "But you're correct—my mind isn't on ledgers today. Shall we discuss the matter later?"

"Of course." Randall grinned back. "And if the wench is even halfway deserving of that fatuous smile, you're a lucky devil."

As Evan neared home, the idea of another gift struck him with vivid clarity.

There must be no gown unfolded with memories tonight. No, tonight she should come to him in sheer purple silk and a whisper of cream lace. His woman, wearing his gown, making new memories that were theirs alone.

Proceeding immediately to the shop of one of the city's most exclusive mantua-makers, he swiftly made his choice. However, when he informed Madame she need not deliver the garment, for he intended to take it with him, she protested she'd be happy to insure it arrived wherever he wished.

Catching the speculative gleam in her eye, he realized the seamstress was consumed with curiosity to discover the identity of his newest inamorata. Instinctively he knew his reserved, dignified Emily would not appreciate having her name bandied about. Cordially turning aside the dressmaker's offer, he paid her well and left the shop.

To be truthful, he found the notion of revealing Emily to be his mistress strangely distasteful. Not that he'd ever flaunted his women, but Emily was different—a treasure he wished cloistered for him alone. He'd not have what they shared be the subject of vulgar speculation by Willoughby and those of his ilk.

What a many-faceted jewel she was, too: elegant and proper as the highest-born lady in that demure lavender gown the first day they'd met; siren last night, her ebony tresses flowing silken over her bare back and full, high breasts, her soft mouth and thighs promising sin and magic.

Just thinking of her hardened him to such urgent need he groaned. How many more hours until dark?

After avoiding his mama's curious glances at tea, he dressed for dinner early and slipped away to his club. Surely he could find someone to get up a game of whist or piquet that would fill the hours until he could present himself back at her shop.

''Ev, well met!'' Brent Blakesly rose to greet him as he entered the reading room. ''Missed you at White's last night. I take it that means your, ah, appointment was successful?''

Evan knew he was beaming; he couldn't help it. ''Completely.''

Brent whistled. ''Congratulations, then! Come—'' he motioned to a waiter ''—let's have some champagne! Though I can hardly credit it—Willoughby was so sure she'd not go down for anyone.''

Evan jerked back the hand his friend was enthusiastically pumping. ''Dammit, don't you dare describe her in such terms.''

Shocked into immobility, Brent simply looked at him. ''Sorry, Ev,'' he said at last. ''I meant no disrespect.''

Shocked himself by the depth of his outrage, Evan made himself smile and motioned Brent back to his chair. ''I don't want this to become common knowledge about London—not a hint of it. If you take my meaning?''

Brent straightened, looking mildly affronted. ''I'm hardly one to go gossiping about my friends. As I thought you'd know.''

''Yes, yes, I do know. Just a reminder.''

''Mrs. Spenser worries for her reputation?'' Brent guessed.

''No, I do. I don't want some idle fool getting the wrong idea and bothering her.''

Brent stared at him searchingly, then shook his head. ''The lady must have made quite an impression.''

Evan let his mind play over the images of Emily in all her guises, and of their own volition his lips curved into a smile. ''She did indeed.''

The champagne arrived, and with a flourish, Brent presented him a flute. "To you," he raised his glass, "the luckiest bastard in London."

After they downed the wine, Evan put a restless hand to his pocket and frowned. "Blast, I seem to have left my watch. What o'clock is it?"

Brent squinted at the mantel clock across the room. "Near on five, best I can see. How about a few hands of piquet before you leave me for the divine Madame? Mayhap I can fleece you of enough blunt to assuage my jealousy."

So strongly did the thought of Emily pull Evan, even the prospect of several hours spent over good wine in the company of his best friend didn't appeal. He knew where he most wanted to be. So why not just go there?

"Another time, perhaps," he replied, deciding on the spot. "I think I'll stop by the shop and make sure the runner is still on duty."

Brent grinned. "Righto, better check. Runners are such an inefficient lot." He ducked Evan's mock punch. "Give the widow my regards—you lucky bastard."

Already halfway across the room, Evan only nodded.

Chapter Five

Quietly entering the salesroom half an hour later, Evan saw Francesca by the office door, Emily bent over her worktable in the room beyond. As the maid's face lit in a welcoming smile, he put a warning finger to his lips and beckoned her.

"Don't disturb your mistress," he whispered when she reached his side. "Will she forgive me if I invite myself to dinner?"

"You honor us, my lord," the maid whispered back.

Grinning, Evan handed her a pouch. "You'll need to make some purchases. I doubt you usually cook enough to feed a healthy man's appetite."

She shook her head sadly. "Not for years."

"Do so tonight. And if there's a special dish your mistress particularly likes, prepare it."

"I know just the one!" Francesca pocketed the pouch, her dark eyes shining. "Ah tonight, such a meal I cook!"

"If 'tis anything like last night's, I may sack my chef and steal you away. Before you go, could you take this upstairs?" He handed her the tissue-wrapped package.

He tiptoed to the office door. Lost in concentration, Emily toiled away unawares. Vases of flowers scattered about the salesroom wafted the subtle but pervasive scent of violets and pansies. Within the small workroom every available surface but the table itself was covered with bouquets. The spicy fragrance teased his nose.

Though he'd not expected her to hide his tributes, he was absurdly touched to discover she'd placed them all around her, some even in public view. Surely she could not be bent on pleasing him only out of gratitude, could she?

Despite the maid's friendliness, he was unsure enough about her mistress's reaction to his unannounced and un-invited arrival that he delayed making his presence known. Silently he settled against the wall, curious, and content to watch her.

A sketchbook sat open on the worktable, a half-finished velvet bonnet on a stand beside it. From time to time she glanced at the book as her long fingers deftly fashioned rosettes of braid and added them to the hat. After completing a final flower, she lifted the bonnet and placed it carefully on her head.

Before he realized what she was doing, she walked to the mirror to inspect it—and saw him behind her in the reflection.

She gasped and spun around. "Lord Cheverley!"

Once again, her beauty seen face-to-face took his breath away. For a long moment, he merely stood, tongue-tied and awkward as an infatuated adolescent.

Quickly she replaced the bonnet on its stand. "I wasn't expecting you this early, my lord."

All the gallant, polished phrases he'd practiced deserted him. "I couldn't stay away."

Groaning inwardly at such gaucherie, he strode toward her. "But I don't mean to interrupt. Please, complete whatever you intended to finish by evening." He halted a foot away, conscious of a strong desire to pull her into his arms. Barely a minute close to her, and already he was lost. He settled for kissing the fingers she extended, savoring the scent, the touch of her skin.

She smiled slightly. "I'm not sure it's possible for me to work with you so near. But Lady Wendfrow expects this tomorrow, so I'm obliged to try."

Could she feel the attraction, that magnetic pull between them, as strongly as he? Evan fervently hoped so.

He stepped toward the table, forcing himself to focus on something other than her intoxicating proximity. "You work from your own designs?" At her nod, he indicated the sketchbook. "May I?"

"If you wish."

To distract himself while she finished, he opened the book, intending to flip idly through the designs. The first image facing up at him riveted his attention. "Why, that's Lady Wendfrow to the life!"

"'Tis easier to design a bonnet that flatters my client if I work from a detailed sketch of her face."

"If you can fashion something to flatter Lady Wendfrow, you're a wizard."

She made a little gurgle of a laugh, the sound so enchanting it momentarily distracted him. "She does tend to wear plumed hats that only emphasize her narrow face, in shades of black that do nothing whatsoever for her coloring.''

''You intend to rectify those errors?'' He pointed to the half-fashioned bonnet.

''Yes. The frame is mourning black, on which she insists, but I've lined the brim and trimmed the sides with peach satin. That soft tone beside her face will warm her skin to cream. And I shall drape the plume more to the horizontal, to broaden her face.''

''By heaven, it might work. Mama said you were a genius. May I look at the other sketches?''

''If you like. I'll be just a few more moments.''

She took up needle and thread and set to work.

While she stitched, he flipped through the book, pausing to study several sketches of the ladies familiar to him. He had to marvel both at how well she had captured their images and at how skillfully each bonnet she'd designed emphasized their best features.

Then he reached the last page and froze.

Emily had caught the sitter at a pensive moment, one hand to her chin as she gazed into the distance. The pale ivory of her hair, the turquoise of her eyes and the wistful, half-smiling expression were so vividly rendered he felt as if his mama might at any moment speak to him from out of the sketchbook.

''This is extraordinary!'' he burst out. ''Please, I must have it. May I buy it from you?''

She glanced over, her hand with the needle momentarily stilling. ''The sketch of Lady Cheverley? Take it, if you like. That bonnet is already finished.''

''I must pay you for it.''

"Nonsense, 'tis only a pastel. Besides, you've already expended far too much for me. If the likeness pleases you, I should be honored for you to have it as a gift."

He hesitated, about to argue the point, but the oblique reference to her indebtedness and the slight lift of her chin alerted him that her pride was at issue.

Give in gracefully, he decided. He could repay her in ways she'd not discover—through Francesca, who, unlike her mistress, seemed cheerfully willing to accept his largesse.

"Thank you, then." He took a knife from the worktable and carefully cut free the sketch. That task accomplished, he looked back to see her hunched over the bonnet, peering at the dark velvet in the rapidly fading twilight.

"Emily, stop. You can't possibly see black thread against black velvet any longer."

'A few more stitches, and 'twill be finished." While he watched in exasperation, she stubbornly bent closer, her nose nearly buried in the bonnet as she attached a final ribbon. At last she knotted off her thread.

"Enough," he said, and put his hands on her shoulders, gently pulling her from the worktable. But at the feel of her flesh under his fingers, he found all his banked passion surging back. He shuddered and went still, resisting the sudden, sharp longing to enfold her against him.

She'd gone motionless as well, and he could feel her muscles tense under his hands. Without thinking, he began to massage her stiff shoulders.

"Ahh," she sighed. "That feels lovely."

"No wonder your shoulders ache, standing in front of that worktable all day," he chided, extending the massage to her neck and upper arms.

"You scold just like Francesca," she said with a giggle. 'Twas so infectious a sound, he found himself laughing, too. She rotated to face him. He looked down into those wide pansy eyes and caught his breath yet again.

Slowly her smile faded. When, helpless, compelled, he lowered her mouth, she raised on tiptoes to meet his kiss.

He kissed her long and longingly, battling the immediate urge to slide his hands to the tempting, tilt-tipped breasts brushing his chest. At last he reluctantly released her. "I've been waiting a century for that."

Her charming bubble of a laugh sounded again. "Indeed? 'Twas nearly six when you left this morning."

"Couldn't have been. It seems an eternity."

She lifted her gaze to his, her velvet eyes holding the slightly startled look of a wild thing disturbed. Then, to his surprise and utter delight, she closed them again and leaned back into his embrace.

"Another glass of wine, my lord?"

Emily had poured half the glass when the hot dish Francesca was carrying in caught her attention. Her eyes narrowing, she gave the maid a sharp look.

"Paella? How delightful," Evan said.

"'Tis Madame's favorite," Francesca confirmed, ignoring Emily's pointed stare. "Also the beef with rosemary, potatoes and minted peas, and the fine rioja."

"Francesca, I'll want a word with you later."

"Aye, mistress." With a curtsey and a saucy wink at Evan, the maid withdrew.

"You mustn't scold her," Evan said. "I asked her to fix your favorites this evening."

"You gave her money," Emily said flatly.

"Of course. I would rather dine with you than anywhere else in London, but I can hardly expect you to regularly feed one large, overgrown male."

"If you are my guest, I can provide for you. Perhaps not paella, rare beef and the finest of riojas."

"Please, Emily, don't pull caps with me. You do a wonderful job providing for your household. Your company gives me such—" he caught himself before uttering the word *joy* "—enjoyment, I wanted to do a little something to express it."

"A *little* something?" she echoed, exasperation in her tone. "My lord, you've already chased away an abusive villain and saved me from being blackmailed a tidy sum monthly for the indefinite future. I think that's quite enough."

"Do you place limits on the gifts you give a friend?"

Lips open as if to pursue her argument, she paused. "No, I suppose not," she admitted after a moment. "Unless necessity compels it."

"Then will you not permit me the same luxury? Please. You have worked diligently for so long. How can it be wrong for a friend to indulge you?"

Seeing that wary look coming back in her eyes, he changed tack. "As for work, I'm impressed by the exceptional quality of your sketches. Did you not say you'd painted portraits while in Spain? Why did you choose not to continue painting here?''

She took a sip of wine. For a moment, he thought she'd ignore the question. Finally, looking away from him, she said softly, '''Twas different in Spain, among strangers. My father was a—a wealthy man. He sent me to an exclusive school. Some of those who would commission portraits here might be his colleagues or acquaintances. Or former classmates of my own.''

She didn't need to say more. All at once he had a searing vision of what her life must have been. Cast out of the privileged world of bourgeois wealth because of her runaway marriage, unacknowledged by her husband's apparently aristocratic family, upon that soldier's death far from friendly lines, she'd found herself utterly alone in a foreign land with nothing but her talent and wits between herself and starvation.

For an individual who had vanquished the dangers she must have faced to return and work as a servant for those who were once her equals would have been intolerable. Small wonder she'd chosen, despite her undeniable talent, to abandon portraiture.

That she had managed to amass enough capital to return to England and begin a business was nothing short of astounding. Stirred initially by her beauty, he found himself even more fascinated by the resourceful, courageous character beneath.

''Will you be offended if I express my admiration for how cleverly you've built a successful business?''

''How could I be? When one lives solely by her own labors, she cannot help but feel gratified that a man praises those efforts rather than her sparkling eyes or raven tresses.''

He stowed that tidbit away for later use. ''I cannot recall ever knowing a woman so completely in charge of her own life.''

She shrugged. ''One does what one must.''

''Was your break with your family that complete?''

''It was absolute.''

''Do you not think they might reconsider, were they to know you are home now, and widowed?''

She laughed shortly. ''My father could not tolerate being crossed. When he realized I had defied him and run away, he was—ungovernable. He forbade my mother to contact me, had my letters to her returned unopened. That he disowned me is certain; I don't doubt he left orders in his will that even after his death, no member of the family attempt to communicate with me. Though, quite typically, he rendered such an order superfluous.''

Her lips twisted in a bitter smile. ''I chanced upon a distant connection in Lisbon a few years ago, and she was astonished to see me. It seems my father told everyone I'd died of a fever the summer I turned sixteen.''

For a moment she stared sightlessly past him. Her voice, when at last she spoke, was a whisper. ''I would have starved in the streets of Lisbon before I would have begged him to reconsider.''

Then the intensity left her and she smiled faintly. ''But enough of that. Can I not pour you some port while I...get ready?''

Instantly the image that phrase conveyed sent the blood pounding to his temples and set his body aflame.

Desperately he tried to reel back the passion he'd been riding all evening on the tightest of checkreins. ''Th-there's no n-need to r-rush,'' he stuttered.

Her purple eyes deepened to smoke. ''Is there not? I find myself rather—anxious.''

She leaned up, and the rest of his noble intentions shattered at the first touch of her lips. With a groan, he gathered her close and tangled his fingers in her satin hair, combing out the pins as he deepened the kiss. Her tongue met his, mated with it, then pulled away to caress every surface of his mouth. His hands slid down to her back, to the buttons on her gown, and jerked frantically at them. The soft sound of renting cloth finally stopped him.

Heartbeat thundering, his breathing a harsh gasp, he made himself push her away. She looked up at him, her lips still parted and her eyes so passion glazed he almost lost control again.

Hands gripping her shoulders tightly to hang on to his dissolving willpower, he dredged up a ragged smile. ''S-sorry! I'm about to take you again like the gr-greenest of saplings. I expect you can't credit it, but I used to account myself a rather slow and skillful lover.''

She smiled, smoky, intimate. ''Oh, but you are.''

''Don't!'' He cupped her startled face with both hands. ''Don't say pretty things you think I want to hear. Tell me what you truly think and feel, or nothing. Promise me?''

''All right.'' A little warily, she drew back. ''Do you wish me to change now?''

"If you want to spare Francesca sewing back on all your buttons." He managed a lopsided grin. "And would you wear this, please? For me?"

He retrieved the package Francesca had brought upstairs for him. After a moment, Emily took it. Some emotion crossed her face and she seemed to withdraw a little.

Had he offended her? "Not that your own gown isn't lovely!" he hastened to assure her, eyes glued to her face. "But I saw this, and couldn't help but envision you...your eyes...the color...." He was babbling, he realized. Shutting his lips firmly, he took a deep breath. "Please?"

"Of course. I'll only be a moment." With a brief smile she gathered up the parcel and walked away.

He hoped she wasn't offended. Later, next time, he would want to undress her himself, placing kisses upon each inch of slowly revealed flesh until she was as hot, as eager, as panting for him as he was for her. But this time, he wanted her to walk out to him as she had last night—wearing his gown.

When she did, the vision was all he'd hoped for. Purple silk framed her shoulders and cupped the lower curves of her breasts like a lover's hands. Cream lace, but a pale imitation of her glorious skin, half concealed, half revealed the swelling mounds themselves and the dark, rigid nipples. The gown overlapped and tied beneath her left breast, then parted along the smooth line of her left thigh and leg as she walked.

She reached him and twirled around. The skirt parted as the light material fluttered in the breeze of her pirouette, revealing the pale skin of her calf, knee and thigh. "Does it please you, my lord?"

"Evan," he gasped, his voice nearly caught in his throat. "Call me Evan."

"Evan," she breathed as she lifted her face to his.

He'd never unwrapped so beautiful a gift.

Taking her mouth hard, he moved one hand to the ties beneath her breast, pulling them free, skimmed the other under the open edge of the gown and down across her satin belly to cup the springy nest of curls. She parted her legs to his insistent fingers and moaned when they entered her.

He slid them in and out, moving his thumb up to caress the small nub hidden above. Flipping the untied gown back over her shoulder, he broke the kiss and moved his mouth to one naked breast.

She shuddered when he filled his mouth with its full-ness, sucked deeply on the nipple. Her arms curved around his head, holding him there, and she moved her hips urgently into the steady rhythm of his fingers.

"T-take me t-to b-bed," she gasped. "Please...Evan."

"Not yet, sweetheart," he whispered against her breast. She reached one hand, feeble, fumbling, toward his trousers, but he caught it, placed it back about his neck. "Later, my darling," he said as he transferred his lips to her other breast and moved his free hand to grasp her tensed buttocks, pulling her more firmly against his fingers.

He quickened the pace, and her nails bit into his neck. With savage joy, he felt it the instant she shattered against him, her soft, gasping cries filling his ears. She sagged, and had he not caught her, would have fallen.

He lifted her into his arms. Her half-glazed eyes, still befuddled, gazed up at him. "Oh, Evan."

He gave her a wolfish grin and kissed her hard, then carried her to the bed, the open, purple silk gown fluttering like fairy wings about them as he walked.

She'd recovered enough by the time they reached the bedroom to insist on undressing him. And got back her own as, after swiftly removing his jacket and boots, she slowed her pace, slipping off his neckcloth and pausing to kiss his neck, chin and ears, then unbuttoning his waistcoat and shirt and tracing her lips down the furred skin beneath. Her tongue playing about his navel, she freed one by deliberate one the straining buttons of his breeches, then stripped the tight garment down to his knees.

He gave a startled cry when she fondled his bared buttocks. And a shock like bolted lightning erupted through him when she took him into her mouth. For a few blinding seconds, he knew only unbearably, unbelievably intense sensation before a series of powerful contractions catapulted him beyond consciousness.

They took it slowly the next time, talking, laughing, kissing between touches. Her caressing fingers never left his body; he explored languidly, tasting, stroking, memorizing every inch of hers, letting passion build until this time they reached oblivion together.

The motion of her arising from the bed woke him sometime later. She caught the hand he thrust out to pull her back and kissed it, nibbling on his knuckles.

''I'm starving,'' she pronounced. ''Francesca promised to leave something for us in the kitchen. I'll fetch it.''

''Let me. You shouldn't carry a fully laden tray.''

She chuckled softly. ''I've carried heavier items, I assure you. No, rest.'' Her hand stayed him when he would have clambered up. ''You don't know where to look, and there's not room enough in that kitchen for us both. 'Twill take but a moment.''

Languidly, she stretched, her naked breasts outlined by moonlight through the balcony doors, then motioned toward the corner. ''There's a necessary behind the screen.'' Tossing on his gown, she tied it, blew him a kiss and walked out.

Evan lay back, watching the sway of hips beneath satin as she exited. He had to be the luckiest bastard in England, he thought with enormous contentment. No— the luckiest bastard in the entire world.

The luckiest full-bladdered bastard in the world. He got up to take care of that, then strolled over to peer at himself in the mirror on her dressing table. He grinned, giddy, and stuck a finger on the nose of his reflection. ''You,'' he told it solemnly, ''are one lucky bastard.''

What a mooncalf he'd become. Laughing, he trailed his fingers down to the table's surface, tracing them over the embossed silver of her hairbrush, a small bottle that exuded the faint but pungent scent of the lavender she wore. How he loved the smell of it on her. He'd buy her gallons of the stuff, so she might wear it always. ''For me,'' he whispered.

Then he noticed a small picture on a stand, and without thinking, raised it to study. A laughing, black-haired, green-eyed man in a red officer's uniform gazed back at him.

Chapter Six

His stomach muscles clenched as if someone had struck him. Fingers trembling, he set the picture down, nearly knocking over the easel.

Sapskulled idiot, he told himself savagely. Whose miniature did he expect to find on her dressing table—the maid's? 'Twas ludicrous to feel this sense of—betrayal, almost, and as for jealousy, 'twas insane. The man was *dead,* for pity's sake!

He cast another sidelong glance at the miniature. ''Well, soldier boy,'' he muttered, ''you may be the hero, but you're no longer here to protect her. I am—and I will. She's mine now, and there's nothing—''

He stopped abruptly. He couldn't believe what he was doing. Ranting. At a portrait. A portrait of a dead man.

He must be losing his mind.

The soft sound of a gasp finally penetrated his abstraction. He turned to find Emily at the doorway, her gaze going from his face to the miniature.

After a silent moment she walked past and set the tea tray on the dressing table. There she stood, her body between him and the table, while the clink of china and the trickle of pouring liquid indicated she must be fixing cups.

''You were right, the tray *was* rather heavy,'' she said over her shoulder. ''Would you like biscuits? And there's a bit of the paella left I thought you might enjoy.''

Smiling, she turned and approached him, a full dish of tea in one hand and the teapot in the other. '''Tis a bit cramped here. Shall we dine in the sitting room? I'll come back for the tray.''

He mumbled something and took the steaming cup she offered, then mutely followed her from the room. But in a backward glance as he exited the bedchamber, he noted the little easel now stood empty.

The tinkle of the shop bell interrupted them as they sat over tea in the office several weeks later.

''That should be Baines with my evening things,'' Evan said, and sighed. ''I must admit, I'm vastly tempted to cry off. I'd rather enjoy Francesca's cooking and listen to you read the next chapter of Miss Austen's novel. That Miss Bennett—'' he winked at her ''—seems just as saucy as you.''

''Indeed? I rather thought I might beat you at chess. Again.''

''You didn't last time,'' he felt compelled to point out. ''Though perhaps 'tis better to face you over a chess-board than be skewered by your violent opinions.''

''What is violent about insisting a sitting member of the Lords should know the facts behind the measures upon which he will vote? Or to point out the enclosure legislation, added to the high prices caused by war, will cause starvation amongst the yeomen farmers who depend upon common land to graze their herds?''

Grinning, he sighed elaborately. ''And what should ladies know about enclosures and grain prices and shepherding?''

''Recall who takes care of herds and farms when husbands and fathers go off to war.''

That reflection sobered him. ''Aye, womenfolk carrying burdens they should not have to bear, as you know only too well. Which is why I must go, despite having to suffer the harangues of dull old government men. Geoffrey leaves London soon and I must decide what to do about those supply figures. 'Tis a puzzle I've not yet unraveled.''

''As I recall, the only puzzle about supplies was how they never managed to arrive,'' Emily said with a chuckle.

''There's that,'' Evan acknowledged wryly, ''but more troubling are the outlays that never seem to balance against supplies purchased.'' He frowned. ''I begin to suspect—but I shouldn't discuss it. Not even with you, my dear, whose opinion would be of much greater value than those of the octogenarians pontificating tonight.''

''I doubt my observations would be of much use. I saw only a tiny piece of the overall campaign, after all. Those who receive intelligence from sources throughout the country surely have a clearer view.''

''To be of much use, intelligence received must be intelligently analyzed.'' Evan grimaced. ''Aside from Old Hooky, whose comments are almost painfully incisive, I fear the civilian detachments spend more time peacocking about and vying for authority than thoughtfully discharging their responsibilities. And if our—problem— turns out to be from causes more venal than simple incompetence, the miscreants should go to the Tower.''

''I wish more in government felt as you! Andr—we always felt the gentry back in England were so far removed from the war they had little conception and less interest in the hardships faced by the troops.'' She inclined her head to give him a measuring glance. ''You are different.''

Her approval warmed him to his toes. ''Not the idle, frivolous dandy you first thought me?''

She gave him a severe look and shook a finger. ''Trolling for compliments, my lord?''

He caught the fingertip and kissed it. ''Unashamedly.''

A mischievous sparkle danced in her eyes. ''Then I must confess I'm fair astonished to discover you do a day's work now and again, when you're not sleeping until noon, visiting your tailor, gambling at your club or drink—''

His hand across her lips halted the flow of words. ''Wretch. I should love to lie abed until noon, could I but induce you to dally there.'' He pulled her closer.

She returned his lingering kiss, then gently pushed him away. '''Tis better I go to my work of a morning and let you tend yours. The country—and our army—need prudent and intelligent men. But I must go let Baines in, before the poor man's attitude sours any further.''

Evan glanced at her sharply. ''Has Baines shown you any discourtesy? I'll sack him this instant!''

She turned her face aside, her ivory skin flushing. "No, you mustn't. I only meant that he—he tires himself, I'm sure, carrying out…errands for you. 'Tis only natural he seems sometimes out of sorts."

As she started past, Evan caught her shoulder. "Stay, finish your tea. I'll take care of Baines." He gave her a little push back toward her chair. "And if you receive any less than the most cordial of words from him in future, let me know immediately."

"Oh, but—"

"Stay." Softening the command by tracing his hand in a lascivious pattern over her derriere, he gave her another push. With an exasperated sigh, she returned to sit in her chair behind the desk.

Evan frowned again as he crossed the salesroom. Baines was well paid to wait upon him, whether at his town house in Portman Square or here. The fact that nearly every day the man had to bestir himself to bring to the shop a fresh change of day and evening clothes for his master was irrelevant. If the lackey had any complaints about the change in routine Evan's new lady had caused him, he'd better get over them. Or find a new master.

After delivering a few terse words that had his employee avowing delight in serving his master however his lordship required, Evan dismissed the man. He dropped a kiss on Emily's forehead as he passed her and climbed the narrow stairs to her bedchamber.

Behind the curtained screen in the corner he struggled to pull off his coat. Why, he wondered for perhaps the hundredth time since beginning to spend many of his evenings here, did fashion require garments so tight one truly needed one's valet to get in and out of them? He certainly didn't want the man about, looking down his long nose at this modest dwelling—or its mistress—with that snobbery as engrained in the service community as it was among their employers upstairs. Even were there enough space for Baines to tender him a valet's service, which there wasn't.

Panting, Evan finally succeeded in stripping off the coat. He tossed on a clean shirt and struggled into his evening jacket, pushing hard to force his arm through the narrow opening. Suddenly his hand broke free, hitting the wall beyond with a sharp crack.

Cursing, he rubbed the offended knuckles. This changing alcove was just not broad enough for a man of his size, nor was the ceiling in the small chamber tall enough. Once again he thought longingly of moving Emily out of these cramped quarters and into a house more worthy of her. One spacious enough to accommodate him.

But how to get Emily to agree to it?

He had to smile wryly at his naive initial vision of settling her in an elegant town house with a discreet staff of servants, carriage at the ready to carry them to the Park or shopping or the theater.

Dazzled with euphoria their first heady week together, he'd proposed just such an arrangement—and received a categorical refusal.

The portrait of injured dignity, Emily had drawn herself up and apologized for offering him accommodations so inferior to those to which he was doubtless accustomed. Though he was exceedingly kind to offer an alternative, the little shop was home as well as business, the best she could afford at moment, and she wouldn't dream of leaving. As for carriages, she needed none, being too busy to go traipsing about, and the theater— She'd stopped, blanching.

Cursing himself for stupidity, Evan had watched her almost physically recoil from the vision of herself on display in some theater box, the beau monde leveling their collective quizzing glasses and buzzing about the identity of Cheverley's latest filly. Before he could attempt to recover, she concluded in a cool voice that a businesswoman rose too early to make indulging in theater trips prudent, though of course she appreciated his thoughtful offer.

Icy calm replaced her initial agitation. It had taken two days and every trick and charm he could summon to finally bring back the teasing repartee and passionate fire he adored. Uneasy at the possibility of alienating her again, he'd not ventured such a suggestion since. Nor protested when, to his huge disappointment, she subtly but unmistakably made it clear she would not accompany him anywhere in public.

Without words, he understood, and without words, accepted that his very proper love could not tolerate being pointed out as his mistress.

A few weeks later he'd forgotten the lesson. Strolling down Bond Street, he'd chanced to see an exquisite silver-lace mantilla set on a diamond-studded comb, and thought immediately of Emily. Perhaps the soldier had bought her such a headdress while she followed him through Spain, but none so fine as this.

Evan's smug satisfaction evaporated the instant she unwrapped it and her fine eyes clouded with dismay.

"You shouldn't have," she'd whispered, essaying a smile that didn't quite succeed.

"You don't like it."

"No, 'tis exquisite. It's just...you have given me so much already."

His irrational jealousy flared, and before he could think he retorted, "Did your husband never bring you gifts?"

She bent her head, fingers rewrapping the tissue about the comb as if the sparkling reflection of the diamonds were a live and threatening thing. "That...that was different," she said at last. "Besides, 'twould look rather out-of-place in the shop."

A pointed reminder she'd not wear it out anywhere—not with him.

Her lingering distress over the illicit nature of their affair was the only shadow in what had otherwise been the most glorious eight weeks of his life.

What a wonder she was! From the first day, she'd continued to amaze him with her talent and intelligence, to mesmerize with her depth and complexity. Nor had the pull of her beauty lessened. Indeed, if such a thing were possible, the attraction seemed stronger than ever.

So drawn to her was he that he'd several times forgotten to attend social engagements at which he'd planned to be present. Of late he'd evaded such entertainments, despite his mama's unspoken concern. Except for an occasional lunch or political dinner, he'd ceased to frequent his clubs. What attraction could some dull ton party, exactly like every other he'd attended a score of Seasons and more, exert compared to the rich delight of his world with Emily?

Beautiful, demure, devilish Emily. Even the thought of her made his spirits, and other things, rise.

Still, he concluded as he had to stoop to tie his cravat at the dressing table mirror, the current situation was clearly inadequate. Not only did he need more room to change clothes without bruising his fists and damaging the plaster, it chafed him to see her living in tiny rooms above a shop—she who should be mistress of a stylish town house equipped with a staff to do her bidding and—without complaint or raised eyebrows—his.

True, he admitted, as her business grew she might well one day earn enough to purchase such accommodation herself, but for the immediate future—

The solution that flashed into his head was so brilliant he caught his breath, his hands stilling on the cravat. So brilliant, so perfect was it, even his proper Emily would not be able to find a flaw in his reasoning.

Excitement speeding his fingers, he swiftly finished the knot. There was, he thought with a giddy laugh, more than one way to move a lady.

Emily was at her worktable, absorbed as usual in the completion of a design, when she was seized from behind and two hands clamped over her eyes. After an initial terrified squeak, she caught at the imprisoning wrists. ''Evan, stop! I've work to finish.''

"It will wait, sweeting. I've a surprise to show you that cannot. Come, Francesca will take you."

"But the shop…the customers—"

"Can return later. Francesca has your cloak and reticule. I'll see you shortly." He leaned over to give her a lingering kiss, then released her wrists. "You know the place, Francesca?" He turned to the maid.

"Aye, my lord. Half an hour, we come."

"Good." Grinning like a small boy inordinately pleased with himself, he strode out.

Totally at sea, Emily followed the maid outside and into the waiting hackney. During the drive, she tried to question Francesca, but the maid would only shake her head and smile, her dark eyes dancing with excitement.

Wherever could he be sending her? Panic flared briefly and died. No, if he were thoughtful enough to honor her unspoken preferences and provide a hackney to convey her separately, rather than taking her up in his crested carriage, surely he was not going to meet her in some public place. And she'd detailed in quite plain, emphatic terms that she neither wanted nor would accept gowns, jewels or other frippery gifts. What could it be, then?

The jarvey left the mercantile district near St. James and headed south. At last the conveyance pulled to a stop on a quiet street before a handsome brick town house.

A liveried footman escorted her up the broad front stairs. Francesca trailing close behind, she followed him through the graceful Adam doorway into a marble entry hall. A smiling Evan awaited her.

"Hush, don't say anything yet." He put a finger to her lips. "Let me show you around."

"But I have work and—"

He silenced her with a kiss. "Indulge me for just a little while. Francesca, there's tea in the kitchen."

With a curtsey, the maid left. Clamping her hand on his arm, Evan proceeded to conduct her through the dwelling, from the reception rooms on the first floor to the spacious parlor and dining room and several bed-chambers above.

It was indeed a lovely house. A lovely little love nest in which a rich man could install his mistress. As they went from room to room, her distress and anger grew until, as he grandly opened a door to lead her into a bedchamber so truly lovely she wanted to weep, she could stand it no more.

Jerking free of his arm, she paced to the window, staring sightlessly at the street outside to keep her voice steady. "I do not want it. I will not have it! Did I not tell you so before?"

"But my dear, I thought you were very satisfied with the growth of your millinery business."

"I will not be—" His words finally penetrated her fury, and she stopped short. "My business? What has the shop to do with this?"

"Everything, of course. What did you think I had in mind? Come, sit."

Before she could think to resist, he took her arm and led her to an elegant Georgian settee upholstered in pale jade satin, tugging the bellpull as they passed. His face guileless as an altar boy's, he turned back to her. "Francesca will bring us tea."

Irritation returned in a rush. "I've no need of tea. I have that business you mentioned to run."

"Which is precisely what we need to discuss. Sit, sit!" Placing both hands on her shoulders, he urged her onto the sofa and took a place beside her.

"Have you not several times said how it pained you to design a bonnet, only to see the effect spoiled by having the silly client pair it with a disaster of a dress? That you would like to create the entire ensemble, from bonnet to gown to half-boots?"

"Well, yes, but I don't see—"

"And haven't you believed—and I share that belief emphatically—that such a business would be even more successful than your bonnet shop, for once a lady was seen abroad in an entirely attractive ensemble, other ladies would flock to have their own toilettes redesigned so as not to be outdone?"

"True, but—"

"And haven't you commented that establishing such an enterprise would require more space—fitting rooms, a workroom for seamstresses and their assistants, a storeroom for fabrics and materials, and a larger design office?"

She began to follow his reasoning. "Yes, I've dreamed of such an establishment, and yes, the shop would offer sufficient space were I to convert the rooms I now occupy. But to make such changes requires a great deal more capital than I possess, or hope to possess anytime soon."

There came a knock and a beaming Francesca entered with the tea tray. Torn between excitement, exasperation and a strong urge to weep, Emily fell silent.

He had not brought her to a love nest. He wanted her to move so she might expand her business.

She dared not admit how strongly the elegant room called out to her, surrounded as she was by the plainness of the shop and its workaday neighborhood. How desperately at that moment she wished she could, in truth, afford to rent this beautiful dwelling.

Her eyes making an awed inspection of the room, Francesca handed her a cup. ''Ah, mistress, is it not *belo!* And perfect for you, yes?''

''Yes. No—oh, I suppose.'' After the maid bustled out, Emily turned to Evan. ''I'm flattered you think such an enterprise could succeed. But not by any stretch of my most hopeful imagination could I come up with the funds to make such a move now.''

''Emily, how do you think enterprises expand? And don't give me that 'idle aristocrat' look. I know a thing or two about business, and few who hope to be truly successful wait upon a venture until they have all the funds necessary. With a vision, talent and courage, they convince investors to advance the cash.'' He paused to take a sip. ''Well, my dear, it just so happens that *I* am such an investor. In several different enterprises. And my business sense tells me that investing in the expansion of 'Madame Emilie' would be a wise financial move indeed.''

She stared at him, the teacup halfway to her lips. ''You? An investor?''

"We aristocrats must make our filthy lucre somehow, since we can't dirty our own idle hands at the business. I've contacts with the City that might astonish you." He chuckled. "You *do* look a bit astonished."

He had to prompt her to sip her tea, so furiously was her mind working. It would be a challenge to design an entire ensemble, all of it conceived with taste and discretion. And it truly did offend her eye when she spotted a client wearing one of her creations with some hideous gown or spencer that nullified the pleasing effects of her hard work.

But to have Evan provide the capital? Would that not just obligate her even further to him? And would he truly have thought to invest in the business, were he not only too transparently interested in getting her out of her quarters above the shop?

His finger under her chin startled her and she nearly spilled her half-cold tea. "Well? Despite that forbidding frown, I defy you to find logical fault in the proposal."

She didn't know how to word her objections without offending him. He bristled at any reference to her indebtedness, and she could read in his hopeful, expectant look that he thought he'd finally found a gift she would be delighted to accept.

"For one, I haven't any idea how much capital I would need, nor how I would go about repaying my—investor. And even should I expand the business, I don't see how I could afford a dwelling as lovely as this."

"Let me show you." Swiftly he crossed to a small writing desk and pulled a document from the drawer. "I've had papers drawn up detailing the amount of the investment, the security involved and the way profit will be paid out. The rental on this town house is figured in with the whole. You can have my lawyer verify it.''

Uncertain, she rose and paced the chamber, stopping before the window. Without conscious thought her fingers reached to stroke the soft velvet of the deep blue drapes. ''It doesn't seem right, somehow, that you—invest in my business. Not when we are—when I...'' Her words trailed off and she flushed.

''As a prudent investor, I choose projects that appear most likely to turn a profit. Why should I refrain from funding you just because we happen to share a more personal relationship? I assure you, both your rights as owner and mine as investor are fully protected in the covenants.''

While mulling that over, she suddenly grew conscious of the softness of the drapery under her stroking fingers. A disconcerting suspicion took form.

She leveled a penetrating look. ''Do rented London dwellings always come so tastefully furnished?''

He shrugged. ''Generally, houses can be let with or without furnishings.''

His air of innocence didn't convince her. ''Velvet drapes, inlaid chairs, satin-striped sofas in the latest mode—I doubt many owners leave such possessions in a house to let. *Did* they come with the house?''

He studied the sleeve of his jacket, picking at some invisible speck of lint. ''I may have given the agent some direction as to what sorts of furnishings would be required.''

"'Some' direction?" She scanned the room again, this time noting in greater detail the arrangement of the furnishings: the wing chair by the hearth with a small portable desk on the table adjacent to the window, just where she used to place hers in various quarters throughout Spain. And the colors—Mediterranean blue, jade, ivory, sunset rose—all her favorites. Her suspicions hardening, she turned back to him. "Did Francesca perchance play a part in those 'directions?'"

"Well, yes, I did consult her. After confiding a bit of my scheme to her, I had her view several houses that were coming available, asking her to choose the one she felt you would like the best, and advise me on the furnishing of it. It does please you?"

She refused to be distracted. "You were so sure you could induce me to agree that you drew my servant into collusion, all without ever consulting *my* wishes?"

"You make it sound as if I were hatching some evil plot," he protested with a smile.

"And if I do not wish to proceed? What will you do about this fine house and its pretty furnishings?" she demanded, growing angrier by the minute. First, to set off on this grand design without even a pretense of consulting her—then to go behind her back and involve Francesca in it! Of all the dictatorial, managing—

His smile faded as he studied her stormy face. "Do you not like it?"

"Like?" she sputtered. "Of course I like it. 'Tis beautiful, as you well know. It's just—"

He strode over to grasp her hand. "I know, Emily! You'll say I was hasty, and presumptuous to arrange all this, even borrow Francesca, without asking you. But 'tis so financially sound and logical a move, one you yourself have several times indicated you wished to make, I did feel confident in proceeding. You work so hard already, I wished to spare you time and trouble. And give you a surprise I hoped would be pleasing. I never meant to—dictate—your actions. If I have offended, I'm sorry.''

Her rampaging anger halted. She *had* expressed the desire to expand her business in just such a fashion. And were she to act on that vision, having this already set up would save her untold hours with estate agents and warehousemen.

She studied his face, which did indeed look sincerely apologetic. If she could not help resenting his highhandedness in executing it all without her consent, she must also acknowledge the loving care he'd expended in trying to assist and please her. A gift perhaps more valuable even than the house itself.

''Once again, you are too kind,'' she said at last.

''Then you will accept the challenge? Begin your business expansion immediately?''

He could not have chosen better words to persuade her. Phrased solely in practical investment terms, she could not, as he had predicted, logically refuse what made such perfect business sense.

''I shall have to consult your lawyer, as you invited. But if the numbers seem in order and I feel certain I can afford to proceed now, then I suppose I must go forward.''

He squeezed her hand. ''You told me once you were pleased to be valued for what you've accomplished.

That's all I was trying to do. In addition to earning my-self a profit, of course,'' he added with a grin. "By all means visit the lawyer, ask your questions, then decide." He brought her fingers to his lips. "More than anything, I want you to be happy."

The deep emotion in his voice was unmistakable, and again, in spite of the caution she tried to impose over her feelings, she was moved. Unable to frame an answer, she allowed him to pull her into his arms.

"I would give you the moon, you know, if you'd only allow it," he said against her hair. "But this is no gift— you've earned it through your own efforts. Don't turn it down solely because 'tis my impetus that makes it happen."

A part of her gratefully accepted his assistance—but another part still resisted. Too often had she been the pawn of controlling men. But he was acting as an inves-tor only, he said. The expansion would be based on a legal document that would protect them both. And the final decision remained hers.

Moving her to arm's length, he smiled, enthusiasm glowing in his face. "I've had all the figures checked and rechecked. As a business decision, you won't regret it. And speaking of business, Madame, your primary stockholder thinks you'd best get back and tend to it. I expect a handsome return on my investment."

He began to walk her across to the door, but before he opened it, she stayed his hand. "Thank you, Evan. For believing in me." And leaned up to kiss him.

It was long, sweet, gentle. As her lips left his and she stepped away, he caught her chin and tilted her face back up, gazing at her with an expression so infinitely tender her breath caught in her throat.

He parted his lips as if to say something, hesitated, then whispered, ''My Emily.''

Whistling, Evan stowed a few more items into the armoire in the bedchamber adjoining Emily's. He surveyed the handsome room, from the brocade hangings to the Chippendale sofa and armchairs, to the imposing canopied bed, and smiled. Even the starchy Baines couldn't fault this dwelling.

Pride swelled in Evan's chest as he recalled Emily quietly assuming command of the small staff Francesca had assembled. 'Twas not the surface courtesy of an employee to his employer they'd extended her; rather, from the very proper butler down to the youngest housemaid, they recognized born-in-the-bone Quality just as he had, and accorded her the deference she deserved.

Yes, the move had been a brilliant idea. Although she'd permitted him to come and go at the shop as he wished, the necessities of running a business had limited his lingering. There'd be no such impediments here.

In fact, were he to install a few volumes from his library in the small study opposite, he could use their town house as a sort of second office. 'Twas closer to Horse Guards, and with Emily gone during the day, 'twould be quieter and less subject to interruption than his own home. An excellent notion, he concluded.

As he placed the last shirt in the cupboard, some of his euphoria dimmed. Emily had greeted his entrance into her fashionable new bedchamber last night with all the warmth he could have wished, and only a slight raise of her eyebrows indicated her surprise when, for the first time in their relationship, he'd joined her for breakfast this morning. Still, he was uncertain how welcome he would be to run tame in the new home into which he'd maneuvered her.

Which was why he'd waited until she departed for work—in the small gig he'd cleverly made sure was part of the bargain—to have Baines bring a week's supply of his things.

It wasn't as if he were taking up residence, after all. It was just so much more—practical to have some necessities here. And 'twas natural for best friends to wish to spend as much time together as possible. She would acknowledge the truth of that, surely.

He dismissed a niggle of unease. If only she weren't so maddeningly independent. He didn't wish her to think he was trying to crowd or dictate to her.

He pulled the last item out of the portmanteau and grinned. Even his prickly, independent Emily couldn't object to a housewarming box of Gunter's finest comfits. Besides, he'd volunteer to eat most of them.

After a moment's reflection, he decided to tuck the box among her lingerie. Let it be a sweet surprise to remind her of him when she dressed next morning.

He walked to her wardrobe and reached in the drawer to push aside the delicate underthings, his hand stilling as the delicious vision of Emily wearing these pale whispers of silk and lace flamed in his mind. That incredible, unquenchable desire only she could evoke suffused him.

It being hours before he could expect to turn that vision into reality, he'd best depart. A bit more forcefully than necessary, he thrust the box into a corner.

A sharp clink sounded from the lingerie-strewn recesses. Drat, had he shattered some favorite keepsake? Impatiently he pawed aside the underthings until something glinted up at him.

The soldier's miniature.

His breath stopped, then whooshed out. Teeth clenching, he slammed the drawer shut.

Chapter Seven

Evan paused on the threshold at White's. 'Twas time for luncheon, and a snug meal might settle his unease.

That Emily still retained her husband's miniature shouldn't be upsetting. One did not just—dismiss such deep attachments. No, he reassured himself, a person of sensibility did not forget so near a relation after the passage of a few paltry years.

He saw Brent Blakesly by the fireplace and his spirits lightened. Chatting with Brent over good food and better wine would quell this restlessness. Smiling, he beckoned.

''Ev?'' Brent extracted his quizzing glass and made a great show of inspecting him as he walked over. ''Well met, my friend!'' Grinning, he held out a hand. ''Haven't seen you in so long, thought you must have turned monk or gone off on some secret mission.''

Evan felt a flicker of annoyance. ''Fustian. I've been—'' he waved a hand ''—working a great deal, I suppose. Besides, one social function seems very like the next.''

''Unchivalrous, but alas, true.'' Brent laughed and took his elbow. ''Come, while we find something to tempt your jaded palate, you can tell me what you've been up to.''

At Evan's noncommittal mumble, Brent looked over. ''Should I not ask?'' He surveyed Evan's face. ''Ah, the affair progresses?''

Despite his current unease, Evan couldn't hold back a smile. ''Wonderfully.''

''You've been off to the country, then.''

''Country?'' Puzzled, Evan frowned at him.

''Haven't you been down to Wimberley to fetch Andrea? I thought—your mama said at the Cunninghams' dinner last month she expected you to do so momentarily.''

An unpleasant pang struck him. Vaguely he remembered his mother pressing him about the matter, but he'd been so...preoccupied of late, he'd scarcely noted the weeks passing. In truth, he realized with a jolt, the Season *would* start soon.

''You are bringing her to London?'' Brent asked.

''Yes, of course. Before he joined the army I promised Richard I'd take care of his sister, didn't I? Besides, it's time she stopped hiding herself away.''

''Indeed. She has such a sunny disposition and charming manners, after a while one scarcely notices the limp.''

''I'll count on you to help me convince her of that.''

''Delighted. When *do* you leave for Wimberley, then?''

Damn and blast. He'd have to move quickly if he meant to give Andrea time to order up gowns and such. He recalled recently discharging a number of bills for his sister Clare, who was also making her come-out.

But how to tell Emily he must leave, and why?

"Zeus, what a frown! Did I say something wrong?" Brent's question recalled him.

"Not at all. Thank you for the reminder. I've been...neglectful. I shall have to depart within the week, I suppose."

Brent laughed. "Now, that's a new one! 'Organized Evan' neglecting something?" As comprehension grew, his grin faded. "Ah. The, um, other lady still occupies you?"

Evan made a noncommittal noise and glanced away.

"And that's who—where you've been hiding away these two months," Brent said quietly, almost to himself. "Thunder and turf, Ev, in all the time I've known you..." An expression akin to shock illumined his face, and the sentence trailed off. "That does make things a bit...sticky."

"Nonsense," Evan replied, more sharply than intended. "There's no connection. Mama will shepherd Andrea and Clare through their debut. I'll merely be called upon to escort them to some very dull parties."

"Naturally," Brent agreed a little too heartily. "Best to have your fill of—other diversions before thinking of getting leg-shackled. Besides, Andrea's known you since the cradle. None of that white-knight, fair-damsel rubbish females seem so fond of. Doubtless she'll turn up some other chap to marry."

Evan found he had nothing to say. Suddenly the idea of a cozy meal, Brent nattering on about matters he'd prefer not to consider at the moment, seemed totally unappealing. "Don't suppose I have time for lunch after all. Capital to see you, Brent."

He turned to leave. Brent put a hand on his arm. "Sorry, Ev. Didn't mean to meddle in your business."

Evan barely refrained from shaking off Brent's hand. "No apologies necessary. Sorry, but I really must go."

"Meet me for dinner later?" At Evan's negative shake of the head, Brent finally withdrew his hand. "Soon, then. I've missed your company."

"Soon," Evan promised, burning to make his escape.

Brent's gray eyes swept Evan's face, concern in their depths. "Take care, old friend."

Evan gave him the edge of a smile and bowed. He felt Brent's gaze follow him all the way to the exit.

Bending over the book, Evan strove to concentrate on the ledger entries. A kaleidoscope of images kept distracting him. Andrea at Wimberley last Michaelmas saying she trusted him to advise her during Richard's absence. Brent in the Member's Room of Whites, shock in his eyes. The devil-may-care grin of a red-coated soldier.

He gritted his teeth at that last. Emily had adored her late husband. Exactly what did she feel for *him?* He pushed the question aside.

He must honor his pledge to Richard and coax Andrea to town for the Season she'd been avoiding. She could find no reasonable objections this year: there'd be his sister and her friends to chatter with, his mama to support her, and himself to oversee and protect them.

Though he would of course fulfill his vow, he had no intention of abandoning Emily. Juggling his personal and family priorities would take a dab of scheduling, but he was a master at that. He meant to enjoy the incredible, unbelievable gift of Emily's body and friendship for however long their affair lasted.

As for Season's end, much could happen in a few months. His fevered passion for Emily Spenser could burn itself out—passion had always done so before. Or, as Brent predicted, some discerning gentleman could look past Andrea's limp to discover the sweet, gentle lady beneath. Some *other* discerning gentleman.

And if not? *You can always marry me, Andy.*

An unpleasant mix of anxiety and foreboding churned in his gut at the memory.

Resolutely he ignored it. His course of action was un-equivocal: he must sponsor Andrea and he must see Emily. There being nothing else he could do to affect it, he'd not spoil the present worrying over the future. Doubtless everything would work out.

First, he needed to fetch Andrea, and soon. How best to break the news?

This afternoon was Emily's last in the salesroom, he recalled. Upon the morrow, she would retreat to her de-sign office in the converted quarters upstairs while her newly hired staff of seamstresses began to turn her sketches into the first complete "Madame Emilie" toi-lettes.

He should bring flowers to celebrate the occasion. Yes, and set Francesca fixing a special dinner. Afterward, when they were both relaxed and replete, he'd inform Emily of the upcoming trip. So calm and independent was she, surely she'd not be upset at his leaving to fulfill a…family obligation. In any event, he'd be back within a few days.

The idea of being away from her even that long brought an unexpected tightness to his chest.

Since go he must, he'd best advance his business at the office. Dismissing a lingering unease, he set to work.

Several hours later, bouquet in hand, he quietly entered the shop. Emily stood at the far corner fitting a bonnet on a customer. As always, the sight of her warmed and soothed him. Not wishing to interrupt, he settled against the wall to wait.

The entry bell tinkled behind him, and a young, smartly dressed matron entered. He watched her idly, the plume on her hat nodding at the corner of his vision as she studied the bonnets on display.

A bobbing jerk of the feather caught his attention even as she shrieked and clasped a hand to her chest.

"Auriana!" the woman cried in accents of delight. "My dear Auriana, it *is* you!"

It appeared she would run Emily over in her eagerness to reach the customer to whom her remarks must be addressed. Before he could pull her out of the impetuous matron's path, Emily turned to the woman and, to his astonishment, extended her hands in a welcoming gesture.

"Dearest Cecelia," Emily said as the woman fell into her embrace. "How wonderful to see you again."

Halted in midstride, he stood immobile as the newcomer pushed Emily to arm's length and inspected her avidly.

"You're as lovely as ever, I see! And how wonderful it *is* to see you, Auriana! When you left us to take Andrew away we lost all contact—no one in the regiment seemed to know where you'd gone—oh, and we were so saddened to hear..." She paused to take a breath, swallowing hard. "Well, you know. Roger has never quite gotten over it. Wherever did you go to after—but, no matter! Now that I've found you, you must come have tea and tell me all your news!"

Before Emily could reply, the customer, who had been regarding Emily and the newcomer with an air of increasing indignation, cleared her throat loudly. "Madame Emilie, however delightful it may be to greet your— acquaintances, I must insist you finish with me first. I have several calls to make this afternoon and cannot wait upon your chatter."

For a moment Emily stood very still, while the newcomer looked from her to the client and back, brow knit in evident confusion. Gently Emily disengaged her fingers from her old friend's grip.

Then, apparently for the first time, she noticed Evan standing just inside the entry. A slight flush mounted her high cheekbones.

He couldn't seem to get words of greeting past the constriction in his throat. Quickly her gaze returned to the newcomer.

"I should love to chat later, Cecelia. Will you not give Francesca your direction so I may call? I'm afraid now I...I must tend to business."

The matron gaped at her. "You—Madame Em—? Oh!" Evidently piecing together the facts, the friend blushed as well. "Yes, you must continue with your w-work. I'll...I'll just speak with Francesca."

The maid appeared at those words, as if she had been lurking near the doorway. Murmuring in Portuguese, she beckoned to the matron. With a final, wondering glance at Emily, the newcomer followed Francesca out.

Head held high, Emily walked back to the client. "Now, Lady Baxter, are these ribbons satisfactory?"

Perhaps it was the shock of seeing her embraced by a stranger calling her a name he'd never heard, or the outrage of Lady Baxter—herself offspring of a merchant who had purchased a titled husband for his daughter—trying to put Emily in her place, but suddenly Evan was blazingly angry.

"Madame Emilie." He strode over and swept her a deep bow. "My mother sends her compliments and wishes to express her delight with your latest creation."

Instantly the client's aggrieved expression turned appeasing. "Lord Cheverley, such an honor!"

Evan inclined his head briefly. "Lady Baxter."

"I'll be with you in a moment, my lord," Emily said, avoiding his glance.

"Silly creature, you mustn't keep Lord Cheverley waiting!" Turning her back on Emily, the client smiled up at Evan. "Pray, do discharge your business first, my lord. I'm in no hurry, none at all!"

"Kind of you, ma'am." Evan accorded Lady Baxter another infinitesimal nod. "But I wouldn't dream of disrupting the work of such an artist as Madame Emilie. I'm quite content to wait. Please, Madame, do proceed."

"As you wish, my lord." Still not meeting his glance, Emily curtseyed.

"I'll wait in your office, if I may." At Emily's murmur of acquiescence, Evan gave her another elaborate bow. "And Lady Baxter." Acknowledging the mushroom's daughter with so insultingly brief a glance the woman's cheeks reddened, he strode from the room.

Still trembling in the wake of strong emotion, he halted by the desk. Then it occurred to him he should continue to the kitchen and intercept Emily's caller. The woman had already yielded up the name of Emily's late husband—information the widow herself had not let slip in all their months together. Mayhap the friend could tell him more.

Before he could move, the bang of the kitchen's back door informed him of the guest's probable departure. Francesca reentered the office alone.

"Tea, my lord?"

"Yes, please." The maid bobbed a curtsey and withdrew as, frustrated, he dropped into the chair behind the desk.

Auriana. The lovely name echoed in his head. Was the woman who so captivated him, his Emily, really named Auriana? If so, how could she not have confided to him so basic a fact as her true name? It recurred to him more disturbingly than ever how little he knew about her. Not her family name, nor her father's profession, nor who or where she had been before becoming an army bride.

Tea to soothe his rattled nerves would be most welcome. Even more welcome would be some answers.

He listened impatiently for the momentarily cowed Lady Baxter to finally take her leave. Even after the tinkle of the shop bell heralding her departure, Emily did not join him. He was about to fetch her when at last, with lowered head, she entered the office.

A few paces from the desk she stopped and looked at him, scanning his face as if to judge his mood. What she saw caused her lashes to flutter down, once more masking her violet eyes. With a deep sigh she walked to the workbench and carefully set Lady Baxter's unfinished hat on the stand. Her fingers were trembling.

"Is Francesca bringing tea?" she asked at last, her back to him.

He could stand it no longer—the need to touch her, to physically snatch her back from another life in which he had played no part, impelled him out of the chair.

With one stride he reached her. "Come, sit. You must be tired." She murmured but did not resist as he urged her to the chair, then seated himself on the desk beside it.

For a few moments after Francesca returned with tea they occupied themselves with that small ritual. Then silence fell once more.

Uncertain how to break it without shouting out the questions clamoring in his head, he turned instead to the half-forgotten bouquet. "I—I brought you something."

He held out the flowers. The action of taking them compelled her to glance up. Her eyes seemed sad, shadowed, he thought with a stab of concern.

"They're beautiful," she murmured. "You shouldn't spoil me so."

"Yes, you're such a greedy, mercenary lady, I might encourage you to extravagant demands—market vegetables, perhaps, or a side of beef." She gave his witticism a brief smile, but did not reply. Forging on, he continued, "I thought the occasion—the retirement of Madame Emilie from the showroom—merited some small celebration."

She bent her head to inhale the sweet violets' scent. Still she said nothing.

He could refrain no longer. "'Auriana'—it's lovely. And it suits you."

Pain flitted briefly across her face. "'Twas like a voice from another life, hearing it. Seeing Cecelia. I've not encountered anyone from my...my days as a military bride since I..." Her words trailed off.

Finally she looked squarely at him. The distress he saw in her face muted the harsh edge of his affront. Instinctively he gathered her into his arms.

For a long moment she rested against his shoulder. Her eyes were moist as she pulled away.

"When my husband died, I had to choose. To turn my back forever on who—what I had been, accept the opportunity offered me and survive, or cling to my pretensions and starve. I chose survival. I thought a new livelihood merited a new name, so I changed mine. Though Emily is my real name, too," she added with a touch of defensiveness. "I was christened 'Auriana Emilie,' after a French relative."

She had not been concealing her past. She had simply made a clean break with a life she could no longer support, that was all. The explanation poured soothing balm over his chafed emotions.

"Will you call on your friend?"

"Yes, I shall call, though I doubt she'll receive me." She took a deep breath. "I am 'Madame Emilie, Shopkeeper' now, no longer the wife of a fellow officer."

The idea of her disdained by one to whom she had once been an equal cut deep. "You are as worthy, nay, worthier than she," he said angrily. "A lesser woman— any other woman—would have expired in Spain, destitute and forgotten. You not only survived, you are flourishing."

"At a cost."

The words were a whisper. And so indisputable, he had no reply to soften the harsh truth of them, fervently as he wished to do so. He drew her closer, offering the warmth and strength of his arms, the only comfort he could give that would not be a lie.

Much later, after they'd shared wine and one of Francesca's flavorful paellas, Emily seemed recovered. When she asked whether he might advise her on some alterations the workmen at the shop were to begin in a few days, he recognized a perfect opportunity to impart his news.

Taking a deep breath, he tried to keep his voice light. "I'm afraid I must leave London the end of the week. Not for long, sweeting."

Did the startled glance she fixed on him contain disappointment? He hoped so, but her cool voice gave no clue. "I see. That mysterious business you do not discuss, I expect. Shall I not see you again before then? I must wish you a good journey.''

Not sure whether to be cheered or piqued by her calm, he continued, ''I shall be able to join you every night before I go, but my evenings once I return will be more...occupied. My sister embarks on her debut, you know.''

''Yes. You must escort her, of course.''

He grimaced. ''I'm afraid so, though I'd rather sit through a hundred dull political dinners than dance a single evening at Almack's.''

He opened his lips to continue, then paused. Need he tell her about Andrea? After all, as he'd remarked to Brent, the two were entirely unconnected, occupants of different worlds whose paths he could insure would never cross. Besides, if he tried to explain, she might misinterpret his care of Andrea, leap to erroneous conclusions—

''Are you sure you will not be—too busy?'' Her question recaptured his attention. ''I should not wish to intrude upon your family duties. I expect I've pulled you away all too often already. Perhaps it would be best if we—''

''No!'' he cried, alarm streaking through him. ''No,'' he repeated more calmly, wiping suddenly sweating palms on his trousers. ''My time will be more encumbered, but not impossibly so. I've no intention of sacrificing the company of my...dear friends, just to support my sister's debut.''

''You are sure?'' she asked quietly.

"Definitely. Now, could you not have the workmen delay? I should return within four days at most. What alterations are they to make?"

As he steered her conversation back to the shop, he damped down the panic that had seized him at her inference of curtailing—or even more unthinkable, ending—their liaison. Later, perhaps. But now? Absolutely *not!*

Still shaken, craving the reassurance of her closeness, he drew her into his arms. "Enough shop talk," he murmured against her forehead, then kissed her. Driven by urgent need too complex to explain, he deepened the kiss, hungry, seeking. Her immediate flame of response reassured and steadied him.

He could do nothing to settle the uncertainty of the future, but the present belonged to them. He would make the very most of it. Gathering her to his chest, kissing her still, he carried her up the stairs.

A few days later, Emily descended from her bedchamber to the dining room. Evan having left on his trip, she was experiencing the now unusual sensation of breaking her fast alone.

He'd already departed when she returned home two nights ago. Dinner had become a dull affair without his amusing conversation, and the evening duller still.

Was it just three months she had known him? Recalling his strong arm around her, his lazy grin, she had to smile. He'd added such a dimension of enjoyment to her hitherto humdrum existence she could almost not remember how she had gone through her days without him.

Or her nights. She'd slept fitfully, missing the warmth of him beside her, missing the lulling aftermath of passion when she sank, sated, to sleep on his shoulder.

Without her quite knowing how, they had become close friends. To her initial surprise she'd discovered they enjoyed many of the same things, from strong tea to Restoration poets to chess. Moreover, a wordless, intuitive communion seemed to link them. Often one knew the other's thoughts before they were uttered, layering over the fiery fusion of passion a comforting bond of camaraderie. Having Evan with whom to ponder, laugh over and puzzle out the events of the day enriched even the most commonplace happenings. As with Andrew.

That casual conclusion stabbed at her breast, driving the complacent smile from her face. How could she have compared this…illicit, temporary arrangement with what she'd shared with Andrew?

Good that Evan had gone away, if she were at the point of drawing similarities that would never be. Even better that he'd evidently not be visiting so often when he did return. Their end was inevitable. Best that she begin sooner rather than later to wean herself from the too-tempting weakness of depending upon him.

Somehow that pragmatic conclusion stole away her joy in the fresh new morning.

Francesca, entering with her tea, caught her expression and frowned. "By the saints, 'tis pining for his lordship you be, and no wonder. But he'll not stay away long, *querida.* Such a sigh as he rode off, like 'twas his soul he was leaving. And his contentment too, eh?" She gave Emily a knowing wink.

Still unsettled, Emily replied more sharply than she intended. "Rubbish. We're neither of us pining. I've my shop to manage and he has business to tend."

Francesca shrugged, clearly undaunted. "Business or no, he will not tarry. For you he has the *amor grande*. 'Tis in his eyes, that look."

Was the earl developing a tendre for her? A thrill darted through her before she angrily squelched that improbable, and ultimately pointless, speculation.

"Ah, you say nothing." Francesca smiled. "But your eyes, too, they tell me of—"

"Hush, Francesca! You talk nonsense."

"Ah, soft, *querida*. There's no shame in opening your heart to another. 'Tis time and more you should do so."

Alarmed at the very thought, she shook her head vehemently. "Even were I ready for such a bond—which I assure you I am not!—'twould be the height of folly to form an attachment to Lord Cheverley. I will never be more to him than his..." Unable to voice the word, she fell silent.

"Me, I think you wrong. Many men have I seen in our travels, mistress, *soldados*, townsmen, great lords. He does not look at you as a man looks at his woman, with lust. No, there is a tenderness, here." She tapped her eye. "Me, I think in a very little, he may claim you for his lady wife."

His wife. A sizzle of excitement seared her at the vision of walking proudly, openly at his side. Sober reality dashed that happy vista.

"Don't be daft, Francesca!" she cried, angrier still at herself for having even momentarily entertained so preposterous a notion. ''The great Earl of Cheverley offer marriage to a shopkeeper? No imaginable quantity of tenderness in his eyes—if such in fact exists, which I take leave to doubt—could ever blind him to the impossibility of such a match!''

''How impossible? Where could he find another with beauty like yours? Fine words—do they not flow sweetly from your tongue like wild honey? Graceful you are as a *cavalo* galloping the *plain,* and—''

''Enough!'' Putting her fingers to the maid's lips, Emily had to giggle, the absurdity of the whole idea easing her agitation. ''Lest, like Narcissus, I fall in love with this paragon myself.''

Brushing Emily's hand aside, Francesca smiled back. ''You make the joke, but 'twill happen. I feel it.''

Emily's humor evaporated. ''No, 'twill not. Ah, Francesca, you are not English, how can I make you understand? Even were I to possess every charm you describe and more, 'twould never erase the taint of the shop. To marry so far beneath him—and despite your 'feelings,' he's given no sign of entertaining such a notion— would mean scandal and ruin for his family. Be assured it will *not* happen.''

Francesca patted her hand. ''And if there were a child? That would change this business of 'matches,' no? The great lord would surely—''

''Don't even think it!'' Too agitated to remain still, she jumped up and began pacing. ''We've been careful, oh so careful. Lord Cheverley cannot marry me and I would rather die than curse a babe with the shame of bastardy.''

An equally humiliating thought brought her to a halt. She turned to point a warning finger at Francesca. "Don't you dare hint of marriage to him! I'll—I'll ship you back to Portugal!"

Francesca held her ground. "You are not so poorly born, eh? Such a match could happen, if you but tell him—"

"We tell him nothing!" Truly alarmed now, Emily seized Francesca's arm with both hands. "You mustn't tell him anything, ever, do you understand? What if he took it in his head to—intervene? We could lose everything! How could you even dream of risking all we hold most dear?"

The very possibility was so awful, so reminiscent of her worst nightmares, that she tasted fear raw and bitter on her tongue.

After the episode at her shop, she'd briefly considered revealing more of her circumstances to the Earl. And swiftly concluded to do so would be dangerously unwise. 'Twas no less so now. She fought panic, a familiar sick, helpless feeling in her gut. Tears welled in her eyes.

"Hush now, *querida!*" Francesca rubbed the whitened knuckles of the hands clutched on her arm. "I am not *louco,* no? Never would I put you or your sweet son at risk!"

Emily took a trembling breath. "No. No, of course you wouldn't. But Lord Cheverley is very clever. If you drop a hint here, a name there, he will shortly manage to puzzle out the whole. So you must say nothing at all. Absolutely nothing, Francesca! Promise me."

The maid sighed. ''Wrong I think it, for truly he is so clever he must discover it in the end, no? But you've worries enough, *querida.* I'll not add to them.'' Making the sign of the cross over her breast, she kissed her raised fingers. *''Promessa.''*

So, too, did Emily fear that sooner or later Evan would discover the full truth of her circumstances. Uneasily she recalled his look of hurt, almost outrage, upon hearing her real name. Well, she'd deal with that eventuality if and when it occurred.

She was about to return to her tea when a commotion in the hallway drew her attention. ''My word, such a racket. Francesca, will you—''

''Yes, mistress, I go.''

Emily had taken one sip when Francesca's gasped *''Mãe de Deus!''* propelled her out of her chair.

''What is it, Francesca? Is someone—''

The spectacle that greeted her froze the rest of the sentence on her lips.

In the early light of dawn, Evan guided his horse into the quiet street before Emily's house. He'd not expected to return so quickly, but Andrea's resistance crumbled after he invoked the magic of Richard's name. As a Season required a whole new wardrobe, little time was lost packing. They'd traveled swiftly, reaching London last evening.

After dropping off his baggage and seeing Andrea settled with his mama and sister, he'd spent most of the night at Horse Guards reading supply dossiers. He really should go home and sleep, but a need stronger than fatigue pulled him to see Emily.

Probably she was awake, but if not, he could slip into bed and stroke her to consciousness. His body responded eagerly to the thought.

Wrapped in that pleasant imagining as he swung out of the saddle, he scarcely noted the yawning housemaid shaking out a feather duster, the hawkers calling out fresh milk and fish, the passing rumble of a heavily laden farm-cart. Then a man stepped under the shadow of Emily's portico—a caller, it appeared.

Curious, Evan looped the reins on a post and approached. An elderly gentleman in a cleric's collar glanced back at him inquiringly. From behind the pastor a darker head leaned out, and he saw—

That face! The face in the miniature—vivid green eyes under dark, arching brows, a laughing curl of lip... A bolt of shock impaled Evan to the step, hand clutched on the railing, thought, breathing, motion all suspended.

Until he realized the figure beyond the cleric was not an apparition, not a tall, broad-shouldered, red-coated man, but a mere boy in nankeens and cap. A lad with the soldier's face. Unmistakably his son.

Emily's son.

For a moment Evan's ears buzzed and he had to gasp to pull air into lungs.

As if from far away, he saw the butler open the door and beckon, heard the cleric speak.

"Sir! Sir, are you quite all right? Drew, help me assist the gentleman inside."

Numbly he stared at the boy's small hand on his sleeve. His feet seemed to be functioning, for with the cleric on one side, the child on the other, he was progressing through the doorway and into the hall beyond.

With detachment he noted the butler's lips moving, the sharp gesture of an order being given, a scurrying housemaid. And the boy gazing up at him, the laughing look replaced by a frown.

His face. That face.

Evan turned away from it to see Francesca, and motionless beyond her, Emily.

For a moment they simply stared at each other.

Chapter Eight

"Mama, what a lovely house! I'm so glad you let us visit!" The lad dropped his arm and scampered over to throw himself at Emily. She bent and hugged him close, nuzzling her cheek against his dark hair.

Holding him to her side, she straightened and looked back at Evan, her face expressionless. "I see you have met my son. And this learned gentleman is his tutor, Father Edmund. May I present to you both the Earl of Cheverley. Drew, make your bow."

"Honored," the cleric murmured, the child echoing an "Honored to meet you, your lordship," and offering a very proper bow. Numbly Evan nodded in acknowledgement.

The pastor looked uneasily from Evan to Emily and back. "Is this time inconvenient, Mrs. Spenser?"

She hesitated but an instant. "Not at all, Father. I am happy to welcome you to *my home.*" She stressed the last words slightly. "Francesca, will you take them in for tea? I had Cook prepare fresh currant cake especially for your visit. I'll join you shortly."

"Of course, Mistress. *Senhor?*"

133

"Ama!" the lad cried, squirming out from under Emily's arm and running to Francesca. She caught him, swung him high and, gesturing at the pastor to precede them, bore him off. Arm in arm the two retreated down the hallway, exchanging a torrent of unintelligible words Evan concluded must be Portuguese.

Silently Emily turned and walked into the front parlor. Silently Evan followed, went to the sideboard and poured himself a brandy.

She waited as he took a swallow. "It *is* my house?"

"Your—of course it is!" Slamming down the glass, he advanced on her, urged her none too gently to a seat on the sofa, then flung himself down beside her. She slid away, crossing her arms as if armoring herself against him.

The shock was still so great, he hadn't begun to sort out his whirling emotions. "Yes, it's your home. You may invite whomever you choose. But why, Emily? Why did you not tell me you have a s-son?" He stuttered over the word.

His son, his mind screamed. *Your beloved husband's son, your cherished lover's son.* A scouring jealousy spiraled up, choking him so he could scarcely speak.

"I thought we were friends, intimate friends," he said quietly. "I thought we knew each other. At least, you know almost everything about me. Not mentioning your change of name, that I can understand perhaps. A trifle. But a son? How could you have thought I'd be uninterested in that small detail? Did you think even knowing about me—us—would corrupt him?"

"Not, it's not that!" she cried. "It's…more compli-cated."

"I would be most appreciative, then, if you would trouble to explain to me the complications."

She sighed heavily. Clasping her hands together, she began in a low voice. "Most of it you know. That I ran away to marry, that the families disapproved. That my father-in-law would not even bestir himself to visit his dying son. When I heard nothing from him then, I thought our connection at an end."

Her face averted, her eyes gazing trancelike into the distance, she continued, "So I was surprised when, several months after Andrew's p-passing, I receive a message from him. 'Send me the brat,' it said. I realized he saw Andrew's death as an opportunity to control his grandson as he had never controlled his son."

She turned to Evan, passionate now as she had been ice before. "The stories my husband told of his boyhood! The floggings, the deliberate cruelty alternating with in-difference. Oh, Andrew laughed with me about it, claimed his papa no longer had any power over him. But I saw his face after he broke the news that he was mar-rying me. In words that must have been the most wound-ing imaginable, his papa absolutely forbade it. I'll never forget how bleak, how…devastated he was. I knew, whatever I must do to avoid it, I could never let that man have our son."

She jumped up, paced the room. "I decided to quickly finish the portrait I was working on and slip away. My patron, Don Alvarez, may the Lord bless him, found me another commission, gave us secret transport and pledged to swear ignorance of our whereabouts to the agents I knew my father-in-law would dispatch when I did not answer his summons. Dispatch them he did, but as they did not speak the language, and friends abetted me, they haven't been able to catch us. Yet.''

The fire seemed to leave her; her shoulders slumped and she exhaled a long sighing breath. ''Eventually I must give him up. When his studies with Father Edmund are complete, when he goes to Oxford, I can no longer keep him hidden. And his grandfather will claim him.''

Evan tried to work through his roiling emotions, tried to focus on facts. ''You think his grandfather will still wish to acknowledge him?''

She looked back at him then. Tears had gathered at the corners of her eyes; one large droplet spilled down her cheek as she turned. ''My Drew bears his name. He's too proud not to acknowledge him.'' Her chin jutted up, her jaw clenched, and she gazed squarely at Evan with the defiance he imagined she would show her absent father-in-law. ''But until then, Drew will grow up surrounded by affection, knowing I am proud of him. Knowing he is loved.''

The fact of her abandoned in Spain, near to starving, her father-in-law knowing of her plight but refusing to assist, suddenly caught in his mind. And flamed instantly to outrage.

''If your boy is some aristocrat's grandson, he should be living in wealth and comfort. As should his mother! Regardless of your father-in-law's opinion of you, if you were his son's legal wife it is only his duty to care and provide for you both. As he should have from the moment your husband died!''

She smiled, a bitter twist of lip. ''No notion of 'duty' has ever intruded between *him* and doing exactly what he wishes. Besides, I think I should rather starve than live as *his* dependent.''

''That matters not. He has a legal, as well as moral, obligation to provide for you. And should be made to do so, if common sense and decency do not prompt him to it.''

She stiffened, then rounded on him. ''My lord, I absolutely forbid you to intervene in this. No one that draws breath has ever influenced my father-in-law to do anything he did not wish. If you think he would listen to your prompting, you delude yourself.''

Evan drew himself up. ''I am neither his son nor a green youth. He would listen.''

''And contact the nearest magistrate to have Drew taken from me! Do you not understand? He is a powerful man. Drew is his legal grandson. It makes my head spin to think how fast he would have me declared unfit to raise my son. Your intervention would only make that easier!''

''But 'tis unnatural and unjust,'' Evan sputtered.

She gave him a long look. ''We have not much ground to stand on in prating of morality. Oh, your friend Mr. Blakesly told me how much you dislike bullies, but you must see your meddling in this would result in disaster. If *he* should ever discover us, my only recourse would be to take Drew and disappear. Beginning again elsewhere would be difficult, but if necessary I shall do it.''

She drew a deep breath and looked at him defiantly. "I swore on Andrew's grave I would not allow his father to brutalize our son as he had Andrew. And I would die, if I must, to honor that pledge."

She faced him, her body taut, her hands fisted, as if...as if she feared *Evan* meant to rip away her security and her son. "Emily, sweeting, I would never hurt you! Or risk having taken from you what you hold most dear. Surely you know that!"

"Yes, I know you would never knowingly harm me. But *he* is out there somewhere, still looking. To challenge him would be to destroy us." She sighed and let her hands go limp, looking battered and weary. "The fewer people who know the truth, the fewer to let slip a name or location, the safer we stay."

As her meaning penetrated, he stared at her, affronted. "You think I would babble out information? I'm glad the Army Department has more confidence in me!"

"No, I don't think you indiscreet! Rather I..." she broke her gaze from his "...I felt there was no need to tell you, that probably our...arrangement would end before I need say anything."

That was even worse than her doubting his judgment and discretion. In two long strides he reached her and seized her hands. "I'm not going to just...go away, Emily! Not now. Not ever!"

She stared at him, her wary, defensive eyes searching his. Slowly her face gentled to a smile. "Oh, Evan. Neither of us can promise forever."

As the second tear fell, he pulled her roughly into his arms, the only reassurance he could give her—or himself. Her words were irrefutable.

Leaving his spent horse in the mews, Evan summoned a hackney to bear him back to Portman Square. He didn't wish to intrude on the little party Emily had promised her son. The stunning discovery of the boy's existence was still too new for him to sort out how he felt about it, much less how he should behave toward the child.

That flesh-and-blood reminder of a hero husband so much more powerful than a miniature tucked at the back of a drawer.

He wouldn't encounter the lad often—Emily had made that clear. She felt it safer for her son to remain in residence with his tutor, she explained, and had no intention of bringing him to live at their—her house, at least not…

She'd left the sentence dangling. Not until he no longer came to her.

Jealousy clawed him again, prowling through a wasteland of hurt, puzzlement—and fear. She had run with the boy once and would again if she felt him threatened. Little as he knew about her, Evan could easily lose her without a trace.

Giving the driver of the jarvey his address, he climbed in. Equally dismal thoughts, irritating as the day-old stubble on his chin, scratched at him as the vehicle lumbered off.

She regarded their relationship as so temporary she'd felt it unnecessary to divulge the fact of her son. Evan had never really considered how long their liaison would last, at the beginning being too dazzled to think, and now…

Had she not felt the growth of their affection? How could she still look on their bond as temporary, a fleeting flash of passion to be enjoyed and as swiftly forgotten?

Too disturbed to remain trapped in the narrow, ill-smelling confines of the vehicle, he banged on the roof. After clambering out to pay the bemused driver twice his normal fare, he paced off.

What did Emily feel for him—and he for her? She seemed to care for him, in the smile that sprang to her lips when he entered the room, the small, tender touches she sometimes gave, the fierce intensity of her passion. But never in words had she vouchsafed any emotion at all.

He couldn't be sure she didn't feel only the pull of lust tempered with a bit of fondness—nothing more. Not the same deep, intense, awesome emotion he felt for her.

When he'd first come to town after Oxford, he conceived a violent attachment to a lovely opera dancer. His obsession, however, dissipated considerably once his passion was slaked, and died altogether after several evenings of the lady's uninformed chatter.

In subsequent years, he'd never again felt that immediate, irresistible attraction to a woman. No lady of his own class inspired him to more than affectionate warmth. By the time Richard sailed off to war, Evan had felt confident in pledging to look after Andrea, having concluded the soul-stirring emotion poets rhapsodized about was simply not in his nature.

Then Emily burst into his life like a shooting star, captivating him from the first moment. Time spent with her had only deepened his initial attraction to a more complex, all-encompassing bond that made the mere thought of another woman distasteful even as it honed the first sharp edge of passion into something purer and more lasting than desire.

A state of being that mimicked every nuance of depth and intensity the most rapturous of poets might have used to describe ''love.''

Emily—his beloved. The words sounded so right together. His heart soared and he laughed in giddy delight.

Emily the middle-class shopkeeper. His grin faded.

Each year a handful of the aristocracy, desperate for funds, married into the ranks of the merchant-princes in a business transaction of lineage for wealth. Such daughters of rich bourgeois were virtually indistinguishable from their better-born peers, attending the same schools, clothed by the same couturiers and living the same socially restricted, idle lives as the daughters of the gentry.

A captain of industry would no more allow his own daughter to work in a shop than would an earl. Evan had never heard of a man of title marrying a woman who actually earned her own bread. 'Twas worse than bad ton, 'twas—unthinkable.

What a clever man, Evan thought, kicking viciously at a flagstone. He'd finally discovered what love was. So clever, in fact, that his passionate affection had been inspired not only by a woman whose own feelings toward him he had no assurance about, he'd managed to fall head over heels for a woman society would never accept his marrying.

The ramifications of that conclusion were so daunting he refused to think further on it. Cursing himself for a fool, he picked up his pace.

A few days later he assisted Andrea, becomingly garbed in one of her new gowns, up the steps to attend her first party. A dinner given by one of his mama's friends, it would be followed by an informal dance and attended only by a limited number of close acquaintances, to ease Lady Cheverley's shy charge into society.

Despite those precautions, Andrea was unusually silent as they made their slow way up the stairs. She'd been subdued ever since her arrival in London, displaying none of her usual animation even when Clare teased her into showing off some of her lovely new wardrobe. And her limp was more pronounced than ever, a sure sign of distress.

A flurry of activity at the office and repeated demands by his mother to escort them to visit various relations before the official presentations began had occupied all his time since his return to London. He'd managed only that fleeting visit with Emily the morning he'd met her son. All the disturbing, unresolved questions raised by that event still roiled uneasily beneath his surface calm, exacerbating his frustration in not being able to break free to see her. His teeth were already on edge at the prospect of sitting through this interminable dinner and a portion of the dancing to follow. At which time, he vowed, come what may, he would go to Emily.

But Andrea needed him now, so once more he buried his own concerns. "Lean harder on my arm and spare your knee, Andy," he murmured. "And don't worry. That shimmery blue gown brings out the bluebells in your eyes and the gold of your hair so well, if I didn't remember the scrubby schoolgirl underneath, I'd think you a princess. So will everyone tonight."

She gave him a brief, strained smile, her face unnaturally pale. "Until I clomp across the floor like some crude mechanical toy. Oh, why did I promise Richard I would do this? I know I'm a coward, but either I shall render them all uncomfortable, like the poor squire and his wife at home who can never think of anything to say when we meet, or they will laugh. Not to my face perhaps, but behind my back. Like the Wimberley village children who throw pebbles when I pass." Her voice hushed to a whisper with the threat of tears. "I'll embarrass you all."

"Those urchins should be switched," he replied, appalled by the casual cruelty she'd encountered. "I daresay here no one will disdain you."

She squeezed his hand, her smile brightening to a pale imitation of the sunny glow he remembered. "Not with my champion at my side, perhaps." The smile faded. "But you can't be with me every moment."

"I don't need to be. Once people know you, they'll love you for yourself. How could they help it?"

But even as he delivered that heartfelt encouragement, his mind furiously searched for ways to reduce her anxiety. One occurred as they reached the top of the stairway.

If walking in front of everyone distressed her, why should she? "Andy, once we've greeted our hostess, I'll help you to one side. Nothing says we must stroll about—I'll bring the guests over to you. The ones worth meeting, of course," he added with a wink. "And when dinner is announced, we'll bring you in toward the last. As most everyone will be at table, your entrance will scarcely be noticed. Agreed?"

The unshed tears in her eyes made them appear even bluer as she looked up at him. "Yes. You are so kind and clever, Evan. No wonder Richard trusts you so."

Uncomfortable under her worshipful scrutiny, he looked away. "It's settled, then. I'll alert Mama and Clare. With my sister's giddy friends around, you'll have time to think of nothing but how silly they all are."

Accordingly, after a quick word to his mother, he busied himself ferrying friends and acquaintances over to the Cheverley party. Actually, he thought wryly, requiring guests to come to *her* only increased Andrea's consequence. After half an hour, he noted with satisfaction, she appeared more relaxed, regaining her color and some of her normal animation.

Just before dinner, as he arranged with a political friend to escort Andrea to table, he noticed a commotion in the group clustered about the Cheverleys. Concerned, he walked over to find his sister enthusiastically embracing a young woman with dancing brown curls and large green eyes.

"Evan," Clare called to him. "Come, you must meet Delia Winstead—quite the best of my school chums! Delia, this is my brother Evan, Earl of Cheverley, but as you can see he's not the least puffed up with his own consequence.''

''A remarkable feat for so ancient a fellow,'' he replied with a grin as she made her curtsey. ''Charmed, Miss Winstead. You've met my mother's ward, Miss Marlowe?''

''Oh yes,'' Andrea replied for her. ''We've called several times, and Miss Winstead has been everything kind.''

Evan noticed the lone soldier standing stiffly by the wall, half-hidden by a knot of guests, just as Miss Winstead gestured to him. ''I've brought someone I especially wanted Miss Marlowe to meet—my brother, Captain Giles Winstead. Giles...''

The green-eyed girl cast a look of appeal. As the soldier, with obvious reluctance, turned toward them, Evan saw that the left sleeve of his uniform coat hung empty. His face was pale and rather drawn, pain lines still etched at his eyes, mouth and brow, as if his injuries were quite recent.

''I must seize the opportunity while I can,'' Miss Winstead confided as the soldier, body rigidly erect as if on parade, approached them. ''Giles only came tonight because our hostess's son is one of his closest Oxford friends. Usually I have no luck at all persuading him to accompany me.''

After introductions were made, bows and curtseys exchanged, their hostess called them for dinner. ''We'll be separated at table, no doubt, but you must talk with Miss Marlowe after dinner, Giles,'' his sister urged. ''Her brother Richard is with the 95th Rifles.''

A flicker of interest flared in the dead gray eyes, swiftly extinguished. "A gallant unit, Miss Marlowe. My compliments to your brother."

'I would very much enjoy speaking with you," Andrea replied. "Richard's letters are fascinating, but so full of fantastical stories I believe half what he writes must be sheer invention. Perhaps you could—"

"I shan't be staying." He flashed his sister an angry look. "I don't dance."

He turned to leave. Andrea reached out and caught his sleeve—the empty one. He froze, then looked pointedly at the white glove grasping the bloodred cloth. Andrea's cheeks pinked, but she did not release it.

"I don't dance, either," she said softly. Looking up at him, she smiled that brilliant, angelic Andrea smile Evan remembered so vividly from before the accident. "Could you not stay? I miss my brother so dreadfully. It would be great comfort to talk with someone who knows—what he faces."

"Giles, please," his sister added in an urgent undertone.

For a moment the soldier was silent, a muscle ticking in his hollowed cheek. If he could resist Andrea's smile, Evan thought, the man had lost more than an arm.

"Very well," he said curtly. "I suppose I could stay a few moments."

"Lord Cheverley, if you please?" His hostess called him to escort in her highest-ranking female guest. As Evan walked off to perform that duty, he glanced back to make sure Andrea's escort had arrived and understood his instructions. He noticed the soldier also waiting with his sister, perhaps employing the same delaying tactic for reaching the table unnoticed he was using to protect Andrea.

After he'd seated his elderly dowager, he looked back a second time to see the soldier halted, an arrested look on his face as he stood aside to let Andrea, leaning heavily on the arm of her escort, limp past him.

A few hours later, aflame with impatience, Evan escorted the Cheverley ladies home. "Yes, Mama, a delightful dinner," he responded as the women handed over their cloaks to the butler. With a raised eyebrow, his mother watched him wave Billingsly away as the man turned to take his coat.

"You are going out?" she asked.

"I imagine you ladies will want a comfortable coze at which to dissect the costume and character of all the guests present. An activity, I'm sure you will agree, you can carry out much more expeditiously without my assistance."

"He's probably going back to that dreary Horse Guards office," Clare said with a groan. "Whatever he can find to occupy himself there for so many hours, I can't imagine. I think he must be doing penance for the crime of remaining safely in England while Richard had to go back to the mud and heat of the Peninsula."

At least part of that assessment struck home with such painful accuracy that Evan grimaced. Before he could reply, though, Andrea spoke up.

"For shame, Clare! You know Evan would have gone, too, had it been possible. Besides, someone of intelligence must remain in England to support the army.

Richard says in his letters that Evan's work with the munitions department is perhaps the most important civilian job here. And he's been neglecting it sorely these last few days to squire us about.'' She smiled at him, that wistful, sweet Andrea smile. ''Don't let us detain you any longer, Evan. And thank you again for—well, you know.''

She gave him a conspiratorial wink and took Clare's hand. ''Come, help me up the stairs. And you must tell me about that young man, Captain Winstead's friend, who seemed to find you so fascinating.''

That earned her a giggle. In a moment the two girls had their heads together as Clare gave Andrea her arm. Evan's mother lingered a moment, however, her keen eyes resting on him.

He stood silent, unwilling to confirm or deny Clare's prediction that he was headed for his office, his desire to quit the house and reach Emily an almost physical ache. Finally his mother said simply, ''Good night, my son.''

''Good night, Mother.'' He bowed and turned on his heel, murmuring in an undertone to the butler as he passed not to keep a footman waiting up for him. As the heavy front door closed behind him, his mother was still at the stairway staring speculatively after him.

With a sigh Emily laid aside the book she'd not been reading for the last hour. It was after midnight, well past the time a shopkeeper who must be up before dawn should be sleeping. Yet an edgy restlessness kept her from slumber.

Evan had not called for four days now, not since the morning he'd arrived to find Drew here. He'd seemed affronted, almost furious at her for failing to confide in him about her son. Was he still angry?

Or was that anger merely a catalyst for the beginning of the end? Or the end itself? Having never indulged in one before, she had no idea how an affair ended. If she'd considered the matter at all, she'd supposed Evan's visits would gradually become less frequent and finally cease, probably with him attempting to give her some sort of lavish farewell present she would firmly refuse.

But mayhap that wasn't so. Mayhap it just—ended, abruptly, with no warning. 'Twas the nature of an affair, after all, that there were no formal ties binding the couple together. And therefore none to sever.

She might never see him again, feel his touch, hear the engaging warmth of his laughter. A wave of bleakness swept over her, so unexpectedly strong it robbed her of breath.

''Emily.''

She gasped at the sound, at first thinking she'd only imagined his voice. Then he stepped into the candlelight. With a little cry, she jumped up and ran to him, the book falling forgotten to the floor.

He caught her in his arms and crushed her close, then cradled her cheek in one hand as he kissed her hair, her forehead. ''Emily, sweeting,'' he sighed against her brow. ''I'm sorry, my darling. If I'd known how much blasted trouble this business of come-outs was going to be, I'd have fled the country.''

His caressing fingers touched the wetness at the corner of her eye and stopped abruptly. Drawing back a bit, he tilted her chin up. "What is it? What's troubling you?"

She swiped impatiently at the tears. "Nothing, now. I'd been thinking you were still angry. That perhaps you wouldn't—come here again."

He stared at her a moment as if her words were incomprehensible. Then his eyes lit with tenderness and his lips curved into a smile. "Ah, sweeting," he whispered. "I'll never leave you, never. If ever we part, it will be you who sends me away."

Dawn was but the faintest promise of light at the east window when an insistent rapping brought Emily out of deep sleep. "Lord Cheverley! It's Baines! Please, my lord, you must come!"

Alarm shocking through her, she shook Evan's bare shoulder. As his eyes opened groggily, Baine's knock sounded again. "Please, my lord, I've an urgent message."

Comprehension dawned and his eyes snapped open. "I'll be right there, Baines. Give me a moment."

Evan leaped out of bed, pawing among the tangle of clothes on the bedside chair for his breeches. As he struggled into them, Emily found flint and lit a chamber candle. With a nod of thanks, Evan took it and strode to the door, opening it just a little so that his body shielded Emily from the servant's view.

"Thank God I've found you, my lord. A messenger arrived nearly an hour ago and set the house in an uproar. He brought you this letter."

Evan snatched the note, broke the seal and held the candle close as he read. ''Dear God,'' he whispered when he'd finished, squeezing his eyes together tightly as though reeling from a blow. Folding the note with hands that now trembled, he took a deep breath.

''Have the stables ready my two fastest horses and pack me a kit. Did you tell my mother where—''

''No, my lord. I didn't tell her ladyship nobbit but that I'd find you. I figured as how you'd be either here or at the office. I tried here first.''

Evan nodded. ''Good. Go, then. I'll want to leave at once.''

''Yes, my lord.'' After a surreptitious glance over Evan's shoulder toward Emily, the valet disappeared.

Evan shut the door. Reaching the chair in two strides, he thrust down the candle and began gathering his clothes. Emily threw on a robe and went to assist.

''Is there anything I can do?'' she asked as she fastened one shirt cuff.

''Nothing. It's Richard.''

''Your friend—the one in the army?''

''Yes. The note is from a regimental surgeon. Richard's been wounded, perhaps mortally. He was evacuated with some other soldiers on a packet that made port yesterday. He told the doctors to contact me. I must go at once.''

''Of course. I'm so sorry.''

Looking up from the boot he was jamming on his foot, Evan opened his lips as if to speak, then swallowed hard instead. He nodded and picked up the other boot.

"Mistress, *está bem?*" Francesca's voice sounded from behind the door.

Emily ran to open it. "Tell Jenkins to saddle Lord Cheverley's horse at once."

Francesca, a shawl wrapped around her nightdress, frilly nightcap askew, peered in at the frantic activity and made the sign of the cross. "*Imediatamente,* mistress."

Emily followed Evan downstairs, helped him shrug on his overcoat. He leaned down to give her a swift, fierce kiss. "I don't know how long I'll be gone. I'll send word as soon as I can."

"A safe journey. I'll be praying for you—and him."

He brought her fingers to his lips briefly, squeezed them, then flung open the front door and disappeared into the night.

Chapter Nine

Evan saw lights at the windows, a groom holding horses and servants hurrying about as he approached his front door at a gallop. Tossing his reins to a stable boy, he leaped from the saddle and ran up the steps.

The entry hall held more milling servants, his weeping sister in the arms of his mother, and Andrea. Stone-faced and tearless, she stood in her riding dress, crop in one gloved hand. "I'm going with you," she said flatly.

"Andrea, dearest, you mustn't," his mother said over Clare's head, continuing what appeared to be a running argument. "'Tis a grueling ride, and you know Evan can proceed faster without you. Reaching Richard as quickly as possible is the most important consideration."

"I may not walk well, but I can still ride better than Evan. Richard's my brother, the only family I have left, and I'm going." She looked over at Evan and raised her chin. "If you won't take me, I'll ride alone."

Evan smiled at her. "I'll take you."

"Evan!" his mother protested, and shook her head. "Oh, very well. But I'm bringing the coach. Someone

153

must be sensible, and we'll need a comfortable conveyance to bring him home, not some ill-sprung jarvey.''

"Then I'm coming, too!" Clare cried.

"I need you to stay and get the house ready." She gave the tear-stained girl a shake. "You'll do that for me, won't you darling? And for Richard?"

Baines appeared at the landing, saddlebag and heavy riding boots in hand. While Evan changed boots, his mama briefly related the news they'd gleaned from the messenger: Richard and several other wounded soldiers had been carried to the Cross and Anchor, tended by the regimental surgeon who'd written Evan. And his case appeared grave.

"I've had the messenger fed and shown to bed," his mama finished as he donned the heavy greatcoat Billingsly held out, and drew on his thickest gloves.

"Good. Fetch my cloak for Miss Marlowe, please," he told the butler, and turned to Andrea. "We'll wrap you up in that. 'Twill be a cold ride. Thank you, Baines. Billingsly, you'll help Miss Clare prepare?"

"Of course, my lord. Godspeed to you both."

Evan gave his mother and sister a quick kiss. "We'll see you at the inn, Mama." He held out a hand to Andrea.

She threw her arms around him and hugged tightly. "Thank you," she whispered. Then she took his wrist, and the two made their way to the waiting horses.

After a long, frigid, punishing ride, during which they stopped only to change mounts and fortify themselves with bread, meat and steaming mugs of tea, they reached the coast. Though he knew she must be exhausted by the pace—he was exhausted himself—Andrea uttered not a word of complaint. There was iron under that fragile exterior, Evan thought with admiration.

They found the well-known inn without difficulty. When Evan helped Andrea to dismount, her lame leg crumpled.

"I'll be all right," she protested as he lifted her. "I'm just stiff from the saddle."

"And no wonder," he said, setting her on her feet gently. "You've been a trooper. I'm proud of you, Andy."

She gave him a brief smile and took his arm. "Let's find Richard."

They were directed to a small private chamber. A surgeon met them at the door. "Lord Cheverley? Thank God you've arrived! And..."

"Captain Marlowe's sister. She will come in, so there's no use telling her she can't. What can we do?"

"Not much, I'm afraid. Captain Marlowe is feverish and unconscious now, though I'm hoping he may come round. He was most insistent that he talk with you."

"And his condition?" Evan asked.

The surgeon glanced at Andrea.

"Tell us straight out. She didn't ride all day to hear it sugarcoated."

The surgeon shook his head. "I can't offer much hope. Quite frankly, I'm surprised he's held on this long. Better let the young lady say her goodbyes."

He heard Andrea's quick intake of breath, and his own chest tightened. This was Richard, the best friend who'd grown to manhood with him, the man with whom he'd gambled and fished and hunted. Richard couldn't be dying.

But the gray-faced, sweat-soaked man sleeping fitfully on the bed looked more like an actor grease-painted with Richard's features than his dearest friend. Shocked, Evan halted by the bed.

Andrea, however, limped quickly over and took her brother's hand. "Richard, it's Andy. I'm here now. Everything will be all right." Over her shoulder she called back to Evan, "Have someone bring cold water and a cloth."

As the day dimmed and night came on, Andrea sat sponging her brother's fevered face and chest, talking, talking in her soft calm voice. The sound seemed to quiet him, for he grew less restless. Finally, just after the candles were lit, he opened his eyes.

"Andy?" A whisper of sound.

"Yes, Richard." She swallowed hard, and one tear spilled down her cheek as she stroked her brother's sunken cheek. "It's Andy."

"Thirsty," Richard croaked. Evan hastened to carefully lift him, gritting his teeth at the muffled moan of anguish even that slight movement caused his friend, while Andrea put a cup to his lips.

"Evan," Richard said, turning his head slightly toward him after he'd lowered the soldier back to his pillow. "Good. Must...talk."

"Rest now, Richard. We'll talk later."

A thin, hot hand sought Evan's and gripped it. "Stay?"

"Absolutely. I'll be here every minute, and in the carriage when we take you home."

The injured man's lips curved into a slight smile. "Home," he murmured, and closed his eyes.

Voices sounded in the hallway outside, and a moment later Evan's mother walked in. Her eyes widened when she saw Richard, and she put a hand to her mouth as if stifling a cry. After a struggle, she seemed to master herself and walked over to Andrea. "Has she eaten or rested?" she whispered to Evan.

"Not since we arrived hours ago."

His mother nodded, then gave Andrea a little shake. "You must have nourishment and get some sleep, my dear. We'll need you strong when we bring him home tomorrow."

"I can't leave him."

"You won't have to. I've directed the innkeeper to deliver a cot. But you must eat, and you'll want to freshen up. I've brought some things. Come, Evan will call us immediately if there's any change."

Stubbornly Lady Cheverley murmured to Andrea until she convinced her to go below for some food and fresh air. After helping her downstairs, his mother returned.

"How is he?"

Evan shook his head, unable to put the doctor's prediction into words. If he did not speak them, they could not be true.

The wounded man stirred, opened his eyes. "Evan?"

Evan bent over his friend. "Here, Richard. Another drink?"

"No. Talk."

"Don't tire yourself. We can—"

"Now. Andrea's...letters. Never...wanted London. Shouldn't...have forced her. Take...her home. Please?"

"Of course. If she wants to go home, I'll take her."

"So...sweet. Needs...good man. If...I die—"

"You won't die!"

"If I die...marry her. Promise."

Evan sat silent. A scent of lavender, the whisper of a voice teased his mind. *Emily.*

Richard grasped his arm, his grip surprisingly strong. "Marry...her. Promise me!"

Evan swallowed hard. "I promise."

The hold on his arm loosened. "Good." The brief flicker of a smile passed over Richard's cracked lips. "Bless you...friend."

His eyes closed again and a sigh shook his fevered frame, as if a great weight had been lifted.

Evan's mother, whose presence he'd totally forgotten, startled him by coming to lean over Richard.

"Is he...?" she whispered, her eyes wide with anxiety.

"No! Just sleeping."

His mother exhaled sharply. "Thank God! I'll fetch Andrea."

The three of them kept vigil through the night. Evan managed to coax Andrea into resting for a few hours on the pallet and persuaded his mother to take a bed in another chamber, but true to his pledge, he remained at his friend's bedside. And as the first birds began to carol in the faint glimmerings of a new morning, with Andrea holding one hand and Evan the other, Richard's soul slipped away.

Andrea sensed it, as he did. She looked up at Evan, her expression bewildered, as if unable to comprehend such a catastrophe could actually occur. Then she laid her head on her brother's chest and for the first time since the messenger arrived, she wept.

As he'd promised, Evan rode back to London in the carriage beside the body of his friend, Andrea, once again stone-faced and silent, at his side. From time to time he reread a part of the letter the surgeon had given him, apparently the last Richard had written before the attack in which he was wounded.

"Damn and blast, Ev, half the boxes in last shipment were empty when we got them! What do those halfwits in Horse Guards think we can fire at the Frogs, pebbles? If we don't get resupplied before our next engagement I'll be down to a handful of shot per man."

Evan refolded the letter and gazed unseeing out the window. The fighting had been confused, one of the other wounded men told him. As usual, the riflemen of the 95th attacked first, harrying the arriving French columns, while the infantry, Brown Besses on their shoulders, waited for the enemy to come within range. But before the distance narrowed enough for the infantry to fire, the riflemen seemed to pause. Misfires were exploding all over, the soldier told Evan, many more than normal. When unexpectedly the French column wheeled and charged into them, the riflemen's fire nearly ceased. The

French mowed through them like a scythe through tall grass.

Had their ammunition been defective, as the misfires seemed to indicate? Had they run short? Did Richard die because some venal public servant abused his trust, selling off the powder and shot that could have saved his life and the lives of many others fallen that day?

I will find out, Richard, Evan vowed silently. *If that is what happened, I'll find out—and the guilty will pay.*

The next two days passed in a blur. With the methodical precision for which he was justly famed, Evan notified friends and family, organized the funeral service, consulted with the solicitors and stood by a stoic Andrea as she received calls of condolence. She greeted mourners with cool calm, and only Evan knew what it cost her fragile strength to present a brave face to the world.

Evenings he spent at the office gathering every detail he could find on the ordering and shipment of ammunition for the Baker rifle, abstracting a dossier of names and contact points. The day of Richard's funeral he dispatched his friend and colleague Geoffrey Randall to Portugal with orders to quietly gather information about each man on that list. "No heroics, now," he warned Geoffrey in a gruff attempt at humor. "Gather intelligence only. I can't afford to lose another friend."

He had time only to send a brief message to Emily, telling her of Richard's death and promising to call as soon as possible. He drove himself to exhaustion as much to prevent himself reflecting on the implications of his new promise to Richard as to keep at bay his trenchant grief.

Andrea wished to leave London, so he must take her home. He could not depart without seeing Emily again, that also was absolute. Beyond those two constraints, he had neither leisure nor heart to think further.

A drizzly rain fell the day of the funeral, for which Evan was grateful. Brilliant blue skies and sun would have grated against the raw wound of loss. The swirling, spiraling mist suited his mood and cloaked the ceremonies in proper solemn dignity. Though Clare broke down in his weeping mother's arms, and he wiped away tears himself, Andrea endured it all dry-eyed, shoulders squared and head erect, her attention never wavering from her brother's coffin. Among the mourners a scarlet slash of coat caught his eye, and he saw Captain Winstead beside his sister, his somber gaze fixed on Andrea.

But when they reached the town house after the service, Andrea fell going up the stairs. As Evan rushed to assist her, the enormous weight of loss finally cracked her calm. Sagging limply in his arms, she began to weep, and no comfort or soothing could reach her. She clung to him, sobbing, as he carried her to her chamber, where he held her sobbing still until at last she subsided to hiccups. As he eased her, barely conscious, onto the pillows, his mama sent him off for food and strong drink while she and her maid stripped Andrea and put her to bed.

Though the food was tasteless in his mouth, he appreciated the sharp, warming bite of the port. A bottle Richard had brought back on his last leave, he remembered with another raw wave of pain. An urgent, desperate desire to be with Emily swept through him, to apply the healing salve of her passion and nearness to the ragged gash Richard's death had ripped in his life. Though he needed sleep, and a shave, he could wait no longer.

He drained the glass and walked out. As he reached the entry to call for his coat, Lady Cheverley appeared on the landing. "Evan, my dear. Can I speak with you?"

Much as he loved her, nearly the last thing he wished at the moment was a cozy chat with his mama.

"Could this wait, ma'am? I'll see you at dinner."

"I shall not require you for long. As you are so *busy* of late—" she emphasized the word "—I should very much appreciate your speaking with me immediately."

Inwardly gnashing his teeth, he gave her the only reply possible. "Very well. I'm at your disposal, madam."

"Are you?" Her face grave, she surveyed him up and down. "We shall shortly see."

With those unencouraging words, she beckoned him up to the sitting room.

He strode in and hesitated before the Louis XV sofa.

"Sit, please." She walked to a side table where tea had been set out. "Should you like a cup?"

"No, thank you, Mama."

She halted, her hands in the process of pouring a cup, then set down the pot. "Very well." In a swish of skirts, she came to sit beside him. "I had hoped never to see the day when you were too busy to take tea with me."

"'Tis hardly that," he protested, irritated. "I've just supped, you will remember. And I *am* busy, so if you could tell me what you wished to say?"

She sighed. ''I expect it's not a good time, but of late there hasn't been a better one. I shall just state it baldly, then, without roundaboutation. Do you intend to keep your promise to Richard regarding Andrea?''

The question caught him off guard. ''W-what?''

''Your vow to marry her. I was present when you promised Richard, you will remember.''

He hadn't remembered. Not sure yet himself how he would reconcile that pledge with his need for Emily, he had no ready answer; exhausted both physically and emotionally, he was ill-equipped to reason it out on the spot. Irritation deepened to anger.

''I shall arrange something. I've always told her if she found no other man to her liking, I would marry her.''

''If she is set upon leaving London, she's unlikely to meet anyone else. You know how she avoids society—''

''She'll be taken care of,'' he snapped. ''I should see to it even if I'd not promised Richard. Sorry, Mama, to be so abrupt, but I'm fatigued and I have pressing business. If you'll excuse me?''

''Another moment, please!'' She held out a hand to stop him as he rose from the sofa. Fuming, almost out of his skin with impatience to be off, with great reluctance he sat.

''I know you're tired—we're all tired. And I hate forcing you to a matter you obviously don't wish to discuss, but 'tis important. Indeed, 'tis crucial.''

She paused, as if gathering her thoughts. Too weary to attempt anticipating them, he gritted his teeth and waited.

''This 'pressing business' that's been so occupying you these past months...it's a woman, isn't it? A woman unworthy of you.''

Totally unprepared for the attack, he found the words leaving his lips before his overwrought mind could judge their wisdom. ''She is the equal of me or anyone!''

Damn and blast, he swore under his breath. He should have ignored the statement, pleaded ignorance. Emily was the last topic he wished to discuss with his mother, even when in full possession of his wits, which he was definitely not at this moment.

''Unworthy of you,'' his mama repeated. ''If she were not, you'd have brought her to me long ago.''

He stared at her, fiercely resenting her prying, resisting her words, but unable to counter them. How could he explain to her his Emily—her courage, her endurance, her charm and fire?

''This is none of your concern.''

''Oh, don't bristle up! I realize you are a man grown, with a life that does not wait upon my approval. Nor, must you admit, have I ever before questioned your...little affairs. But this is different, I can feel it. This is...serious.''

She paused, as if waiting for him to speak. Having nothing he wished to say, he remained silent.

Lady Cheverley sighed. ''You will not make this easier, will you? I am sorry to meddle in a matter you obviously consider none of my business, but I must ask. Just what are your intentions in regard to this...lady?''

Having no clear answer to that question himself, he held on to his rapidly fraying control with an effort. "No disrespect, Mama, but I repeat, this is *not* your concern."

"You can hardly argue that the welfare of our family and your sister's future are no concern of mine."

He stiffened. "And you, madam, can hardly believe I do not keep a watchful eye over both."

"Do you, Evan? Have you, these last three months? Tell me, this lady whom you so admire—would she be deemed your equal in the eyes of the world?"

"The world is a shallow and cynical place, Mama. In any arena that judges true merit she would."

His mother sighed deeply. "Oh my son, I wish we lived in such a place. But we must deal with the world as we find it. Can you be considering—marriage?"

When he made no immediate denial, she drew in her breath sharply, her eyes widening in alarm. "Then it is more serious even than I feared. Oh, my dear son!" She leaned over and imprisoned his hands between her own. "Can you not see what effect such a dreadful misalliance would have on your family? On Andrea? On your innocent sister?"

"Mother, I think this has gone far enough—"

"You must listen! You *will* listen!" She hung on to his hands as he attempted to pull away, waiting until, anger raging so fiercely he could barely prevent himself from jerking free and stomping out, he at last reluctantly met her gaze.

"Speak your piece, then, and have done with it."

"Andrea would make you an unexceptional wife, though I am not set on her, should you prefer another of your own rank and station. Despite her limp and lack of fortune, I feel sure we could fulfill your pledge to Richard by contriving another suitable match. But if you were to disgrace the family with a misalliance such as you seem to be contemplating? Oh, Evan! For myself, I care nothing. But what of Andrea and Clare—what would happen to their prospects were you to make us outcasts from polite society?''

He tugged at the hand she still held, struggling to contain his fury. ''I believe I know enough what is due my name not to make a misalliance. Nor do I see at present any need to marry at all. I'm hardly in my dotage, Madame.''

''Let's suppose, then, that you maintain an informal but long-term...alliance with this lady. What if there should be a child?''

He felt a flush hotter than anger stain his cheeks. ''How irresponsible do you think me?''

''Oh, Evan, no protective measures are completely effective! Just consider—should your...precautions fail, could you stand aside and see your babe by a woman for whom you obviously care deeply born out of wedlock? Can you swear to uphold your duty to the family even then?''

For the first time he thought of Emily bearing a child. A child to displace her fixation on the soldier, *his* child of her body, the body he worshipped every night they lay together. *His son.*

And realized with unshakable certainty he could never give up such a child, never allow him to be born a bastard.

The conviction must have been written on his face, for his mother shook her head silently. "You see how it would be. Oh, my darling, I am sorry it will cause you pain, but you must break with her. You must! Now, Evan, before something...irreversible happens."

That she was correct, that she was forcing him to face the full implications of an undeniable, unpalatable truth he'd never before considered, made his guts churn with impotent fury. Break with Emily? The very notion sent a lance of agony to the core of him.

First Richard, now Emily? One could lose only so much of one's self and go on. Writhing inwardly, he tried to twist out of the dilemma.

"Have I not always done what is necessary?"

"Then you must break with her and form an attachment elsewhere—with Andrea or another, it matters not as long as she's suitable. Only a formal betrothal will prevent your resuming...inappropriate bonds. My darling, I know this is the worst possible time, with us all still in agony over Richard, but later you'll be grateful you took the proper course." Her eyes pleading, she squeezed his hands.

Hardly able to bear her touch for the rage churning in him, he jerked away. Speaking softly, lest the howling beast within break free to rant at her, he said, "Dare you *presume* to instruct me in my duty?"

She flinched at the harshness of his tone, tears starting at the corners of her eyes, lips trembling. But she held his gaze, implacable.

"If you know your duty, then do it."

With a growl he flung himself to his feet. "Very well. If I must marry someone *suitable,*" he snapped, giving the word savage emphasis, "then it might as well be Andrea. I'll propose as soon as she's recovered enough to hear me. You shall have your socially approved wedding. But ask me nothing more."

She grabbed at his arm. "Dearest, I didn't mean—"

"Unhand me!" he barked, ripping his sleeve free.

Weeping openly now, fingers to her mouth, his mother nodded. Without a backward glance he stalked out.

Chapter Ten

Despite his bone-deep weariness, instead of riding or summoning a hackney Evan set out for Emily's town house on foot. He needed time to sort out his ragged emotions and decide what to do.

A few blocks of pacing were enough to convince him, much as he frantically tried to devise some rational alternative, that his mother was indeed right.

He couldn't marry Emily. Doing so would irreparably damage his sister, for no family of stature would wish to align itself with one so lost to what was due its name and lineage. Andrea would likely not marry, either, unless he wed her. There was no other way to preserve honor, to honor his vow. *Ah, Richard,* he thought, bleeding inwardly, *how could you ask this of me?*

How could he wed Andrea and not lose Emily?

They could remain friends, could they not? He could stop by, consult with her, share hopes and plans....

It wouldn't be the same. He would no longer be free. And their time, their precious time together would be even more restricted than it had been since Andrea's arrival.

Marrying Andrea was the right, the only honorable course. Since there was no acceptable alternative, he would do so. Why, then, did it all feel so wrong?

Once he did his duty, he would be more at ease, lose this sense of impending catastrophe. Andrea would make it easier—they had always been friends. That in his current frame of mind he had to struggle not to view even the innocent Andrea with distaste he would not dwell on. He pushed the whole detestable vision of a forced marriage from his mind.

For the short, sweet infinity of the next few days, until Andrea recovered enough to entertain his proposal, their relationship could continue as it was. He could watch Emily at tea, curving her little finger over her cup as always; tease her into that throaty gurgle of a laugh; fence with her sharp wit; cherish the touch of her hands and lips, the deep satisfaction of their intimate joining.

Before he lost the privilege forever. That stark realization sucked the breath from his lungs.

It was unthinkable. It was inescapable.

He closed his eyes for a moment, marshaling the remains of his waning strength. Extinguishing further thought of so unspeakable a future, he forced his weary mind to a scarcely more palatable problem.

How was he going to break the news to Emily?

He toyed with the notion of delaying the announcement. After all, as Andrea was prostrate with grief, he could hardly rush her with a proposal for several days at least. That she would accept his proposal was nearly certain, he knew, swiftly extinguishing a flare of hope.

Could he not savor these last few days with Emily?

It would be unfair to conceal his imminent change of status, he concluded reluctantly. Emily had the right to know, to prepare herself—and to help him think of a way to salvage as much as possible of their life together.

That last thought was the only faint glimmer of hope he could glean out of this whole dreadful business.

He halted before her door, awash in yearning for what could never be. Then, chastising himself not to waste another second, he mounted the steps.

As he'd never mentioned Andrea, the news he would shortly deliver must come as a shock. Would Emily greet it with tears, pleas that he not marry another, vows of devotion? Or the cool pronouncement that to all things there is a season?

Raising his hand to knock, he took a deep breath. One way or another, he was about to find out.

Humming to herself, Emily arranged sandwiches and biscuits on the tea tray. Well pleased with the progress of her seamstresses, she'd returned home early today. She'd be able to report to Evan that ''Créations Madame Emilie'' would soon have its debut.

She expected that, as her primary investor, he'd greet the news with enthusiasm—though she wasn't sure. His brief note, in a nearly illegible script so unlike his usual precise penmanship, spoke of the depth of his grief over his friend's death. Vividly she remembered reeling from such blows, and poignant tenderness swelled in her breast. She longed for him to come to her, that she might let him talk it out, offer sympathy and wifely comfort.

The thought caught her up short. Cheeks heating, she reminded herself yet again, as she seemed to have to do with increasing frequency of late, that she had no right to intrude into his personal life. Such instincts were best firmly squelched, lest she slip into viewing her role as something it was not nor could ever be.

She heard his distinctive step in the hallway and a smile sprang to her lips. A gust of raw, rain-scented wind, memento of the wintry storm that had plagued the city all day, blew into the room with him.

His face worn and bestubbled, he came and drew her immediately into his arms. Compassion for his evident distress flooding her, she held him close.

He moved her to arm's length, but instead of releasing her, bent to place gentle, lingering kisses on her brow, her eyelids, her cheeks, her chin. Finally he claimed her lips in a kiss so infinitely tender her guarded heart beat faster and a melting warmth spread through her.

Rather than extending his kisses into the interlude such ardor seemed to promise, he drew back, his hands resting lightly on her shoulders. "My sweet Emily."

'Twas so difficult sometimes to maintain her distance—but she must. Swallowing the "My darling Evan" that sprang to her lips, she reached instead to brush some errant raindrops from his dark hair.

"I'm so sorry, Evan."

He opened his lips, then closed them and acknowledged her condolence with a short nod.

"Should you like tea?"

With a little sigh he released her. "Yes, tea would be good." He walked toward the sofa, halted, paced to the window and stood staring out at the street.

She regarded him with concern. What could she say or do to help? Words, she knew, were meaningless at such a time. Instead, she brought him his tea.

"Here, drink this." She touched his cold fingers. "You seem chilled—'twill help warm you."

"Emily, I...I shall have to leave town shortly."

Conscious of a sharp disappointment, she nodded. Settling his friend's estate, probably.

"I see. Will you be away for long?"

"I'm not sure. We'll...need a mourning period."

"You must take all the time necessary," she said, trying to damp down the hurt that he evidently chose not to seek her solace. "Grief can neither be ignored nor quickly mastered."

Still standing, his gaze on the far distance, he took a sip. "When I do return, things...will have to be different. I...I shall be engaged."

She was stirring her tea when the import of his words exploded in her mind like an unexpectedly tossed firecracker. Her heart stopped, the spoon dropped from her nerveless fingers and clattered against the saucer.

As the shock waves of meaning spread, her hearing dimmed, her eyesight blurred, she felt at once hotly dizzy and piercingly cold. She had the sensation of falling before Evan's firm hands grasped her.

"Emily! Emily, are you all right?"

His words penetrated, barely. Taking deep, unsteady breaths, she locked her vision on small details and willed them to remain in focus. The teacup that lay shattered on the carpet where she must have dropped it. She should call Francesca to mop up...

Then Evan was lifting her, carrying her to the sofa.

"Emily, sweeting, I'm sorry! I shouldn't have just— blurted it out, but I didn't know how to tell you."

He laid her down, but with trembling hands, she pushed back to a sitting position. He took a seat beside her.

"Please don't be angry with me, my darling." Evan chafed her cold fingers, kissed them. "Taking this step has nothing to do with any change in my feelings for you! I'm here now, I'll always be here for you, just as I promised. Anything you wish, anything you need, you have but to say it and 'twill be yours, I swear it. Please believe me!"

He gazed at her, face strained, his eyes desperate. "I've a duty to Richard—to his sister, Andrea. Her horse fell on her in a hunting accident several years ago and nearly crushed her leg. She's a lovely girl, but shy, un-comfortable and fearful of strangers. Our families have always been close, and I'm all she has left. Before Richard died, I...I promised I would marry her."

Emily's numbed brain was finally beginning to func-tion. "Yes, of course. I understand." Over the rapid beat-ing of her heart and the faintness that kept trying to over-whelm her, she endeavored to tell herself this was right. Sooner or later it would have to end.

Did it have to be so soon?

He drew her into his arms, kissed her fervently. "Things do not have to change between us, though I'll not be able to be with you as oft as I have. I'll have to be more discreet in my visits, but—''

As his meaning slowly penetrated her still-muzzy brain, a second shock struck her. She seized his caressing fingers. ''Evan, of course things will change! You cannot think that I...that I would... No, 'tis not possible.''

''Sweeting, it's not what I wish, either, what I would want for us. I know the...circumstances are distressing to you. But nothing would be as distressing as losing you altogether.''

Could it be he did not understand? That he thought his engagement—his *marriage*—would have no effect on their relationship? Had her coming to him given him that erroneous an impression of her?

The chilling thought focused her. She pulled her hands free. ''Your marriage must mean the end of our—friendship, Evan, surely. There's no other way. I've...sinned with you already, for which I'll owe a lifetime of penance. I will not be an adulteress. I cannot.''

He looked from the hands folded on her lap to her set face. ''You would send me away?'' he asked, his tone aghast, disbelieving. ''Refuse to see me again?''

She said nothing, unable to trust her voice to reaffirm the truth that cut like a saber's slash into her heart. But if she did not stand firm now, she sensed the force of his persuasion and her own treacherous longing would sweep her into actions that would lead to self-loathing and destruction.

''Does what we share mean so little to you?'' he whispered at last.

The anguish in his eyes echoed his tone, but she made herself meet his gaze firmly.

"Marriage vows mean more. 'Tis a holy promise, Evan, given before God, to love, cherish and keep thyself only unto one other. I would not wish you to break such a vow, could not live with myself were you to break it with me."

He remained silent a long time, as if her words were so difficult he must struggle to comprehend them. "We shall have to part, then?"

"Yes."

"Permanently?"

"Yes."

"And there is no way, no circumstance under which we might be together?"

Tears scratching at her eyes, she shook her head.

"Even as friends...my dearest friend?"

'Twas as if a giant fist had clamped around her chest, squeezing, squeezing ever tighter. "Oh, Evan, could you truly pledge to meet me just as a friend?"

"I would pledge the world and everything in it not to have you tell me goodbye."

The despair in his voice so closely mirrored her own she could bear it no longer. Clamping her lips together to hold back the words she must not say, she threw herself into his arms.

He crushed her close. Driven by the gale of imminent farewell, the sparks that always glowed between them ignited to a mutual hunger as elemental and irresistible as the forces driving them to part. Breathing her name in a sigh, he carried her to bed.

Their first coupling was fierce, frantic, the next so sweetly tender Emily felt she would weep. Afterward, again by mutual unspoken desire, they did not go down to dinner, did not attempt to play cards or chess or even exchange the candid, incisive commentary about current happenings that normally formed an enjoyable finish to their day.

Instead, they remained holding each other close, conscious of the mantel clock steadily ticking away the precious minutes and hours of their last time together. At length, the street noises outside faded and Emily dozed.

Sometime in darkest night she woke to Evan's touch. With lips and hands he cherished her from the crown of her head to her toes, lingering where he knew her to be most exquisitely sensitive—her nipples, the soft cleft of her thighs—and bringing her to blindingly intense release. Then slowly rebuilding the tension again to couple her pleasure with his own.

Afterward, in the lightening dawn, still joined, Evan turned them to the side, then laid one hand between her chest and his.

"You feel it?" he whispered. "Even our hearts beat as one."

The tears started as he left the bed to dress. Fisting them away, she rose as well, threw on a dressing gown and sat silently watching him. She should assist him as she had since their first night, but a listless languor held her motionless.

Her chest tight in that squeezing grip, she felt her heart match the tick of the mantel clock, each beat seeming to chip away at something deep inside.

Buttoning his last cuff, he turned to face her. "This is it, I suppose. For a few days. Then we shall have a month or so before the...event takes place." He squeezed his eyes shut, took a shuddering breath. "A month...and then eternity."

His words finally penetrated her lethargy. "A month? No, Evan, that cannot be. As soon as your lady accepts you, you are bound to her. Regardless of when the wedding occurs."

"That fierce conscience of yours cannot give us even another month?"

Dying a little with the word, she uttered it anyway. "No. I cannot. I'm sorry. Probably even last night was a mistake."

His head snapped up, his whole body instantly alert. "How can you say that? How can you feel anything—*anything*—for me, for us, and call what we shared together last night—for the whole of the time we've known each other—a *mistake?*"

His affronted tone nearly broke her resolve. "Oh Evan, did you really think there was a place in this world where an earl and a shopkeeper together would be right?"

"I thought we made it right."

It was never right—but oh, how precious you are, she thought. But now that he was to marry, what good would it serve to admit tender feelings she shouldn't have allowed herself to develop in the first place? Emotions that might encourage him to attempt dissuading her from the end she knew they must make.

No, better that he stay angry, better for him—and for her—to make the break swift and irreversible.

"We both knew from the first our time together would be brief. Now we should acknowledge it was... *pleasant*—" she uttered the insultingly tepid description with a slight tremor "—and move on."

He stared at her as if she had spoken in tongues. *"Pleasant? Move on?"* he echoed furiously. "To a new novel, a new bonnet...a new lover?"

She swayed with the force of his derision, but somehow it reinforced her resolve to deal the final blow.

"Whatever is suitable." Summoning some inner reserve of strength, she stood up and made him a deep curtsey. "May I wish you and your wife very happy, my lord."

His lip curled, he raised one hand, and for a moment she thought he would strike—or seize her. Then, exhaling in a ragged rush of breath, he straightened. His voice, when he spoke, was barely a whisper.

"So be it. Thank you for your kind sentiments, *Madame.*" He swept her an exaggerated bow. "And let me add I will earnestly endeavor to forget you with as much dispatch as you seem eager to dismiss me." Turning on his heel, he walked out.

After the echo of his retreating footsteps faded she staggered to the bed, collapsed on the edge with arms wrapped tightly around herself, eyes closed. *This is better, this is better, this is better.* To admit how enormous a loss his leaving was, how trenchantly deep the pain, would be to acknowledge an emotion that spelled disaster to any present or future peace of mind.

Must it have ended had she revealed her full identity at the outset, before his friend's death? But even though her birth was better than he assumed, she was still un-recognized by both her husband's family and her own, still virtually penniless, still engaged in trade. Any one of which factors would make her unsuitable to be his bride.

Nor in the midst of all his protestations of devotion had he ever hinted he desired her for *that* role. The only role she could in good conscience fulfill.

No, as parting was inevitable, better sooner than later, she told herself.

Of course it hurts, she soothed. *Losing a friend, a very dear friend, is never easy. You will get through it. You've survived worse.*

She'd almost convinced herself when Francesca entered. But when, after one glance, her friend gasped, *"Mão de Deus!"* and gathered her close, the fierce, body-racking sobs welled up and broke free. For a very long time she could not make them stop.

At midmorning, after he'd forced himself to down a Spartan breakfast and tea that might as well have been hemlock, Evan went to check on Andrea. He found her still abed, pale, but awake and composed.

"I'm glad you stopped by before leaving for Horse Guards, Evan. I wanted to thank you for..." She swallowed hard. "Well, for everything. I hate to ask anything more, but—could you take me home?"

Despite his own anguish, her distress moved him. "Of course, Andy. As soon as you feel strong enough."

"I'm ready, whenever you can break away. I want—I need to be home." She bit her lip, obviously struggling for control. "Maybe then I won't be so afraid."

He came to the bed and took her in his arms. "Don't be afraid, Andy. I'll take care of you." Recognizing the moment, he sucked in a breath and made himself say the words. "I'd like to take care of you always. Will you marry me?"

She pushed herself back and studied his face.

"Are you sure, Evan?"

Evading that question, he said, "I already asked you once, you'll remember."

A smile lightened her face. "By the lake at Wimberley years ago. You made me a wedding ring out of daisies."

"Yes. But you haven't given me an answer." His heart beat faster with crazy hope she might refuse.

"I'm sorry I'm so weak." Was it an apology? She smiled again, tremulously. "If you're truly sure you want me, then yes, of course I'll marry you."

The words struck his heart like a deathblow. Numbly he took her hand and kissed it. "You honor me," was all he could manage in reply.

Several weeks later Evan sat at Richard's desk in the library at Wimberley. He'd sorted through almost all his friend's papers; the solicitor had called yesterday to inform him the will should go to probate.

Evan needed to return briefly to London, to finish estate details and check at Horse Guards. Though he'd received courier mail, he was anxious to see if headquarters knew any more about the progress of his friend Geoffrey's mission.

London. Emily.

Savagely he crushed the wave of longing, as he had on each of the innumerable occasions it had seized him these past weeks. Emily was quite content to be on her own again. She'd made that point brutally clear.

"Evan, may I come in?"

Startled, he turned to the doorway where Andrea stood. "Of course. Come, sit with me."

Slowly she approached with her awkward, uneven gait and took the armchair beside the desk. "I'm afraid I have another favor to ask. I know it's quixotic of me, after practically dragging you and your family out of town, but the fact is I...I want to return to London."

Again, that instinctive leap of anticipation. Again he squelched it.

"You needn't go back, Andy. I do need to return, for a few days at least, but Mama can accompany me and arrange all the wedding details."

"No, I want to come. I thought being here at Wimberley would be better, but it's not. Oh, Evan! Everywhere I turn, I see Richard—his horses, his books, his hunting rifle. Even that silly rapeseed blooming in the meadow he insisted we t-try...." She broke off, struggling with tears.

Once again he gathered her close. "Of course I'll take you back. You needn't go out or see anyone if you don't wish to."

"Actually, I think I should prefer going out. Not to balls or parties, of course, but you never took me to

Hampton Court or to Astley's or the theater. I have friends, too, who can help...divert me. I don't have to worry now about making a good impression on gentlemen or their mamas.'' She looked up to smile at him. ''Now I have you. I'm just sorry I'm such a bother.''

He looked down at her gentle, guileless face. He should say, ''Nonsense, you'll be my wife soon, I want to care for you.''

The best he could do was, ''You're never a bother.''

Her smile widened. ''Thank you, Evan. You're so good to me. Well, I shall start to pack!''

He gave her a chaste kiss on the cheek. Not seeming to mind that lack of ardor, she patted his hand and walked out.

If they were to depart soon, he'd best finish these papers. But as he worked, though he struggled to banish them, two words kept thrumming at the back of his mind. *London. Emily.*

Chapter Eleven

Emily sat at the desk in her new office, previously her bedchamber, and gazed over at the sitting-room-turned-design-studio where the first completed toilettes hung.

Her clients had responded with enthusiastic praise and a number of advance orders—in cash. She gazed down at the sum she was about to insert in her money pouch and sighed.

She ought to be delighted with herself and the business. In a detached way she was. In her head she could acknowledge satisfaction that her trust in her design instincts had been well placed.

In addition, she was able to bring Drew to spend the weekends. Having her son's company for two whole days rather than the Sunday afternoon to which she had been rationed since their arrival in London—what a joy it was. She had no reason to be melancholy.

If her shop continued its progress, within a year she would be able to repay Evan in full the sum he'd initially spent to rescue her. Ah, Evan.

Her glance traveled the room. Here, in this chamber, he had first carried her to bed. There by the balcony door he had undressed her, to let the moonlight painting her body show him where to kiss, he'd said.

Her face flushed; a tingling began in her nipples. It seemed that, once awakened, desires long dormant refused to return to slumber.

But less carnal reminiscences were no better. In the next room, where seamstresses now toiled, where her designs now hung, they had dined and chatted and laughed together.

A dull pain vibrated through her. She pressed a hand to her chest. The sorrow was lessening, truly it was. It was just that everything here reminded her of their beginnings.

It was even worse at her house—their house—where she knew every item of furniture, every rug, plate and vase, had been chosen by him to please her. Where they had dwelled together a few precious months in such total contentment.

Damn and drat! She sprang up in exasperation. She was becoming a maudlin, whining weakling such as she despised.

She needed a change, something to refocus her mind.

Her restless glance fell upon the post Francesca had brought earlier. In it a playbill caught her notice. Announcing the premiere of a most excellent presentation of Will Shakespeare's *King Lear,* it boasted the renowned Mr. Hampton in the title role.

Hampton in *Lear.* The notion generated a spark of interest. And theater—she'd loved attending plays in Lisbon. Her father-in-law was still absent; Francesca had just checked. Why not treat them to a night at the theater?

Would Evan attend? She wasn't sure if he'd returned to London yet. He enjoyed Shakespeare, she knew. Warmth spread through her.

A little fear chilled it. What would he do, should he be present and see her?

The unease swiftly passed. 'Twould be in neither his best interests nor hers that he acknowledge her. If he were present, he'd most likely be with his betrothed.

She stifled a pang. *You will not,* she told herself sternly, *attend the theater solely on the ridiculous notion that you might, for a few moments, be able to watch him.*

In any event, 'twas just as like he'd not be there. Even to a family in mourning, London offered innumerable other entertainments.

Should he chance to be present, she would not gaze at him, anyway. Certainly not. She'd go for the play itself and the revitalizing change in routine it offered.

Smiling, she called Francesca to see about obtaining tickets. And told herself her rising excitement was merely the anticipation of seeing Mr. Hampton play Lear.

From her seat among the lower tier of chairs Emily gazed about her with awe. She'd not been in a public assembly in so long, the sheer volume of sound, color and motion mesmerized her.

In the pit just below, a group of flamboyantly dressed bucks lounged among a diverse assortment of shop boys, clerks and ill-clad ruffians she strongly suspected must be pickpockets. The scent and smoke of candles mingled with the odors of perfume, nosegays and unwashed bodies. Then one of the lounging men caught her eye and winked.

Alarmed he might interpret her glance as encouragement, she jerked her gaze away and up to the boxes above. Perhaps she had been unwise to sit here. She'd feel safer had she been able to afford a box.

But she'd have hesitated, even were she able to afford it. What would she do if she claimed a box—and saw Evan enter the one next door? The very idea caused a shudder.

Besides, she thought as she watched the beautifully clothed, jewel-bedecked Upper Ten Thousand drift in amid laughter and called greetings, the few among society who knew Madame Emilie, hatmaker, would surely not approve her seating herself among them.

For the first time since Andrew's death she felt the full force of her social isolation—friendless among the bourgeoisie she had joined, banished from the society of her birth. Being isolated in Spain had been natural—she was a foreigner. In England, she had until this moment been too preoccupied with survival to spare a thought for position.

Nonsense, she told herself, ripping her gaze from the upper levels and transferring it to the stage, where a herald was announcing the opening festivities. Years of foraging about Spain on her own had taught her how to send any potential heckler to the rightabout. And her grip on survival was still not firm enough that she waste time in maudlin reflection over her proper place.

A blur of motion in an upper box caught her attention, and a shock of awareness jolted through her. Though the arriving gentleman had his back to the stage, adjusting his lady's chair, she knew immediately it was Evan.

He turned toward her. For the briefest moment her gaze clung to him, tracing every detail of that dear familiar face. Did his eyes seem shadowed, the lines at the corners of his mouth grim? Or was that merely an effect of the flickering torchlight?

Then she forced her gaze away, before the unconscious, irresistible pull that telegraphed his presence alerted him to hers. She would not have him discover her staring up like a ragged waif begging alms.

By the time the ringing in her eyes dimmed and her tumultuous pulse calmed, the first act was nearly over. With determination she focused her attention onstage.

Though still acutely conscious of Evan in the corner box, she managed to immerse herself in the play. As the actors exited for the first interval, however, she stirred uneasily.

She should observe the crowd, she told herself. Anything to hold her attention and prevent her succumbing to the nearly overwhelming desire to look up.

Could she not dare one quick glance? Just to see if the lady privileged to become his bride was fair or dark, if she seemed kind? He deserved a wife with a warm heart, who would fill his home with gladness.

So intent was she on her inward struggle that the touch on her arm made her jump.

"'Evenin', lovely lady," said a slurred voice at her side. "Beauty such's you shouldn't be sittin' alone."

A powerful odor of spirits hit her nose. She wrinkled it in distaste, recognizing at the same time one of the most persistent of the Corinthians who had been wont to drop by her shop—Lord Willoughby? Suddenly she wished Francesca had not firmly refused to accompany her mistress to a play whose Shakespearean language she could not fathom.

The inebriated man was followed by several others who crowded close around her. She tried to step back, but the narrow aisle allowed no retreat.

"See who I've found, lads," Willoughby said. "Our little shopkeepin' beauty, all alone and pinin' for company." Laughing, he took her arm.

As she tried to shake it off, another dandy stepped to her other side. A liquor glaze on his face, he grasped her shoulder with one unsteady hand. "Gotta kiss for an old frien', sweet'eart?"

"Find your own tart, Baxter." Willoughby gave his rival a push, to the hilarity of the watching group. "I've been waitin' for this little morsel a long time."

Anger and a gathering panic rose in her throat. Without Francesca she was alone against them. One of these drunken ruffians she could handle, but four?

What right had they to spoil her enjoyment with their boorish insults? Harnessing her rising indignation, she wrenched her arm free. "I do not appreciate your presence, sir. Kindly remove yourself."

"She don't sound too friendly, Willoughby," one said.

"Needs a lit'l more charm," Willoughby replied, pulling a coin from his waistcoat. "This'll sweetin' her tongue." Grabbing her shoulder, he pulled her to him and made as if to jam the sovereign down her bodice.

In anger as fierce as her fear, she prepared to deal him the roundhouse punch her husband had taught her. Before she could swing, her tormentor was seized by the throat and yanked away, the coin tumbling from his fingers.

"*Kind* of you to watch out for my guest, Willoughby, but as I've returned, further assistance is unnecessary."

To her infinite relief, the dark-haired form of Evan's friend Brent Blakesly moved to her side. Positioning himself between her and the loitering bucks, he surveyed the men with a hard, unsmiling gaze. "'Evening, gentlemen."

Willoughby rubbed his throat. "*Your* guest?"

"If you care to dispute that, I'll be happy to oblige," Brent replied. "Not, of course, at this moment. Excepting yourself, there is polite society present." He made a quick gesture to the surrounding boxes. "Unless you'd like to provide the entr'acte amusement?"

For a moment, face creased in a scowl, Willoughby stood fast. But as he met Brent's implacable gaze, his own faltered. He looked away.

"I thought not." Turning his back on the group, Brent offered Emily a smile. "I'm sorry your visit to the theater was marred by these oafs. Won't you stroll with me and see if I can reverse that bad impression?"

He held out his arm. Grateful, she took it. "Thank you, Mr. Blakesly. Some cool air would be most refreshing."

The press of people prevented further conversation until they reached the lobby. He guided her into a space in the far corner and stood guard, back to the milling crowd.

"Thank you again for your kindness. I don't think I could have discouraged those gentlemen without a most embarrassing scene."

Brent grimaced. "No gentlemen there. I'm so sorry you were disturbed. Reflecting on it, I believe I must look Willoughby up later and teach him some manners. However—" a grin softened his face "—though it hardly excuses his behavior, I must warn you that so beautiful a lady seemingly unescorted does attract attention."

Was there reproof in his tone? "Francesca was to accompany me, but at the last minute found the prospect of Shakespeare too daunting. 'Twas not wise to come alone, I suppose."

"I find Shakespeare a bit daunting myself. But if you will permit, I would feel easier if I might escort you for the remainder. 'Twould be my privilege as well."

His unassuming courtesy touched her. "Thank you again, sir. I should be privileged to accept."

Her gratitude at his rescue helped ease the awkwardness she would otherwise have felt at being squired by a man so nearly a stranger. And his tall presence beside her not only put to rest any fears of a repetition of the unwelcome attentions she'd encountered, but distracted her from the compulsion to gaze back up at a certain box.

She ended by enjoying the play much more than she'd anticipated. The awkwardness did not return until, as they walked out to the street thronged with carriages and theatergoers, he offered to escort her home.

"A jarvey would most likely get you there safely, ma'am. But the streets at night can be dangerous, and I'd never forgive myself were something to happen en route."

She had to admit she'd been a bit anxious herself. There seemed no course but to allow him to accompany her.

She held herself stiffly at the far edge of the seat, but he made no attempt to draw close. Indeed, he continued his commentary on the play, plying her with questions so absurd she knew he was trying to set her at ease.

She couldn't truly be easy, especially not when they reached her house. Her discomfort increased after he escorted her up the stairs and into the entry.

Despite his kindness, she must make certain matters clear. After dismissing the footman, she turned to Brent.

"Mr. Blakesly, I'm most grateful for your assistance." She gave his hand a quick, firm shake. "However, you must realize I do not generally..." she fumbled for words "...accept a gentleman's escort. Or keep company with one."

He smiled. "Then I am doubly lucky."

Did he take her full meaning? Flushing, she steeled herself to continue. "I know you are a friend of Lord Cheverley. Excuse me for being so blunt, but you must understand I will not, under any circumstances, undertake another...relationship such as I had with him."

She felt heat down to her toes. Despite the humiliation of so baldly stating the matter, she forced herself to meet his gaze, make sure he'd comprehended.

A self-deprecating smile twisted his lips. "I'm no grand lord like Evan, to offer costly inducements. Nor, frankly, would I want to." He met her gaze squarely.

"I'd be lying if I said your beauty left me unmoved. But I also enjoy your company. Your wit, your very lack of flirtatiousness. I truly wish to stand your friend."

His face grave, he raised one hand. "Upon my honor, I would never do you the insult of suggesting something...else." He paused, as if to give her time to judge his sincerity, then added softly, "Is your life so busy you have no room in it even for a friend?"

She searched his face and could find only honesty. She recalled the comfort of him standing by her at the theater, the comfort of having someone with whom to share the evening's enjoyment. Though caution urged her to refuse, a lonely longing kept her silent.

A friend. Dare she allow it?

"I...I don't know."

"At least you haven't refused." He grinned, which combined with the dusting of freckles on his nose the bright lamplight revealed, made him appear younger. Not threatening. "Do you ride? If you followed the army, you must be a bruising rider."

Memory of some of those "bruising" rides brought a smile to her face. "Indeed."

"I'm a bit of an enthusiast, I admit—'tis my only extravagance. If you enjoy it, I've a mare in my stables I think would be perfect for you. And I ride early." He held up a hand to fend off that probable protest. "'Tis the only time, before most of London is stirring, for a good gallop."

Oh, how tempted she was. A country girl born and bred, she'd always loved horses. Selling off Andrew's cattle had been one of the most heartbreaking tasks she'd faced.

"'Tis excellent exercise, and the morning air very beneficial," he coaxed. "But I won't push you. Send me a message any time, Curzon Street, Number 15. Now I should leave you to your rest." He swept her a bow.

He would not coerce her. That simple fact alone nearly prompted her to accept on the spot. But when she opened her lips, he put a finger against them.

"Say nothing now, please. A refusal would cast me into the dumps, and an acceptance so excite me I should not sleep a wink. I need my rest, too, you know."

As he watched her, his teasing look faded. She could feel the tension between them build. Slowly, slowly, tracing her lip as he went, he removed his finger.

Before her alarm escalated into retreat, he seemed to shake off the mood. He caught up her hand and kissed it briskly. "Good evening, ma'am. I will sleep in hope."

Someone to laugh and ride and chat with—no strings attached. Bittersweet longing filled her. "So shall I."

Bowing again, he walked out. She wandered to the window and watched as, whistling, he strolled away in the flickering gaslight, leaving her to ponder with bemused appreciation his wit and kindness.

A friend such as that might be just what her aching heart needed.

Hampton as Lear, Evan thought as the carriage approached the theater. Shakespeare always revitalized him, and Lear certainly fit his mood. Thunder and turf, he was tired of pasting a smile on his face.

It's getting better, he told himself, repeating the litany with which he'd extinguished all other thought these past weeks. Maybe soon, in a million years or so, he'd actually believe it.

As always, he clung to long-engrained rituals of civility to get him through. See his mama and Clare and Andrea out of the carriage, make way for them through the throng to their box, arrange chairs for the best view.

Andrea. She was in looks, her pale blond beauty shown to advantage in the cherry gown his mama had chosen. Mercifully, she demanded little of him, seeming content to spend most of her time in his mama and sister's company. But then, they had always been friends. *Friends.*

As the time for their nuptials slowly approached he found it increasingly difficult to express even that limited emotion. He dared not allow himself to feel, lest the caged beast of rage and despair escape to ravage all around him.

Grateful when the start of the play relieved him of the task of manufacturing more light chatter, he fastened his gaze on the stage.

The lyrical cadences did soothe, allowing him to lose himself in the play for a time. As the interval began, he kept his eyes focused downward, delaying as long as possible the necessity to resume polite conversation.

A commotion among the lower seats caught his attention, and in the next heartbeat, he saw her.

Emily! She never went out in public, yet it was unmistakably her. And the group of rowdies surrounding her were Willoughby and his loutish friends, unmistakably accosting her.

Rage brought him instantly to his feet. But before he could race to her assistance he saw Brent step in, shoulder Willoughby aside, say something that caused the group, with obvious reluctance, to disperse.

Bravo, friend! he exulted. And watched intently as a moment later, Brent led her out.

Was she upset, shaken? He must know. Suddenly aware of the curious stares of his family, he mumbled something disjointed about spotting a friend, and pushed his way from the box, nearly running in his eagerness.

He didn't pause until he reached the lobby. Stopping to scan the crowd, he located them in a corner. Brent stood protectively before her; Emily, head lowered, seemed to be listening to something Brent was saying.

Something amusing, evidently. The hint of a smile curved her lips.

Evan took one step to go to her before sanity returned. What could he say or do? Any acknowledgement from him would call down on them the worst of the gossipmongers, evil weaselly minds intent on ferreting out every detail.

Even with Brent her presence was attracting some notice. Though as an undistinguished younger son with neither great fortune nor elevated title, Brent was able to do as he pleased with little comment from the ton.

Unlike himself, whose every word and gesture would be noted. No, he must not go to her.

And had to clench his teeth and curl his hands into fists to keep himself from it.

Ah, how beautiful she was! If he could not hear the timbre of her voice, inhale the spice of her lavender scent, he could at least feast his eyes on her, trace his hungry glance through her glossy locks, across her smooth cheek and down the column of her throat, embrace her with his gaze as his arms ached to do.

Focusing on her with longing so sharp it squeezed the air from his lungs, he finally realized despite his mama's admonition that with time, his sacrifice would seem easier, despite his own determination to ''move on,'' he'd only been deceiving himself.

He would never forget Emily. To his last breath he would carry her with him, under his skin, in his blood, feel the beat of her heart like his own, just as he had the last time they lay together.

Close his eyes and he could hear the music of her voice, feel the smoothness of her satin forehead as he tapped it teasingly when making a point in some argument....

A passerby jostled him and he stumbled back, flattening himself against the stairwell as the lobby crowd began returning to their seats. Obscured by the press of people, he stood watching as Brent took her hand, led her away.

Not until the lobby stood empty, the custodians looking at him curiously, did he slowly climb the stairs to his box.

He ignored the searching glance his mama sent him upon his tardy return. With only a slight change in the angle of his chair, he could see Emily. Through the rest of the play he watched them, the dip of Brent's head as he spoke, her upturned face in reply.

Her father-in-law must still be absent if she judged it safe to go out. But she shouldn't be sitting there among the crowd, subject to the insults of any lounging buck. Simmering anger stirred again, and with anticipation he resolved to search out Willoughby and challenge him to a highly satisfying bout of fisticuffs.

She should have a box available the rest of the Season, to use whenever she wished. He'd speak with Manners about it on the morrow.

The frozen lethargy in which he'd moved, trancelike, this past month began to crack. He ought to have Manners check on the progress of her business as well. And why not instruct the lawyer to transfer the deed on her house into her name? Set up an account for her son's education, another with a tidy sum to see her through any future financial difficulties. So she'd never again need to seek assistance from another or—his eyes rested on Brent—incur debts she felt obligated, one way or another, to repay.

During the rest of the play he savored the sight of her, not jumping into his own waiting carriage until the hackney—he frowned a bit when Brent followed her into it—bore her away.

Then for the first time in five weeks a genuine smile curled his lips. Tomorrow at opening of business he'd visit the lawyer. Then wait to hear every detail of how the very independent Mrs. Spenser responded to his gifts.

*   *   *

Ten days later, Mr. Manners sat with a glass of Richard's port and recounted his interview with Emily.

"Quite a determined lady, and looking to be very successful," the lawyer told Evan. "I think you shall see a handsome return on that investment."

"I'm glad of it, but about the box—what did she say?"

Mr. Manners turned to him, his austere face almost…smiling. "She wished me to convey her appreciation, but said she could not put you to such inconvenience."

"You told her the box was already rented and will stand empty if she does not avail herself of it?"

The solicitor's smile broadened. "Aye, I did. And assured her that the box being now in her name, she and she alone could determine its use."

"And?"

Mr. Manners cleared his throat. "She asked if my wife and I enjoy the theater."

Evan laughed. Damme, how long had it been since anything had stirred him to genuine amusement? Chuckling as well, Mr. Manners produced a ticket from his waistcoat pocket and waved it. "I remonstrated, but as she remained adamant, what could I do but thank her most kindly?"

"And the house?"

Mr. Manners sipped his port. "She insisted she could not accept the deed. I finally convinced her her acceptance is irrelevant. Once the title had been conveyed, the property was legally hers whether she wished it or no, to use or dispose of."

That prospect had not occurred to him. "Do you think she will sell it?" he asked, loath to lose any link to her.

"No, quite the opposite. She assured me she considers the dwelling her home. However, she insisted she must continue to pay rent until such time as she reimburses the purchase price of the property."

Evan's lips twitched. How he wished he might have spied upon this interview! He could see her, back ramrod straight, chin up and eyes shining as she proudly declined largesse he knew no other woman would conceive of refusing.

"You told her that was unacceptable, I trust."

"Actually, no." The lawyer paused to take a sip. "I told her she might continue to pay rent through my office."

Evan's humor faded. "By no means, Mr. Manners! You know I would never permit—"

The lawyer held up a hand. "Hear me out, my lord. If it makes the lady feel easier, why not let her establish what amounts to a savings fund? You must know she vowed she'd not touch a penny of the other trusts you established. In any future difficulties, she might be more likely to approach me if she thought I managed monies she herself had accumulated. Of course, her deposits could then be...augmented as you desire, the increase discreetly credited as interest."

Evan's smile returned. "Small wonder, Mr. Manners, that my family has always been so pleased with your services."

The lawyer bowed. "My privilege, Lord Cheverley." Setting down the empty glass, he turned to the door.

"Thank you for your kind hospitality, and naturally I shall keep you informed of any developments."

Evan rose and offered his hand. After a startled moment, the lawyer took it. "Thank you, Mr. Manners. I can rest easy now, knowing she will be protected."

The lawyer paused on the threshold. "I must admit, when first you broached this project to me several months ago, I thought it most ill-advised. But Mrs. Spenser is not at all what I expected. A most…extraordinary lady."

Longing coiled within Evan, a familiar ache. "Aye."

After the lawyer departed, Evan looked over to the painting he'd hung over his mantel. Pots of lavender glowed in a mist of morning sun that shimmered over a stone sundial and spilled splotches of warmth on an old deacon's bench.

The scene beckoned every time he looked at it, inviting him into the garden—Emily's garden at the shop.

Just before she removed to the new house, knowing she'd be moving the picture, he'd baldly asked for it. He'd placed it first in his office at the ministry, but after their…break, he'd transferred it here.

Since he'd brought Andrea to London to stay with them he'd established his library as his personal retreat, the one place in the house he allowed none but the cleaning maids to enter, refusing permission even to his mother.

How many hours, ostensibly employed in business, had he spent gazing at that painting, scoured by memories?

Returning unexpectedly, he'd once caught his mama at the open door staring at it. She'd walked quickly away, no doubt sensing the curt words of dismissal he'd not have been able to prevent himself uttering.

He brought his mind back to the conversation with Mr. Manners, replaying every detail.

The new venture was prospering and she'd secured an impressive number of advance orders. No problems with the house or shop, as far as Manners knew.

Evan had, God help him, even pressed the solicitor to comment on her gown and appearance. After one speculative glance, as if wondering about his client's sanity, the lawyer recalled she had worn something in lavender and appeared pale but self-possessed.

Evan sighed. As energizing as it was to be able to talk about her, Manner's descriptions were far too sketchy.

How he missed her still. Even the prosaic discussions they had held over evening tea about the details of the day he recalled with poignant fondness. He dare not allow himself to remember anything more intimate.

Just how did he think he was going to steel himself to take Andrea as his wife?

Pushing away that unanswerable question, he thought once more about the new business.

There were many details the lawyer had not thought to ask. The advance orders were a clever idea, one he'd not considered, he thought approvingly. Should she hire an additional seamstress, or would those now engaged be sufficient to expeditiously complete the volume of orders?

He could send Manners back again, but those answers would surely generate other questions.

The idea electrified him the moment it flashed into his head. He was her primary investor. He had considerable, if secondhand, business experience, much more than his solicitor. Why should he not pay a call himself? Strictly business, of course.

The Pandora's box of suppressed longing bursting open, he jumped up, possessed of an urgent desire to seek her out.

Struggling to retain perspective, he forced himself to sit down. He should send a note—but no, she might not wish to receive him, and once formed, the idea of seeing her so possessed him he doubted he could bear a refusal.

Dropping by during business hours would be unexceptional. She met with other people of commerce during that time, why not her primary investor?

His glance flew to the mantel clock and he cursed under his breath. Already too late to set out today.

How many hours until start of business tomorrow?

He sprang up again, paced the room and came to rest beneath the little painting. Thank heaven he was not promised to escort his family anywhere tonight. He might remain safely in his sanctuary.

Or mayhap visit his club. Filled now with an edgy restlessness, he found the book-lined dimensions of this room too confining. If it hadn't been coming on to night, he'd have headed to the park for a gallop.

He'd visit his club.

That sojourn was marginally satisfactory. Dinner was tolerable, he supposed, though he tasted none of it, after which he won several hands of whist without recalling a single moment of the play. Had gambling, drinking, the endless political gossip always been this much of a bore?

But near midnight, as he tooled his curricle north from St. James, his hands seemed to take on a life of their own. Without conscious decision, they guided the bays west around Hyde Park, then south again toward the river.

To a small, elegant townhouse.

He pulled up the horses, gazing at the lamp glow in the window. His heart commenced to pound.

He'd see her tomorrow. Surely he could wait that long. 'Twas unwise, no, 'twas insanity to try to see her tonight.

Would she even admit him?

Before his mind finished the thought he found himself looping the bay's reins to a hitching post. He mounted the stairs, listened to the reverberating bang of the door knocker. Scarcely breathing, he waited.

Chapter Twelve

Emily gaped at the sleepy footman, the book she'd been reading sliding from her grasp. "Lord Cheverley is below?"

"Aye, mistress, and desires but a word with ye."

A starburst of contradictory reactions exploded in her head, as if a match had been tossed into a box of fire-crackers.

How dare he intrude upon her peace, uninvited, at this hour? 'Twas preposterous, presumptuous in the extreme.

Why had he come? Was he hurt, in some need? Anxiety fired through her fury.

Had he broken off his engagement? An eager longing overshadowed all the others.

Nonsense. She tried to extinguish the spurt of excitement. Even had he done so their relationship was over. There was nothing between them that could not better be conveyed by letter.

"What do you wish I should tell him, ma'am?"

Attention recalled to the waiting footman, she tried to marshall her scattered wits and reply.

He was here, just below in her parlor, a few minutes' walk down a short flight of stairs away.

Without conscious volition she rose, patted the mystified footman on the sleeve as, still speechless, she passed him and moved to the stairs.

Then she stood before the parlor door, dizzy with anticipation and dread, thoughts still flitting about in her head like a flight of demented butterflies.

He shouldn't have come. Why had he come? *Dismiss him. Speak just for a moment. No, 'tis madness—send him away.*

Taking a deep breath, she walked in.

He was staring out the window. Though she entered soundlessly he must have sensed her presence, for he turned.

Body tensed, fists clenched, he examined her from hairline to the tips of her slippers, his intense gaze mesmerizing her. The powerful, instantaneous attraction that had always existed between them drew her irresistibly closer.

A foot away she made herself stop, clasped her hands together lest she reach up to touch the tiny lines beside his eyes, the cleft of his chin.

She opened her lips to order him out, and said "Why?"

"Please, don't send me away yet! I wanted—I needed to talk with you. For a moment only. About the business."

Business? She glanced at the clock. "'Tis hardly the hour for a business call."

Did he flush? "Yes. Sorry. But I talked with Manners about the...the shop this afternoon and I could not wait."

The shop. How could she concentrate on income, disbursements, supplies with him but a touch away? She made herself focus on the fire beyond him.

"W-what did you need to discuss?"

"Manners said you'd taken advance orders. How many? Do you anticipate needing additional help?"

For the next few moments she struggled to harness her muzzy brain to extract intelligent answers for the smattering of questions he fired at her. Then silence fell.

The question seemed to pop out of her still-disjointed thoughts. "This house—you bought it for me at the very beginning, didn't you?"

He smiled slightly. "Yes. Are you angry?"

"Not any longer." She raised her chin. "I'm purchasing it, you know."

His smile broadened. "I can always use another good investment. And—I've wondered about it but Manners wouldn't tell me—is Spenser your real name?"

"Part of it."

"So if you were to...disappear, I'd not find you."

"You'd have no need to."

"Need," he repeated, and sighed deeply. "Ah, Emily."

She shouldn't look back at him. The business discussion had ended. She should simply bid him good-night.

But despite that wise counsel, her gaze lifted. A poignant tenderness welled up, and for a moment she gave herself over to the pleasure of studying each dearly remembered line of cheek and lip, the angle of brow and jut of chin. And his eyes, ah, the beautiful midnight blue depths of his eyes.

So focused was she it took her a moment to realize he was approaching, his hand moving toward her.

''Don't—''

''Please! Please, Emily. Just one touch. Then I'll leave, I swear it.''

No, no, no, the rational voice in her head shouted. *Not closer. Not touching.*

But her feet wouldn't move, her word of protest rusted in her throat. She could only watch his hand descend.

''Emily,'' he whispered.

She closed her eyes as his fingers traced gently, so gently over her brow, her temple, her eyelids, her cheekbones, around her chin. She sensed more than saw his head move toward hers.

''You mustn't,'' she tried to say, and caught the glancing touch of his tongue on hers. Had he crushed her against him, demanding, insistent, she might have shoved him away.

But the kiss was gentle, too, so full of the same wonder and aching need she felt herself that her arms moved instead to encircle his neck and of her own will draw him nearer.

Ah, here she belonged, close against his chest. Here her ragged incompleteness was smoothed whole, here and here alone she found peace.

Then he was lifting her into his arms.

''One touch,'' she gasped. ''You said one touch and you would leave.''

''I thought I could. I was wrong.'' Kissing her fiercely, he clutched her tighter and mounted the stairs.

Emily sat propped against her pillows watching Evan sleep beside her, fighting the tenderness that constricted her chest.

'Twas daylight now, time to put an end to midnight madness, to this ill-advised reunion that changed nothing.

That he was not yet married was a feeble sop to her conscience. Being but days or weeks from it, he was as good as married, and their night together inexcusable.

As soon as he woke she would tell him so, force herself to make him leave.

She hoped he would doze a very long while.

All too soon he stirred. As his eyes opened, he saw her and a smile of pure joy illumined his face. ''My darling,'' he whispered, and drew her into his embrace.

Despising herself for her weakness, she let him. Just this one last time she would lie beside him enveloped in the blessed comfort of his closeness. One last time before facing a future whose absolute bleakness she dare not contemplate.

He stroked her cheek, the wispy tendrils of hair at her temple. ''I've missed you so, sweeting. Every day and night and hour since we parted. I tried to convince myself it was for the best, that it must be. Not until last night did I realize how wrong I was.

''We'll have to be careful, of course. I shan't be able to come to you every evening, and 'twould not be prudent for me to acknowledge you in public. Perhaps I shall lease a country house—'twould be easier to get away for a few days outside of London, and…''

Get away? See her? The words jarred her to alertness. Could he possibly think—

"No!" She pulled away abruptly and sat up. "What can you be imagining?"

"I know none of the—circumstances have altered. But after the hell of these last weeks, surely you believe as I do that we must be together. Sweetheart, 'tis a sorry crumb of a loaf, but better the tiniest crumb than none at all."

He could rationalize his own conscience—and just dismiss hers? Once again seize control of her life and think to dictate what she would do?

She fed the fortifying anger. "No, Evan. You've so much power, you think you can control me and by your wishing it, change the rules of conscience? It's not that easy."

He stared at her a moment, disbelieving, then shoved himself upright as well.

"Easy?" he repeated. "Do you honestly think anything about you, about us, has ever been 'easy'? Do you think I don't realize in doing this I sully my honor as well as yours, bend or break the solemn oaths I've pledged? But not to do so condemns me, us, to the unspeakable existence we've suffered these last seven weeks. In the depths of my heart I cannot believe what we share is wrong. 'Tis far more than lust, you know that! Bah, I'm no philosopher, to sort out reasoned arguments. I just know that what we have together is pure and precious. Can you deny it?"

She dare not admit a feeling her self-respect demanded she smother.

"Call it what you will, 'tis still wrong."

He wants to dictate, just like Papa and Andrew's father, she thought, trying to refire her anger. *Don't let him.*

"What right have you to dismiss my honor, as if only yours mattered? I'm not a plaything, to toy with as you choose."

"No, you are not. You are the center of my world, my universe. I can't conceive of a future without you."

His impassioned words flamed through her, scorching her weakening defenses. She must marshal her pitiful reserves and end this before he reduced them to smoking ruin, before she went mad. Or even worse, succumbed.

"Those of lower status learn early they cannot always get what they desire, or turn wrong into right by wishing it. 'Tis a difficult lesson, my lord, but I think you must learn it."

He stared at her, his face inscrutable. At last he spoke, his voice near a whisper. "After I've beggared my honor and bartered my pride, you will still send me away?"

He must never return, she must never see him again. She could not withstand a repetition of this. She forced herself to utter words that would make it so.

"Let us not spoil the past with unpleasantness. You've been most generous, for which I thank you, but the bald truth is I don't require your assistance any longer. For you I have been a useful convenience. But 'tis time to move on, so let's not confuse the issue with pretty words."

She could not look at him and withstand the hurt she knew she'd find in his eyes, in every stiff line of his outraged body. She kept her face averted.

"Convenient?" He spat out the word, then uttered a harsh bark of laughter. "Aye, madam, no more pretty words." He leaned over and seized her.

"Tell me, my heart, my darling," he snarled as he forced her down on the bed, pinned her with his body, "tell me this is just 'convenient.'" Holding her head prisoned with one arm, he kissed her mouth and throat roughly, scouring her with his lips, his stubbled face.

As his lips descended, though, their touch altered, became taunting, seductive. "Tell me," he whispered hoarsely as kissing deep, nipping gently, he assaulted her collarbone, her chest, "tell me you feel nothing."

She wanted to resist, to reinforce with her body the lies of her lips, but, battered by her own anguish and his, she lay helpless, reserves exhausted. Tears came, welling in her eyes and dripping down into her hair. When his lips reached her breasts, when with infinite cherishing skill he played upon those sensitive nerves, she broke completely, bringing her limp arms up to cradle his head.

At her touch he shuddered and went still. His arms slid around her shoulders and he bound her to him in a long, fierce, breath-stopping embrace, his face searing her chest with hot wet heat.

The sudden coolness struck her when he sprang up. Swiftly he gathered his clothes, then turned to face her, his eyes stark.

"Deny it to yourself, but never to me."

He turned on his heel and strode from the room.

* * *

She knew not how long she lay immobile. She concentrated all her will on taking one slow steady breath after another, shutting out everything else. To think at all would be to scream in agony.

Gradually the chill of the unheated room penetrated, each faint stir of breeze frosty over her damp eyes and moist hair. With shivering fingers she reached down to cover the frigid wetness at her belly. And touched the small cold pool of his tears.

After a period of fitful slumber, Emily roused to a knock at her door. Francesca peeped in.

"Mistress, Senhor Blakesly calls. Do I let him in?"

Emily turned to peer at the mantel clock. "Heavens, Francesca, why did you not wake me sooner?"

The maid stared at her a moment, a gentle sympathy in her eyes. "I sleep lightly, *querida.*"

Francesca knew. Heat washed Emily's face.

Ever practical, the maid wasted no time in recrimination. "Do I tell him stay, or go?"

Emily tried to focus her rattled thoughts. Had she promised to ride with him?

The very morning after the theater trip, Brent had stopped by and repeated his offer of a mount. Unable to resist the dancing, spirited beauty of a mare he'd brought, she'd accepted, and now several times a week they rode together. Being able to lose herself in the simple pleasure of a hard gallop did much to ease her ever-present restlessness.

Brent had stood by his offer to be her friend as well. Though she recognized desire within the warmth in his eyes, never did he hint of a closer relationship. Unique among the men she'd known, he did not attempt to dictate, a fact that was gradually relaxing her wary reserve. Witty, calm, attentive but not dominating, he let her, as he'd promised, set the tone and timing of their meetings.

Sometimes she asked him to stay for breakfast after their rides, and twice she'd accompanied him to the theater. Struggling as she was to contain her sadness and desperate longing, she could not help but appreciate his steady, undemanding presence.

She was quite sure she'd not agreed to ride this morning. What else would bring him here at so unfashionable an hour? Good friend that he'd been, if there were some trouble she should help. Despite her physical and mental exhaustion, she pushed aside the bed linens.

''Tell Mr. Blakesly if he can wait a few moments, I will join him. And bring tea, please, Francesca.''

Brent was standing by the fireplace when she walked in some moments later—exactly, she recalled with a pang, where Evan, bathed in moon glow, had stood last night. She felt the fraying threads of her control loosen again and jerked herself from memories she must never again indulge.

''Good morning, Brent. This is a pleasant surprise. What brings you here—no trouble, I hope?''

He turned then and studied her face. ''Should I not rather ask you that?''

She gave her head a tiny shake. Her wits were so scrambled this morning, it took her a moment to puzzle out his meaning. ''W-why should you think there was trouble?''

He said nothing for a time, continuing to subject her to close scrutiny, as if searching for—what, she couldn't fathom. Finally he said, "I brought a new mare to town yesterday for you to try." He uttered a short laugh. "As a surprise. I brought her by early this morning, knowing you are usually awake, and...and saw Evan leaving."

Shame, embarrassment and regret swirled in her. She wanted to explain, to apologize, but how could she excuse the raw truth he had seen?

"I can't imagine what you must be thinking of me. All I can say is—"

"Please, don't!" He captured one hand and kissed it. "I think you the most beautiful, talented, courageous woman I've ever known. Nothing, absolutely nothing could happen that would change that opinion." He looked away. "'Twas my belief, however, that Evan had—relinquished his claim."

"We parted weeks ago. But last night he stopped by unexpectedly, and we—" She broke off, flushing.

"He forced you? The blackguard, I'll—"

"No, you mustn't think that of him! 'Twas my fault as much as his."

Shame heated her cheeks, but remembering that night ignited flames of another sort all over her body. Curse her for a fool, she still wanted him. She still missed him.

She closed her eyes, fighting the insidious longing. Then opened them and made herself continue. "'Twas only last night. I knew 'twas wrong, but..."

"Do you love him?"

She mustn't, couldn't love him. "No. But he is still...very dear to me." The truth, surely. "Regardless of that, our...association is over, quite finally. I do not expect ever to see him again.''

The heaviness that descended on her chest as she spoke those words was merely fatigue, she assured herself.

''You are certain that is what you want?''

Want? No, but conscience permitted no other course. ''Yes.''

Brent released a long, slow sigh, almost as if he'd been holding his breath. ''Then he will never bother you again. I give you my word on it.''

A stab of foreboding pierced her. ''You mustn't—oh, please do not speak of me to Evan! There's no need, I assure you. I would not wish to sow discord in your friendship.''

''Hush, now.'' Smiling, he put his finger against her lips. ''If there be discord, 'twill not be you who is the cause. You...you do still wish to see me?'' Though his tone was casual, his body tensed as he awaited her answer.

He really did forgive her. More than that, though she had just given him ample cause to despise her, for some reason he still wanted her for a friend. She blinked back a prickle of tears.

''Should I not rather ask you that?''

His eyes lit and his smile turned brilliant. ''Then I believe we are scheduled to ride tomorrow. Perhaps if I'm especially witty you'll ask me to stay for one of Francesca's marvelous breakfasts. But now you must get to the shop.''

''Yes. I shall see you tomorrow, then.''

He took her hand, but rather than brushing it with his lips, he turned it over and placed a lingering kiss on her palm. He raised to her violet eyes dark with emotion. ''Thank you.'' After a brief bow, he walked out.

She didn't deserve Brent's fidelity, she thought guiltily as she watched him leave. But the soothing balm it offered was immense.

He really ought to forget her, Evan mused as he stared up at the little landscape. In a fit of anger upon his return after their bitter parting, he'd yanked the painting from above his library mantel.

Later that day he'd rehung it. Her words had been meant to wound, to rip a final breach through their accord and cauterize it beyond hope of mending. He understood that intuitively, once the blindness of hurt and outrage faded, understood why she had spoken thus.

But he could not believe her. To some resonant note deep within him she still played the resolving chord, a harmony beside which disdainful words were as the thunder of a passing storm outside an unbreachable fortress, irrelevant, unable to cause harm.

Her resolve to remain parted he did believe. She was right; 'twas for the best to uphold honor and fulfill duty. If behind that facade of fortitude the inner self suffered, he must be man enough to endure.

He would bury himself in work and think on her as little as possible. And if late at night he drifted back to the library to gaze at her landscape and cherish their memories, should he not be allowed some small reward for soldiering through yet another endless day?

The sound of a throat being repeatedly cleared finally pulled him out of meditation.

"My lord, Mr. Blakesly to see you."

He'd been so busy upon his return to town, he'd not seen his friend since Richard's funeral. With pleasure he extended his hand to the tall figure entering the library.

"Brent, good to see you! It's been too long."

Brent halted a pace away. His face unsmiling, he glanced at Evan's outstretched hand and, arms held stiffly at his sides, made him a short, stiff bow.

"I've not come for a visit, *my lord.*" He gave the courtesy scornful emphasis. "I've but a message to deliver."

Surprise at the rebuff held Evan speechless for a moment. "Message?"

Eyes narrowed and jaw set, Brent leaned until his face was but a few inches from Evan's. "You call yourself a gentleman? You celebrate your engagement—notices in the press, small elect gatherings among the ton. Then under cover of darkness slink away to treat Emily as your *whore!*" Face contorted with anger, he spat out the word.

Shocked, shamed, Evan could think of no reply.

Brent exhaled an explosive breath. His voice, when he continued, was cool, his face deadly calm. "Well, no more. Sooner or later I intend to marry Emily, if she'll have me. And married or not, as God is my witness, if you ever go near her again I'll kill you." He made an elaborate bow. "Your servant, my lord."

Brent turned on his heel, began to walk away. Finally finding his voice, Evan strode after and halted him with a hand to the shoulder. "Marry Emily? How can you? 'Tis impossible!"

Jerking free, Brent whirled toward him. "I'm not the mighty Earl of Cheverley, with duties owed a portrait gallery of ancestors long dead. To think I used to envy you that title and wealth." He gave a short, mirthless laugh. "My family may squawk, but duty in the Blakesly line falls on Cousin Edward. If they wish to see me and my children, they'll treat Emily with the respect due my wife. And should it come to a choice between her and the cut direct from the ton, I swear to you I'd have the ring on her finger faster than you could blink."

Brent to marry Emily? *His* love, *his* secret joy? Corrosive jealousy and anger born of weeks of repressed longing fired to instant rage. "You cannot marry her. I forbid it!"

Brent tensed as if to throw a punch, then relaxed. "You *forbid* it?" He laughed shortly. "You forfeited the right to say anything months ago. This time, see that you remember that fact, for I assure you, my warning is no idle threat. Stay away from her, Evan." He bowed again, curtly. "My regards to your mother and Andrea."

Before Evan could remonstrate further, Brent strode from the room. Fuming, Evan followed, but at the door, reason returned and he halted.

There was nothing he could or should do. Brent was a good man; he'd take care of Emily. She deserved that, deserved someone fine enough to recognize her excellence, someone willing to brave the scorn of the ton to claim her.

Why did the mere thought of someone else touching her burn in his gut like acid?

Perhaps because their shared memories were his most precious possession. The idea of yielding her to another, even a man as worthy as Brent, was like having the most cherished part of himself ripped out.

Yes, he wanted Emily comfortable, appreciated and cared for. He just could not kill the hopeless longing that he be the man to do so.

A few days later, Emily sat over her portfolio at the desk in her old office. In the wake of that disastrous night with Evan, a lingering depression bore down her spirits, from which even Brent's quiet, thoughtful companionship couldn't entirely distract her.

Dear Brent, whose words still spoke of friendship but whose assiduous attention and increasingly ardent glances were growing ever more like a courtship.

With a pang of guilt, she couldn't help wishing, bruised as she was in body and spirit, for a continuation of their straightforward camaraderie. Anything more was beyond her just now.

At least here at the shop, adding detailed notes to her sketches, she could accomplish something useful. She did find solace in perfecting her designs, directing the busily stitching seamstresses, did feel satisfaction watching what began as visions in her head turn into gowns whose sale would buy a safe future for herself and her son.

She heard the entry bell ring. Francesca was in the kitchen fixing her soup and tea, so the newly hired shop girl met the customers at the door. From the corner of her eye as she studied a sketch Emily noted them enter, heard the murmured greetings.

She had but to add a few more instructions and the riding dress would be complete. Long, slender, its cap-sleeved pelisse trimmed with epaulettes and gold braid, the gown was a feminine interpretation of Andrew's army uniform. She smiled, remembering the stir she'd created the first time she'd worn a similar garment out riding in Portugal. "Daughter of the Regiment," some of Andrew's fellow officers had said, teasing her.

Ah, Andrew. She rested her head on her hand as shame swirled up to color the old familiar burden of grief. Praise God you cannot see me now....

A shadow fell across her, followed by two hands that seized hers hard. "Auriana! Blast it, woman, I've been the length and breadth of Spain hunting you!"

Fear shot through her and she looked up so sharply little stars of light marred her vision. Not until a moment later did her eyes focus enough for her to recognize a dearly familiar face: her brother-in-law, Major Robert Alan Waring-Black.

Chapter Thirteen

"Rob!" she cried joyfully. "Whatever are you doing in England? And out of uniform? I thought you still with Wellington's staff!"

"No. I took a hit a few months after Andrew was wounded—but 'tis a long story. Ah, Ari, how good it is to see you!" He wrapped her in a hug.

She hugged him back, then grasped his hands. "'Tis wonderful to see you, too, Rob."

"Robert?" A tall blond woman entered the little office. Her startled gaze went from Emily's face to the hands her brother-in-law still held, and lingered there.

After giving her fingers another squeeze, Robert released them, but left one hand resting on her shoulder, as if to reassure himself she was truly found. "Natalie, my dear, only see who I've discovered. Auriana, may I present to you my wife Natalie. Nat, this is my brother's elusive widow, Auriana."

Andrew's wild, carefree scapegrace of a brother married? 'Twas hard to conceive. "Delighted to meet you, ma'am—and congratulations."

"Thank you." The tall woman nodded but did not smile. Her eyes returned again to her husband's hand at Emily's shoulder. "So you are the lady we've been tracking over dusty roads in every manner of poorly sprung conveyance for half a year?"

"You've been searching for me?" she echoed, astonished.

At his wife's frosty tone, Rob only laughed. "'Tis a good thing I was forced to sell out. I'm afraid my Nat would never have made a soldier's bride. And how could you not expect me to hunt for you as soon as I was able, dear friend, my brother's wife, the woman who tended my wounds and pulled me back from death?"

He released her shoulder and his tone lightened. "You'd covered your tracks well, though. We'd only just begun to make progress, but I'd given Nat my word after six months I'd bring her home."

"Mistress, *que barulho,*" Francesca said as she backed into the room, heavy tray in hand. She turned, spied Robert, and her face lit. "Roberto, *meu amor! Como está?*"

"Francesca!" Robert sprang over, dispensed with the tray and enveloped the maid in a hug. In a rapid spate of Portuguese the two exchanged greetings. Then, wrapping one arm about Francesca, he walked the maid over and put his hand back on Emily's shoulder.

"Come to the town house for tea. You must send for your things and stay with us. And where is my imp of a nephew?"

The town house? Chill foreboding dampened her joy. "We cannot! Your papa would never...where *is* your papa, Rob?"

A look of bitterness passed over his face. "Papa? You do not know? Indeed, we do have much to discuss."

At that moment the new sales girl came to the door, her hands full of hats. "I fetched these bonnets from the window, Lady Maxwell. Would you like to inspect them? And his lordship?"

Slowly Emily turned toward Robert. "His *lordship?*"

Robert gave her a rueful flicker of a smile. "At your service. Papa and your dear eldest brother-in-law both died of the same fever last winter, God rest their black souls. And as Alastair's wife never managed to pop out a son, the honors of the estate fell upon lowly me." He laughed shortly, the sound not pleasant. "Is that not rich? They are both writhing in their graves, I'm sure."

Too surprised to utter a word, Emily merely stared. Her father-in-law dead. Dead, no longer a threat to her. *He cannot take Drew.* Her son was safe.

While her rattled brain tried to absorb that incredible information, Robert's austere face softened to a grin. "But enough of that—I'm hungry for my tea. Pack up the tray, Francesca. In the carriage you can begin to tell us all your news. And explain how I spent seven months scouring every alley and byroad in Spain only to find my precious lost sister-in-law in a London shop."

A week later Emily reclined upon a satin-striped settee in the sitting room of an elegant guest bedchamber at Maxwell's Rook. In true military fashion, Rob had overridden her protests that she could not possibly leave London with her collection incomplete, and had carried all of them—herself, Francesca, Drew, his tutor and the tutor's family—off to the Earl's country estate. She needed rest and fresh air, he insisted, and they all needed time to become reacquainted.

She'd barely had a day to turn over her sketches to the chief seamstress, gather clothes and scribble a note to Brent before Rob packed them up and bore them off.

With staff officer efficiency, Rob arranged for every comfort—baskets of food and pots of tea for the carriage, hot bricks for their feet, warm meals and heated private chambers at every stop. Sometimes, when she'd catch a glimpse of him in profile, he reminded her so keenly of Andrew that her heart turned over. She wasn't sure whether it was balm or torture to be living in his house.

Aye, his house now. 'Twas the first time she'd seen the inside of Maxwell's Rook, but she vividly remembered her only previous glimpse of the crenellated fortress set high on a hill, the mullioned windows of its Elizabethan wings gleaming like feral eyes in the near darkness.

Andrew had left her at the gatehouse, the gatekeeper and his wife fussing over the intended bride of their forbidding master's much-loved youngest son, while Andrew went to inform his father of their upcoming marriage.

She would never forget the look on his face, cold and scarred as those ancient stone towers, when he returned with his father's refusal. After scarcely a word, he'd ridden off with her. Neither had ever looked back.

'Twas a moment before she realized Rob must have entered, for he stood at the foot of the sofa gazing at her.

"Thinking how much has changed?" he asked softly.

"Y-yes. How different it was six years ago."

"Aye. We were both on the run from Papa, fellow outcasts—he for marrying you, me for buying us commissions in Wellington's army. Disowned for fighting the French instead of dutifully hunting heiresses to swell the family coffers. We swore a blood oath the night after your wedding, Andrew and I—did you know?"

She shook her head. "We vowed to watch out for each other—and you," he continued. "All for one, and such." His amused voice grew serious. "I mean to honor that vow."

"Rob, I'm enjoying my holiday, and 'tis wonderful for Drew to be part of a family at last, but I cannot remain here, hanging on your coattails. You know what I've become. 'Tis not fitting for a shopkeeper to be living with the Earl of Maxwell."

"You are family, Ari. Come, I know how difficult it is to accept, especially for you. Going from your father's household to the catch-as-catch-can atmosphere of an army on the march, and then—" He took a deep breath. "I cannot imagine how you scraped along after Andrew was wounded, after he... But wait a moment."

Holding up a hand in a restraining gesture, he walked over to rummage in the drawer of the nearby desk.

Remembering the days of short rations, haphazard shelter, odd dinners concocted of army grain, foraged fowl and confiscated French wine, she had to smile. She'd been sometimes terrified, occasionally hungry, but never bored during her vagabond life with Andrew. Whatever happened, she'd had his voice to tease her out of annoyance, his arms to snuggle in at night, his unfailing love to give her courage, to make every sacrifice, every hardship worthwhile.

Her smile faded as Rob handed her an object he removed from a large leather portfolio.

"Andrew's pistol! Where did you get it?"

"From the local lord near the village where he's buried. Don Alvarez would have nothing to do with me until I convinced him I had no ties to Papa. I bought back several items."

Assailed by memories of the last time she'd seen it, with shaking hands she took the weapon. "Thank you, Rob. I'll save it for Drew."

Close her eyes and she could hear it still—the shallow huff-pant of Andrew trying to draw breath into his damaged lungs. She'd hoped to carry him to medical treatment, but by the time they'd reached the village nearest where their party had been ambushed it became evident to move him further would be to kill him outright.

So they'd stayed. Sometimes the villagers, sympathetic to the plight of the English soldier and his lady, would leave food on their doorstep—eggs, milk, once a chicken tied by a cord on its leg to the door knocker.

Despite that her small store of funds was soon exhausted. She'd sold her jewelry first, then Andrew's horses and rifles. Then the pistol.

Tears welled up and she swiped them away. "He complained so little, though I knew he was in constant pain.

One day he begged me for this that he might end his life and release us all. I was so glad I'd already sold it.''

Silently Rob took several other items from the satchel and laid them on her palm.

''His insignia,'' she whispered, touching the glittering bits of braid, gold and silver lace with a reverent fingertip. Each pin and ribbon, epaulette and fastener had meant food, blankets, fuel for their tiny fireplace. ''I sold the last gold button from his tunic to pay for his funeral,'' she murmured.

''There's one thing more,'' Rob said, his voice strained as he handed it to her. A thin gold wedding band.

Her vision blurred as she took it, held it up to read again the familiar engraving: ''Today and forever—Andrew.''

''I didn't want to sell it, I swear! But it's all we had left.''

''I know that, Ari! I'm not blaming you. I know you had to be one meal from starvation to have parted with his ring.''

Still she felt a need to explain. ''I used the money for paints for Don Alvarez's portrait. Later, when I...I had more funds, I tried to buy it back, but the goldsmith said some purchaser, a stranger, had already taken it away, he knew not where.''

''Don Alvarez had an agent purchase all Andrew's things, apparently. I suspect he wanted to give them back to you for Drew as a wedding gift but you...didn't fall in with those plans. Only by insisting Andrew's son should rightfully have them did I convince him to sell them back.''

Slowly she slid the ring on her finger. "Thank you, Rob. For finding it. For f-forgiving me."

"Damn, there's nothing to forgive!" he exploded. "You should never have been reduced to that! 'Tis all Papa's fault, and your hard-headed father's. Well, *I've* the money and power now, and I mean to see you have everything that should have been yours from the beginning. Wealth, comfort, your proper place in society—

"Don't even say it!" He held up a hand to forestall her protest. "I care not if you mucked out stables and serviced the whole French army. Andrew would have wanted you restored to society, to the place you abandoned for him. He would have insisted. Can you deny it?"

That being unanswerable, she gave him none.

"I know how you feel," he continued, his tone coaxing now. "How I felt myself at first. As if it were somehow a betrayal of all we'd fought for, a capitulation to Papa, almost, to enjoy being comfortable and wealthy. But such reservations are silly. We are what our character shows us to be—fine clothes, elegant dwellings and deep pockets are not the true measure of a man. Is that not one of the principles over which we fought with Papa?"

"I suppose. But the world is more likely to share your father's opinion of me than yours."

"We'll just have to change it then, won't we? Because I won't give you up, Auriana. I've lost Andrew. I won't lose you as well. You and Drew are my family, and you stay."

A family. A place to belong. How long had it been since she had known either? While she had Andrew the lack had not mattered.

She recalled happy days in Portugal and Spain, Rob talking and laughing, sharing their frugal meals. She thought of bringing Drew permanently into such a community of caring. Rob was offering what despite her deepest love she could not otherwise provide for her son.

Emotion clogged her throat as Rob held out his arms. Tears blinding her now, she came into them.

After a moment he released her. Emily looked up—into the face of Rob's wife. From the unhappy expression on her pale countenance, Emily knew she had witnessed their embrace.

Rob casually draped an arm over his wife's shoulder. ''Nat, I've been telling Ari she and Drew must make their home with us now.''

Was there a moment of hesitation? ''Yes, of course. *Blood* relations—'' Rob's wife stressed the word ''—belong together.''

And Emily was a connection, linked to them only by marriage—was that what her sister-in-law was implying? Tempting as it was to accept Rob's offer, she'd not do so at the cost of his wife's hostility.

''Natalie, you must make him see that a shopkeeper— a *former* shopkeeper,'' she acknowledged, at Rob's immediate protest, ''does not belong in the household of an earl. 'Twould cause no end of comment and embarrassment.''

Her sister-in-law opened her lips, then closed them. ''I'm sure Robert knows what he wants,'' she said at last.

"I cannot impose so disgracefully on your kindness. Besides, I rather enjoy running the shop, and my house in London is perfectly charming."

"Keep the shop—you can still design," Rob offered. "Or go back to painting portraits—you've a dab hand at that. But here or London, with us you stay."

He gave his wife's shoulder a shake. "Come, Nat, you must help me convince her. We'll see you established among the ton, never fear. Nat's not yet been formally presented as my countess, but—ah, I have it! We must give a grand ball and introduce you both together!"

Emily's jaw dropped and Natalie looked stricken. "Present me? Rob, you've taken leave of your senses!"

Perhaps the devil-may-care soldier hadn't been entirely tamed, for that dangerous sparkle that in times past had heralded some act of recklessness was gleaming in his eyes. "I'm Earl of Maxwell now. You are my sister-in-law, widow of a soldier who died fighting for England. Who has better right to mingle with society's elite?"

"And what of the London matrons I waited on, who bought my hats? You think they will invite me into their drawing rooms or call in mine? I'd be a laughingstock, Rob. They would never—"

"Maxwells have defended England since the days of the Conqueror. I may be new to the title, but I daresay none will dare snub *me*."

Emily clamped her lips shut, realizing too late that deferring to the opinions of the ton leadership, contemporaries of his detested father, was the last thing Rob was likely to do. No, he'd relish forcing them to meet him on his own terms. Which perhaps he now had the power and influence to effect—though she'd as lief not be cannon fodder in that battle. Nor watch her innocent sister-in-law suffer for choices she herself had made.

"Of course they will welcome you," she soothed. "'Madame Emilie,' who painted portraits in Spain and sells hats in London, is quite a different matter. I'd certainly not be invited anywhere upon my own account. And the whole business must excite gossip and speculation that cannot help but be painful to Natalie. You cannot ask it of her."

"Ah, my Natalie's game for anything, aren't you, sweet?"

Her sister-in-law was twisting one pale blond lock. Her glance darted from Emily to her husband and back. Moistening her lips, she said in a colorless voice, "I'll do whatever Robert wishes."

"That's my girl." Dropping a quick kiss on his wife's cheek, Rob walked to the door. "So, there are no objections. You must excuse me—some bloody papers to sign. I've brought Hampstead—you remember him, Ari, my aide-de-camp who lost an arm at Vittoria?—to be my secretary. Dashed good business, this being an earl. I've found positions for half a dozen men from the old regiment. As for the presentation, I'll get Ned cracking on logistics and invitations and such. Everybody who is anybody in London will be there."

Rob clapped his hands, his expression gleeful. "Tear it, wouldn't I love for Andrew to be here when we welcome all our rackety army friends to Papa's marble mausoleum of a town house?"

Still chuckling, he left the room. Natalie made as if to follow, but Emily reached out to stop her.

Despite Rob's insistence, 'twas all too apparent her sister-in-law was less than thrilled with her presence. Family for Drew or no, she'd not stay unless Natalie was able to accept them. Better to settle the matter forthwith, before the industrious Rob got his plans too far in train.

"Please, will you not stay for tea? We've had little chance to chat, and I'd very much like to know you better."

Natalie looked as if she wished to refuse, but was too polite to do so. With obvious reluctance she replied, "Certainly," and took the chair Emily indicated.

"First, I wanted again to extend my good wishes on your marriage," Emily said a few moments later as she handed her a cup. "The Rob I knew was ever a charming rascal, but absolutely adamant about wishing never to wed. You must be a very special lady to have changed his mind."

Surprise widened Natalie's china blue eyes. Obviously taken aback, she fumbled, "Th-thank you, I suppose. Though I must protest I am not in any way out of the ordinary."

"On the contrary. Rob described your journey, and I assure you I know exactly what sort of amenities an English lady can find in the villages you passed through. To have survived that odyssey with sanity intact you must be both resourceful and possessed of an excellent sense of humor."

Natalie's stiffness thawed a trifle. "It was indeed an...adventure," she allowed with a slight smile.

Impulsively Emily reached over to clasp Natalie's hands. "I'm so happy for you both! Rob is very special to me, one of my dearest friends, and I always wished he would find the right lady to love."

Natalie's smile faded. "He certainly cares for you. I heard nothing for months but stories of beautiful, intrepid, resourceful Auriana."

Emily groaned. No wonder her sister-in-law suspected her a rival. What a great dolt Rob was!

"Oh dear, how very tiresome of him. Military gentlemen, as you've doubtless discovered, like nothing better than to prattle on about comrades and campaigns. I suppose because with death all around, the bonds one forms with one's companions become particularly strong."

Natalie merely nodded. Emily paused, considering. The lady obviously resented Emily's hold on her husband, which was only natural. How to convince her now of what time would prove—that Emily posed her no threat?

Again, perhaps 'twas best to speak frankly.

"Forgive me for being direct, but I know you must be concerned about my relationship with Rob. I can only pray you believe that, though he is Andrew's brother and the two are somewhat alike, my feelings for him—and his for me—are entirely fraternal."

For the first time, Natalie looked at Emily squarely, her eyes searching Emily's as if trying to assess the veracity of that claim. "I should like to believe it."

"Another fact about military men I'm sure you already know—once they determine a course of action they are devilish difficult to dissuade! But despite Rob's intention to take us in, I shall not permit it unless I feel you genuinely agree, not just acquiesce to Rob's persuasion.''

For the first time Natalie gave a genuine smile. ''He does tend to order one about, as if one were a soldier in need of direction.''

Emily laughed. ''Indeed! I suspect you've already discovered wifely ways to deflect those commands. If necessary, we shall stand firm together on this. I'll not dissemble—more than anything, I wish my son welcome here. But I'll not intrude myself—not at the cost of your comfort.''

There, she had said it. What happened next depended on the coolly lovely lady sitting opposite.

Emily made herself wait patiently as Natalie silently gazed at her, apparently pondering her answer.

'Twould be sufficient if Rob acknowledged Drew, Emily thought, invited him to Maxwell's Rook or the London house upon occasion. She could manage alone—had she not done so all these years?

She closed her eyes and tried to squelch the hope Rob's rash invitation had engendered that the child-bride who'd been cast off at sixteen might finally come home.

''Auriana—Ari.'' She opened her eyes to find her sister-in-law smiling. ''I may call you Ari, may I not? Since it seems you will be living with us permanently. And not just to please Robert. Perhaps 'tis foolish for me to welcome into my home a lady so highly esteemed by my husband—and so beautiful into the bargain. But he is right. You are family, you and your son, and with us you must stay.'' Natalie held out a hand.

Smiling back tremulously, Emily took it. "Thank you. I hope we will be friends as well. But 'tis enough for you both to acknowledge me quietly. This plan of Rob's to introduce me—'tis madness! You must help me talk him out of it. You've been in society. You know my gaining acceptance would be nowhere as easy as Rob envisions."

Natalie sighed. "No, not easy. Robert told me your parents are dead. Have you any other family?"

Emily shook her head. "No one else. Since Mama died a year after my marriage, and Papa never relented, he went to his grave leaving any more distant relations thinking I'd died. 'Twas what he told everyone, apparently, after I ran away with Andrew."

"You have none who could vouch for you, then? Stand with Robert as your sponsor at a presentation?"

"I'm afraid not."

To her surprise, Natalie threw back her head and laughed. "Oh, dear—'twill be a truly desperate undertaking! A single-handed frontal attack on the ton to shatter opinions, gather support here and reinforcement there—almost like a campaign in the army he so loves."

Emily nodded. "Exactly what I fear. Except 'tis likely to be your status and reputation under the gun as well as mine. I couldn't permit you to suffer on my account. No, we must convince him to drop this."

"Perhaps…" Natalie rested her chin on her hand and looked at Emily, her eyes narrowing. "But I'm not really the pudding-heart I might first have appeared. If you are the lady you both claim you are, 'tis only right you regain your place.

"Besides…" Natalie quirked one eyebrow and grinned, dimples flashing in a mischievous look that gave Emily a glimpse of the charm that had lured her skittish brother-in-law into parson's mousetrap. "I'm not so sure I wish to discourage him. True, gaining society's acceptance may be all but impossible. Launching my dazzling sister-in-law into close proximity with single gentlemen, however, one of whom Robert might eventually deem sufficiently wealthy and distinguished to take over her care, might just be the best solution for us all."

"You think to marry me off?" Emily said with a laugh. "How Machiavellian! But even did I wish to remarry—" she felt a pang and dismissed it "—gentlemen are as concerned about their family's consequence as ladies. I've been a shopkeeper, right there in London! I'm afraid my receiving an honorable proposal is about as likely as my being sent vouchers to Almack's. And the humiliation to us all should a presentation fail! No, I will not even attempt it."

"Perhaps it would fail. But think of the benefits to your son should it succeed."

A protest died on her lips. It was undeniable that a mother returned to the ton, no longer isolated in the shop, would do more to ease her son's path than any other factor save his recognition by the Maxwell family. The risk of personal humiliation was nothing compared to the gain such acceptance would win Drew.

'Twas her most vulnerable point, and Natalie obviously recognized it. In helping with the presentation, Natalie would be a heroine in her husband's eyes, championing his brother's maligned widow and aiding her to make an advantageous second marriage. At worst, she would earn his gratitude by risking personal harm in standing by the outcast. Assuming her husband's love was more important to her than anything else, as Andrew's had been for Emily, either way Natalie would gain.

Machiavellian indeed. Emily's admiration for her sister-in-law's cleverness and courage ratcheted up another notch. Bowing to force majeure, she said, "I suppose I must reconsider, then."

"Splendid! I'm sure you'll not regret it." Natalie linked her arm with Emily's. "However, unless we wish to be dragged along with whatever mad scheme Robert devises, we'd best plan a campaign of our own."

Chapter Fourteen

Wet and weary, in the early evening drizzle a few weeks later Evan finally pulled up his tired mount by London Bridge. He'd left three days ago to ride to the coast and meet Geoffrey Randall, afire with impatience for a first-hand report on all his good friend and assistant had learned in the Peninsula. But Geoffrey never arrived. After waiting a day and interrogating every packet captain who made port, he'd found no trace of the man.

Deeply troubled, he urged his horse onto the bridge. He needed a hot bath, dry clothes and food before he returned to Horse Guards and tried to untangle the puzzle. Had Geoffrey not received his missive? Stumbled on new information too important to leave without pursuing? Or had something more ominous occurred?

Anxious as he was to pursue the problem, with Randall hundreds of miles away the small delay required to refresh himself would make no difference. But as he turned his horse north toward Mayfair, a submerged but ever-present yearning drew him to Emily's street.

He could ride by—'twas a public road. Filthy and bestubbled as he was, he'd not be tempted to stop in. Not that she'd ever permit that again, anyway.

239

Yet as he slowed his mount to a walk and saw the familiar landscape silhouetted against the dusky sky, a thrill of anticipation licked through his veins.

It faded as he reined in by the front door. To his surprise, the windows were dark. Curious. He was about to ride off when he noticed through the darkening gloom that the knocker was off the door.

For a moment, shock held him motionless. Could the staff have taken it down to polish? He could not conceive that she would have left London. Where would she go? As far as he knew she had no family, no friends beyond the military wife who'd once stumbled into her shop.

A more unsettling reason for her absence occurred, and he drew in his breath in alarm. Had her dreaded father-in-law finally found her? If the man had carried her off, was it to make amends for his previous ill-treatment—or would he wrest away her son and abandon her, alone and destitute in some distant village?

Early in their liaison, curious about the background of the woman who so captivated him, Evan had pressed Mr. Manners to discover more about her. A short time later the man informed him he had found no aristocrats with the family name of ''Spenser'', nor did anyone of prominence in the City recognize the name. He'd offered to dig deeper, but hoping eventually Emily would confide in him, Evan had not pursued the mystery.

Desperate to know she was safe, he wished now he'd persisted. How could he find her?

He might ask Brent her whereabouts—but he'd save that as a last resort. Gossip might help, he concluded. If Emily's father-in-law occupied the high position to which she always alluded, his discovering a long-lost grandson would surely elicit talk. Evan needed dinner, anyway, and would just as soon avoid his family and the inevitable inquiries his return would engender. He'd slip home for a quick wash and change of clothes, then proceed to White's.

Mercifully, none of his close acquaintances were present and Evan was able to dine alone. He could idle about the gaming room for an hour or so, see what he could glean, and then proceed to Horse Guards. Arming himself with a deck of cards, he went in.

Soon after, a group of young dandies entered in a rush of laughter and loud voices. One of the newcomers, a man Evan knew from Oxford, saw him and approached.

"Evening, Cheverley. Haven't seen you in a dog's age!"

Over the obligatory handshake, Evan replied, "Family business, Braxton. Dull stuff, I'm afraid."

"Isn't it always? Now, me and the bucks—" he grinned and indicated the noisy group now settling around several card tables "—always find some amusement. Say now, did I not read in the *Times* that you're getting leg-shackled?"

At Evan's nod, he continued, "Congratulations, then. My sister's being fired off this year—you must bring your betrothed to her ball, right?"

"Your sister's ball ain't going to be the one to catch," one of Braxton's friends remarked as he joined them, bottle in hand. "Everyone's agog to see the Earl of Maxwell's little 'surprise.'"

Braxton held his glass up to be refilled. "Indeed! Now, there's a story! 'Tis his mistress, I'll bet—and so I've wagered. You stood some blunt yet, Cheverley?"

Listening idly, his eyes scanning the room for more interesting company, Evan replied absently, "Wager?"

"Aye. Haven't you heard? Seems the old Earl of Maxwell—now there was a bad bargain of a man—and that nasty pup of his, Alastair, both got carried off by a fever. Title fell to the next younger son—Robert, I think the name is. Went haring off to the army a few years back, displeased the old Tartar and got himself disowned. Anyway, the banished son was riveted to some prunes-and-prisms nobody last Season before Maxwell's honors fell in his lap—"

"But you're leaving out the best part, Brax," his friend interrupted. "Not only is Maxwell claiming he'll sponsor the grandest ball of the season—"

"Stubble it, Wilton, I'm gettin' to it." Braxton put up a hand to forestall his friend. "What tears it is the fellow's also going to present another female, the widow of his younger brother, he claims. And not just any old meek, mild dowd in black. This gel's reported to be beautiful enough to take the dazzle off every Diamond in this year's crop. Most incredible of all, though, until a few weeks ago, she was—you'll never imagine—"

"A shopkeeper!" Wilton inserted triumphantly.

Evan had been half listening, but those words recalled his attention with a start. "What did you say?"

"Unbelievable, ain't it! But all too true," Braxton replied. "Why, my own mama's bought hats at her shop. 'Madame Emilie' she was callin' herself then."

"Did you ever hear the like!" Wilton exclaimed. "M'father says even old Maxwell, unpleasant as he was, didn't have this much brass."

His heart commenced pounding and his head felt so light he wasn't sure he was hearing correctly. "W-who did you say the lady is?"

"A shopkeeper, of all things! Of course Maxwell's saying she's not really a shopkeeper. That she's—hear this, now—the long-lost daughter of a duke! The Duke of Suffolk, he claims."

"Some fairy tale, eh?" Wilton scoffed. "Mama knew the old duke, and she said the daughter died years ago. 'Course, the old duke's dead now, and the new one's a distant cousin who didn't grow up with the family, so can't vouch for the girl. Convenient for her, ain't it?"

"I still place my money on her being his mistress," Braxton stated. "Must be some hot bedmate to have him so swoggled he thinks he can perpetrate this outrageous a hoax. And his poor wife! Humiliating, even for a country nobody."

Evan couldn't speak, couldn't move. Earl of Maxwell. Disowned brother in the army. Widowed shopkeeper. It all fit—fit too perfectly to be coincidence. It must be true.

Then the last bit of information sank in. *Long-lost daughter of the Duke of Suffolk.*

Through his numbed brain he tried to recall every scrap of information Emily had ever divulged about her father. That he was wealthy, powerful. That he opposed her marriage to a younger son. That he commanded her absolute obedience and would not tolerate being crossed.

Evan had always assumed the man was some wealthy captain of industry who wished his daughter wed to either an equally rich bourgeois or a nobleman whose family countenanced the match. Yet everything she had told him of her upbringing fit perfectly the image of a duke's runaway daughter.

That instinctive grace and air of command, too inborn to have been veneered on by some ladies' academy. Her independence, her fierce refusal to submit to anyone. Even her real name—Auriana Emilie. What English bourgeois counted a French aristocrat among her relatives?

It had all been there, all the pieces, and he too blinded by her current position and his own prejudice to see it. He had agonized over her status, dismissed outright the prospect of marriage. With the daughter of a duke, who from birth had outranked him.

Through the roaring in his ears he heard the conversation continue.

"How he thinks to pass off such an adventuress is beyond belief—" Braxton was saying, "—but you can bet everyone who can wrangle an invitation will be there. Can't wait to see Sally Jersey and that dry stick Countess Lieven give the filly the cut direct."

"Aye," Wilton chimed in. "'Twill be the best show since old Earl Simpson tried to bring his opera singer to Lady Wetherby's ball. You're attending of course, aren't you, Cheverley?"

Speech was still beyond him. Evan merely nodded.

"Come on, Brax, there's a table getting up. You, too, if you'd like, Cheverley. No? Well, later perhaps."

Clutching his bottle in one hand and Braxton's elbow in the other, Wilton led his friend away. ''What's wrong with Cheverley?'' Evan heard him say as the two walked off. ''Looks devilish queer, don'tcha think? Not sickening with something, is he?''

He was still staring at his trembling hands when the anger hit.

All those weeks they had shared thoughts, dreams, every physical intimacy. He had agonized over the decision to break with her, a break that might have been unnecessary, had he known who she was. He could have held off proposing, begged his mama's assistance in keeping his vow to Richard by finding some other worthy man to appreciate Andrea's gentle excellence. He would have tried something, everything, before taking the step that now rendered a union with Emily forever out of reach.

Why had she never told him?

It appeared she had been reclaimed by her husband's family, would be presented with their backing and surely, eventually, be accepted. Having been a shopkeeper would hurt, that was true. But only the very highest of sticklers were likely to exclude forever the daughter of a duke.

She would be entering the society he frequented. He might see her at any number of routs or dinners or parties.

And the household of the Earl of Maxwell, with her included, would surely be sent an invitation to his wedding.

A short time later he found himself at his office without remembering a step of the way. With steel discipline he forced his mind to the urgent matter of Geoffrey Randall's disappearance.

Another friend dispatched to the fray of battle while he remained behind. *Dear God, don't let Geoff end up as Richard did.*

His stomach soured at the thought and he focused instead on relentlessly examining every shred of information. Hours later, exhausted and disheartened, he had to admit he'd drawn a blank. No one at Horse Guards, nothing in any recent communication, gave him any clue to his assistant's whereabouts.

Finally he gave up. It had, he concluded with bitter irony, been quite an evening. In honor of all he'd learned, he decided to return to White's, where he immediately ordered a bottle of brandy. And then another and another, until for the first time in the history of his membership, the Earl of Cheverley had to be carried home unconscious.

The morning of Robert's grand ball Emily sat with Brent in the drawing room of the Maxwell family's London town house. She still could not quite believe she now resided within the austere marble-fronted walls she had so often this last year hidden in the shrubbery of the park to scrutinize for signs of occupancy.

"Nervous?" Brent interrupted her thoughts. "You shouldn't be. Rob and his army friends will be there, and me, of course. Not that you'll have need of our influence. Which," he added with a self-deprecating smile, "is fortunate since I wield little of it. But the rich and powerful of London have only to see you to recognize the truth of who you are.''

Rising from her armchair, Emily sighed and walked to the window. 'I wish I might believe it, but I'm afraid I rather think it will be a disaster. Oh, I've tried to talk Rob into letting me out of this! But even after we called on my mama's Aunt Augusta, who made it quite clear that though she admitted us to her drawing room she had no intention yet of acknowledging the connection, he's refused to let me withdraw. Why can he not see Natalie deserves her own presentation, free of the taint of scandal I bring?''

''Perhaps.'' Brent came over to stand beside her. ''But having you reside with them without presenting you would seem an admission the family doesn't really believe you to be Suffolk's daughter. Better to unite and strike boldly.''

''I suppose. Since Rob's invited every person of importance in London, they can watch the bold strike fail together,'' she added with asperity. ''Oh, I care not for myself! Rob's sponsorship alone will be enough to secure Drew's future, and as for me—I'd hardly weep over rejection by a society I've never known or needed. But Natalie…''

Emily swallowed hard. One of the many blessings of being discovered by Rob was getting to know her sister-in-law. The tentative accord they'd reached that first day had grown, once time had proven Emily had no designs upon Rob, into a deep and true friendship Emily had come to cherish.

"Military men! They ever know what is right upon every occasion. I swear, if this presentation turns to disaster and my blameless sister-in-law finds herself ostracized because of me, I shall never forgive Rob!"

"Your blameless sister-in-law would never forgive herself were she not to stand beside you." Natalie's voice came from the doorway. Her blond hair shining, her face serene, she came swiftly to give Emily a hug. "Stop worrying! I predict you'll be *un succès fou,* and your only regret will be the ballroom isn't large enough to contain more of your admirers."

While Emily sniffed in patent disbelief, Brent replied, "I must be happy for the small stature of the room, then. Once she's besieged by men of larger rank and fortune, I fear 'Lady Auriana' will no longer have time for those who knew her as plain 'Emily.'"

The wistful note in his tone brought her up short. Impulsively she put a hand to Brent's cheek. "Not have time for those who befriended me when I was but a shopkeeper, rode with me, dined with me? I will always be Emily to my friends—how could you imagine otherwise?"

Brent covered her hand with his own, pressed it into his cheek. Heat flaming in his eyes, he whispered, "How glad I am to hear it."

Uncomfortable under his ardent gaze, she lowered her own. Behind her, Natalie cleared her throat and the now-familiar mischievous expression sparkled in her eyes. "I'll leave you two. Don't forget you're coming to dine before the ball, Brent. And wait until you see Emily's dress! Her design's exquisite—she looks not like a duchess, but a princess! Well, I've a thousand things yet to do. See you at dinner.'' Blowing them a kiss, Natalie walked away.

''I should help.'' Emily tugged gently at the hand he still held. ''But before I rush off, please let me emphasize again, if I haven't yet made it sufficiently clear, how much your kindness and support have meant. Thank you, Brent. You shall have my friendship always.''

He placed a light kiss on her hand before releasing it. ''I hope for a good bit more, you know. But for now, 'tis enough that you'll promise not to forget me in the flood of suitors who will shortly be vying for your attention.''

Emily smiled wryly. ''Once the gentlemen discover that I not only designed hats and waited upon customers in a shop, but intend in future to continue at least the designing, I doubt there will be a trickle, much less a flood of suitors. Especially once I return to my own house. I've been humoring Rob by remaining here until the presentation, but I've been mistress of my own establishment for too long to live in another household, even with my family. In any event, I've no interest in marrying again.''

Grinning, Brent released her hand. ''We'll see about that. But no more now. How does Rob feel about your maintaining the business?''

''Rob?'' She chuckled at the memory. When she'd warned Rob she would not have her creative efforts relegated to the genteelly acceptable ones of china painting and needlework—perhaps secretly hoping the fact would dissuade him from presenting her—he'd surprised her by agreeing. "He's ever been the rebel, even more so than I. His first response was that Lady Auriana Spenser Waring-Black of Suffolk can do what she damn well pleases. His second was that he hoped I'd earn enough from the enterprise to support expanding his stables."

Brent laughed. "Don't you know? Shabby-genteel Mrs. Emily Spenser could be cut for wearing the wrong style of dress, but Lady Auriana, the Duke's daughter, could dance in her petticoat and be called merely 'eccentric.'"

"We shall see. 'Tis by no means sure the ton will believe me to be Lady Auriana. After all, even Great-aunt Augusta doubts my veracity. But enough hand wringing." She lifted her chin. "I am who I am, and so be it. Whatever happens, I just hope Natalie will not be hurt."

"Until this evening. Promise me at least one waltz."

"If I'm snubbed, I expect you shall have them all."

"I may hold you to that."

She shook her head at him and turned to go. He caught her hand, though, and a little reluctantly she let him kiss it again.

She watched Brent thoughtfully as he strode out. He'd hinted his intentions long before the fickle shift of fate had set her on a path to possibly regain her birthright. She had no doubt his regard and his desire for a closer connection stemmed from sincere affection alone.

If only she could return that affection. He was kind, attractive, witty, devoted. But though she treasured his friendship, her heart was still fixed on another.

Who must be thinking heavens knows what about her. And intelligent as Evan was, he had by now undoubtedly pieced together the stories and determined that the scandalous impostor—or long-lost relative, depending upon which version of the story one favored—was her.

She had almost sent him a note describing the circumstances that had brought her from the design studio above the Bond Street shop to a bedchamber in the Earl of Maxwell's town house on St. James Square. Almost, but after their bitter parting, she couldn't be sure he would be interested enough to read it. Besides, he was soon to be married, and she had no right to intrude upon his life.

But the shivers that set her trembling when she thought of standing in the receiving line tonight came not from worry over possible rejection by the ton, but from wondering whether a certain nobleman would put in an appearance. And what she would do or say to him if he should.

Chapter Fifteen

With each turn of the carriage wheels as they crept along with the crowd approaching the Earl of Maxwell's town house, Evan's spirits sank lower. 'Twas all he could do not to snap at the ladies, who were attempting to enliven the tedium of the slow journey with some conversation.

Had he been able to manufacture an excuse to avoid going this evening, he would have done so. However, with all London clamoring for admittance, to have refused to escort his mother, Clare and Andrea to the ball that, whatever its outcome, was sure to remain the most talked-about event of the Season, would have been thought extremely odd.

Even more so since Lady Cheverley knew he was acquainted with the lady, having collected bonnets from her at the shop on several occasions. To have expressed no interest whatsoever in seeing the former shopkeeper in her vastly changed circumstances would have engendered more speculation than he wished anyone to entertain.

Paradoxically though, much as he dreaded it and as fiercely as his anger at her still burned, he probably would not have been able to stay away. He had not seen her since the morning of their bitter parting. He was willing to suspend all his grievances just for a chance to gaze for a few moments upon her face.

How pathetic, he thought savagely. After all this time, while she went on with her life without even the courtesy of a note of explanation, he still ached for her.

"How well did you know the young lady who claims to be Lady Auriana?" Andrea was asking his mama.

Groaning inwardly at the unwelcome shift in the conversation, Evan turned his face into the corner and tried not to listen.

"Rather well, actually. Strikingly beautiful and a wonderful designer. You've seen me wear several of the bonnets she fashioned—the pale blue velvet and the pheasant-feathered shako?"

"Why, yes. How lovely they are, and so flattering. Do you think she can truly be the Duke of Suffolk's daughter?"

His mama laughed. "I think that more likely than some of the other absurd rumors I've heard—that she is the *chère amie* of Lord Maxwell, or an impostor hired to try to claim some of the late Duke's wealth."

"Did you never suspect she might be—other than she seemed?"

"Not really. Though she did ever possess an air of elegance and the presence of one used to command. I attributed it to her having fended for herself as a soldier's wife and widow. Of course, I knew her as a shopkeeper, and I suppose we all accept what we see."

"Do you really think the Patronesses will cut her? Lady Barbara's daughter told me the reason most of the guests are coming is to see whether Lord Maxwell's consequence is sufficient to win her acceptance, or whether she'll be publicly humiliated."

Humiliated? Would it come to that? Jolted from his resentment, Evan didn't notice the carriage had finally halted until a footman let down the step. Emily's story was so clearly true he had not considered the possibility that she might be rejected. All his protective instincts were roused.

They took their places in the long line winding up the stairs to the ballroom. Here in the brighter light of the candles, Evan tried to keep his face turned away from his mama's sharp eye, and blessed the babble of several hundred voices, which made it easy to avoid conversation.

They were halfway up the stairs now, almost within sight of the figures in the reception line. How would she look? Serene, cool, self-possessed as ever despite the threat of social disaster?

Over the wrench of his heart, he had to smile. The valiant Emily he knew, who'd withstood Josh Harding's bullying and earned her bread in a foreign land, would hardly quail at facing down a passle of idle aristocrats.

He saw the painting before he saw her. Above the landing behind the reception line hung a large oil of two men in uniform. He recognized at once the black-haired, green-eyed man on the left as her late husband. The soldier standing beside him, his hair lighter but his features unmistakably similar, must be the brother, the new Lord

Maxwell. Though a portrait, the painting was most unconventional, for the figures were not posed formally against a heroic backdrop, but lounging against the railing of a verandah, pelisses unfastened, a breeze from a brilliantly blue sky disordering their hair.

The style was unmistakably Emily's—the same vivid pure colors, sharp contrast and casual positioning used in her husband's miniature. And in her landscape of the lavender garden hanging in his town house library.

The guests behind him were murmuring. He realized the line before him had advanced while he stared, transfixed.

As his mama was still.

Lady Cheverley's eyes were riveted on the large oil, a look of incredulous dismay growing on her face. Before he could think to turn away she glanced over at him. ''God forgive me,'' she whispered.

He jerked his head toward the limping Andrea, concentrated on assisting her up several more steps. Until he could no longer avoid looking upward.

At the head of the line stood the brown-haired man from the painting, a lovely blond lady beside him, and in profile beyond them—Emily.

She was aglitter in silver, like a midnight star. His gaze rose from the dazzling dress to her slender neck, her pale cheek—and froze, all other details ignored.

Her throat and ears bare of jewels, the only ornament she wore was a comb supporting a gauzy lace mantilla that whispered over her dark hair. The diamond-studded comb and mantilla he'd given her the first weeks they were together.

He didn't remember ascending the rest of the stairs, nor what reply he mumbled to his host and hostess's welcome. Then he stopped before her.

"Miss Marlowe, Lady Cheverley," she said, extending her hand to his mama. "How good to see you."

"How good to see you so well, my dear. And what a beautiful comb. 'Tis Spanish, is it not? A gift of your late husband?"

"No." For the first time she turned and looked at Evan directly. He felt it as always, that immediate connection, the little thrill darting through every nerve. Her glorious wood-violet eyes scanned his face as she murmured, "'Twas a gift from my dearest friend."

Did her gaze hold the same hungry intensity he knew his must? His heart accelerated, the noise of the party faded to a hum as if only the two of them were standing there, a bare touch apart.

"Lord Cheverley." She said his name in her low-pitched voice. And she smiled. All his anguish, heartache, anger melted away in the brilliance of that smile.

"You'll save me a waltz, Lady Auriana?" he heard himself asking.

She nodded. The press of waiting guests forced him on.

He was halfway across the ballroom before his mind began to function again. Whatever had possessed him to ask her to dance? He'd intended to do his duty by his mama, Andrea and Clare, and after the inevitable greeting, scrupulously avoid Emily. 'Twas idiotic to torture himself by holding her casually in front of a roomful of people.

Nonetheless, as he made himself go through the familiar ritual of escorting the ladies to a chair, arranging refreshments, greeting acquaintances, all he could think was that in a very few moments she would be in his arms.

Every nerve vibrated with awareness. He had come. She hadn't been sure he would, wondered if he would somehow avoid meeting her again.

She had to force her glance from following his slow progress through the crowd as he escorted his party off.

Was he still angry, as he had been the morning she'd sent him away? Hurt that she had kept her past secret?

But she had revealed nearly everything save only her name and birth. He must know that, when the whimsy of fate had taken her life and spun it upside down, she had not dared contact him. And if he hadn't, he should now. She'd worn the comb for him.

When his mama asked about it, had anything like understanding dawned in those stark eyes? She could not tell, but…he'd asked her to dance. A waltz, where under cover of the movement, he could hold her close. Would he take that opportunity to congratulate her good fortune, or chastise her for not confiding in him?

Rob introduced another arriving guest to her, and she dragged her attention back to the receiving line. The ballroom was already crowded, and if the success of an evening were judged by how much of a ''crush'' it became, this ball was certainly successful.

However, the greetings of the assembled guests had been cautious. Though they acknowledged her title as introduced, the speculation in their glances—and the overly familiar gleam in the eyes of some of the supposed gentlemen—made it clear their initial approval was qualified.

Who is she really? Emily could almost hear them thinking. *Shopkeeper or duke's daughter? Lost relation or impostor? Widow or whore?* She clenched her teeth.

An almost palpable atmosphere of anticipation hung in the air, the attendees obviously waiting to see the reactions of those high-born leaders of the ton whose approval was essential to her success. None of whom had yet appeared.

If those doyennes of society stayed away, 'twould not matter how many others attended. Her presentation would fail and the Maxwells' social position suffer accordingly.

The thought made her indignant. She cared naught for herself, but how dare those haughty women slight Natalie?

Nearly an hour later, Rob insisted she leave the receiving line. As he waited for the eager officer he had called over to take her in to dance, he patted her hand reassuringly. ''I'll summon you when the Dragons arrive. Chin up, the evening's just begun.''

She was not so sanguine. But though a part of her mind simmered with outrage and another part made polite conversation with the officer, every nerve hummed with anticipation that soon the hand at her waist, the voice murmuring in her ear, would be Evan's.

The dance ended. Her partner remained to chat as the orchestra struck up the next selection. A waltz.

Out of the throng she spied Evan walking toward her, his face grave, his deep blue eyes mesmerizing hers until at last he reached her side.

A mumble of words, a bow, and he offered his arm. As she laid her hand on his sleeve the spark of contact made her heart skip a beat. A tingle of flame raced from her fingertips up her wrist, her shoulder, her neck.

Neither spoke as he led her out. One hand slid up her arm to clasp her wrist, his other encircled her waist and drew her close as he swept her into the rhythm of the waltz.

Though he seemed rigidly unresponsive, the burn of his hands upon her, the arousing heat of his torso brushing hers, the solid presence and achingly familiar scent of him intoxicated her. Right, wrong, duty, obligation—all fell away as she abandoned herself to the embrace of the dance. With a deep, shuddering sigh, for just an instant she allowed her head to rest against his shoulder.

His hands on her clenched. Then he brushed his lips against her hair and she felt more than heard him whisper, ''Oh, Emily.'' His hand on hers twisted, splayed her fingers apart and intertwined them with his own.

He swung her into ever-faster spirals. The velocity of the turns flung her against him the whole length of her body, from leg to hip to chest. She leaned into him giddily, but 'twas his nearness rather than the circles that made her dizzy.

After the upheavals of the last few weeks, reclaiming a role she'd abandoned so long ago it felt foreign, as if she were a ghost resurrected in the wrong body, this was solid and familiar and *right.* Here, in his arms, moving as one with him, she'd come home. She clung to him and wished the waltz would never end.

But of course it did, although they danced until the very last note, earning a spatter of applause from the laughing couples around them. Once more offering her his arm, he led her off the floor.

But not immediately back to the chairs. Rather, he made a circuit of the room, as if searching for a particular party. She was about to question him when at last he spoke.

"Why, Emily? Why did you never tell me who you were?"

He was still angry, she thought with a pang of sadness. "What difference would it have made?"

"What diff—" He sputtered and halted to look at her. "All the difference in the world, as you must know!"

"How so? Oh, Evan, if Rob had not chanced to return, I'd still be Madame Emilie working in her shop. Even now, 'tis highly doubtful I'll be accepted. I'd not even have attempted it had it not—"

"Evan, well met! I see you've stolen the belle of the evening. You'll hand her over for the next dance?"

A smiling young man with slightly protuberant eyes, his gaze on her offensively familiar, blocked their path. "Not to you," Evan replied baldly. "Sorry, Axelrod, she's promised elsewhere. If you'll excuse us?"

Evan bore her away before the man had a chance to dispute the matter. "We can't talk here. Meet me. Green Park tomorrow morning at seven."

She bit back an immediate acquiescence. "I doubt that's wise. My status may be—altered, but yours is the same. You're still the Earl, still engaged—"

"Emily, please. Don't you think you owe me some explanation? Or did I mean that little to you?"

She looked up at his face—and regretted it. The bewildered hurt she saw there robbed her of a safe, circumspect lie.

"N-no," she replied shakily. "You meant a great deal."

"Meet me then. Just this once. Please, Emily."

'Twas madness to entertain the thought. But the allure of being alone with him, even in the public venue of the park, of being able to fully explain all she had felt essential to keep hidden, was too seductive. With every cautious instinct for self-preservation screaming "no," she murmured, "Yes."

He closed his eyes briefly and exhaled in a rush of breath. "Thank you," he whispered. He opened his lips as if to say more and halted abruptly, his gaze focusing on something behind her. "Lady Auriana," he said, made her a crisp bow and walked off.

She whirled around to see Brent standing rigid, hands clenched into fists, staring with narrowed eyes at Evan's retreating back.

She thought she heard Brent swear softly, but then he smiled down at her and held out his hand. "Rob sent me to fetch you. Guests are arriving he felt you must greet."

"G-guests?" she stuttered.

"Yes." His smile widened to a grin. "Lord and Lady Castlereagh, Princess Esterhazy and Lady Jersey. Come. We mustn't delay your triumph."

Consternation gripped her for a moment. "Or catastrophe," she muttered. But what matter to her whether she be patronized, accepted or shunned? Raising her chin, she took his arm. "Let us not keep the Great Ones waiting."

Natalie cast her a relieved glance as she and Brent approached them. "Ah, here she is! Lady Ingraham, may I present to you my sister-in-law, Lady Auriana Spenser Waring-Black, widow of Maxwell's younger brother, Captain the Honorable Andrew Waring-Black."

Beyond her, Rob was greeting a large party, among whom she recognized Lady Jersey. Emily took a deep breath and inclined her head. "Pleased to meet you, Lady Ingraham."

The stout woman before her subjected Emily to a head-to-toe inspection. Her lip curled, as if she'd seen something unpleasant. "We may have met before," she said in a loud, carrying voice. "I believe 'twas when you waited on me at your shop."

Rob and the other guests froze. In the sudden silence Emily heard Natalie's gasp of distress, and her temper flared. Holding on to it with an effort, she replied evenly, "Perhaps so. I do not recall."

"Making gowns now as well as bonnets, isn't that right? How clever! I expect you stitched up the lovely little silver thing you're wearing all by yourself." She turned to look accusingly at Rob. "*Interesting* company you keep, Maxwell. You might have a care for your consequence.''

The woman took a step, obviously intending to walk past Emily without acknowledging her by title—an unmistakable cut. In midreply, Rob's calm voice faltered.

At the stricken look coming over Natalie's face, Emily forgot the ball, the milling crowd of spectators, the good impression everyone was so eager she make.

You bitch, she thought. *Who do you think you are to try to humiliate my family?*

With one imperious hand she grabbed the matron's sleeve, halting her. ''Robbins.'' She raised her voice to hail the butler who was announcing guests at the door. ''Would you be so good as to have someone fetch Lady Ingraham's cloak. Not having found the company to her liking, she wishes to depart.''

The matron looked from Emily's hand grasping her arm to her face, jaw dropped in shock. Before the woman could speak Emily gave her a none-too-gentle shove. ''Immediately, if you please, Robbins. The only one more gratified by her swift departure than her ladyship will be me.''

The barest hint of a smile flitted across the butler's face before he bowed low. ''At once, Lady Auriana.''

Still furious, Emily turned her glare from Lady Ingraham, whose face was turning an alarming shade of puce, to Lady Jersey and the other notables standing breathless at Rob's elbow. ''Is there anyone else who wishes a cloak brought now? If so, please speak up. I should not wish my servants discommoded a second time.''

For a moment no one said a word. Then a tinkling laugh issued from behind the people crowded about Rob. "Lord and Lady Maxwell, Auriana, forgive me for being late." The group parted like the Red Sea before Moses as, leaning heavily upon her cane, Emily's great-aunt Lady Augusta, Dowager Countess of Doone, moved slowly forward.

To Emily's astonishment, the old woman came over and kissed her on both cheeks. "If she don't sound like her papa to the life! Though I swear, you've a bit to go to be as dismissive as Stephen. Sally—" she turned toward Lady Jersey "—you remember Stephen's glare! My nephew by marriage, the late Duke of Suffolk," she explained to the avidly listening crowd. "Don't this little chit have just the look of him?"

Emily found herself subjected to inspection by a pair of shrewd dark eyes. Evidently she passed, for the woman hailed as "Sally" walked forward to take her hand. "I most certainly do remember," she replied with a shudder. "When I was but a giddy young girl, someone dared me to try to tease him into a dance. The Black Duke turned that glare on me and I declare, I expected to be turned into a pillar of salt upon the spot."

As the bystanders laughed, Lady Jersey took Emily's arm and steered her toward the rest of her group. "Now, you must let me present you to a few friends."

"Mind you bring her by later to chat with this old lady, Sally," her great-aunt admonished. "She's got Stephen's quick wit, too, and as such is likely one of the few people worth talking to at this demned caper-party.

Now, Maxwell, find me a comfortable chair. These old bones don't like standing about in a draft.''

Rob grinned. ''At once, ma'am. Martin, see Lady Augusta to a chair by the refreshment room.''

Impulsively Emily turned back to give the old woman a hug. ''Thank you, Lady Augusta, for coming to my ball.''

''Turn me loose, child, 'fore I break somethin','' the old lady protested. ''And it used to be 'Auntie Augusta' to you, missy.''

The vague outlines of a memory focused. ''No, 'twas 'Auntie August,' was it not? As a child I thought how delightful it was you'd been named for a month.''

The old woman's imposing face softened. ''Aye, I remember, too,'' she said. Then jerked her chin up and tapped her cane on the floor. ''Come along, young man! I'm weary for that chair.''

In the early hours of the morning Emily at last sought her chamber. The ball had succeeded well enough. Her great-aunt's recognition laid to rest most of the speculation about her parentage and relationship to Rob. However, since she'd defiantly replied to Lady Jersey's pointed inquiry that she had and would continued to design gowns and bonnets, the matter of her mercantile connections would still stand between her and full acceptance.

Vouchers to that Valhalla of acceptable breeding, Almack's, would likely never be forthcoming, nor would she be included in invitations sent by the highest sticklers. But as long as Rob and Natalie did not suffer from their connection to her, and her son's future under Rob's sponsorship was secure, she was content.

She fell into bed, exhausted, but sleep eluded her. In a few bare hours it would be dawn. Though prudence, safety and discretion all clamored against it, she intended to keep her pledge. When morning broke, she would ride to the park and meet Evan.

Chapter Sixteen

After dozing fitfully, Emily finally gave up and rose before dawn. She astonished the sleepy groom by appearing at the stables with the sky still black. Even now, pink and coral light painted the eastern sky, and 'twas just bright enough to ride safely.

Edgy and restless, she turned her feisty mount into Green Park and signaled the mare to a trot. 'Twas an hour or more before she could expect Evan. The broad expanse was empty, it being still far too early for the nursemaids with their charges or the cowherds with their flocks to make an appearance. Perhaps, as soon as it was fully light, she could indulge in a nerve-steadying gallop.

But as she turned the first corner, she saw him farther down the carriageway, mounted on his big black. She pulled up sharply, her heartbeat leaping as her horse halted. He kicked his stallion forward.

In the privacy of the deserted park and under cover of semidarkness she let her eyes devour every detail as he approached. The minute movements of his knees and muscled thighs as he guided the horse. His strong hands gripping the reins. The jut of his jaw, the arrogant tilt of chin, and finally the blazing blue of his eyes.

He dismounted and walked toward her, obviously intending to hand her down. She took a shuddering breath.

'Twas idiocy—she should never have come. Never, for though fatigue no doubt contributed to the haze in her brain, she could muster no rational thought. All the tidy reasoning and moral certainties filed away in neat array seemed beyond her power to summon.

She only knew she was aware of him in every sense and nerve. And that all she wanted was for him to take her down into his arms and kiss her.

Neither spoke as he reached to help her dismount. She stifled a gasp when his hands finally touched her, closed her eyes to savor the feel of each separate pad of his fingers gripping her waist.

''You're trembling,'' he said, his voice husky as he set her on her feet.

Lost in watching his lips, she couldn't reply. Syllables swarmed about in her head, a hive of disturbed bees, but she could not capture them, shoo them into words. She could only stand staring mutely at him.

''Sweet Emily.'' A whisper, brushing her ears like silk. He raised his gloved hand to her face, caressed her cheekbone with the chamois of his knuckles. A soft sound escaped her and she leaned into his hand.

He grasped her chin and tilted it up, his eyes searching. Forced to meet that gaze now at close range, she could only hope her own would not betray her longing.

A vain wish. Uttering her name in a cry, he pulled her into an embrace so tight she could not breathe, then eased his grip a fraction to kiss her forehead, her eyes, her cheeks and finally her lips. To her shame, she kissed him back with equal fervor.

Finally, when she was nearly too dizzy to stand, he pushed her a breath away within the circle of his arms.

''Sweetheart,'' he whispered, ''you—''

A sharp whistle and the ''baugh'' of a cow warned of impending arrivals. Reluctantly they stepped apart.

Reason, and with it outrage at her current behavior, slowly resurfaced. Trying to hang on to both, she bent to retrieve the reins of her grazing horse. Evan did likewise, and in unspoken accord they fell in step side by side.

''You have been well?''

''I have Rob and Natalie to help me now. And with my father-in-law dead, I no longer have to hide.''

''I'm glad of it, and delighted you shall be esteemed by society as I always felt you deserved. But Emily, I must know. Taking an assumed name to evade your father-in-law I understand, but why did you never tell me who you are?''

She paused, considering how best to explain an action he clearly found inexplicable. ''First, 'Spenser' is one of my given names, if not a surname. Then there's the simple fact that I've been plain 'Auriana Waring-Black' for so many years I scarce think of myself any longer as 'Lady Auriana.' And there was pride. I endured a surfeit of commiseration about 'how the mighty have fallen' during my army days. Since you'd expressed pity enough at the hardships I faced after Andrew's death, I suppose I could not bear the thought of engendering more. Or chance fueling the outrage you'd previously voiced at the injustice done me. You'd already shown yourself ready to barge off in pursuit of Andrew's father.'' She gave him a wry smile. "So, at the risk of angering you again, I felt the less you knew, the safer Drew and I would be.''

He'd been listening patiently, but at that he exclaimed, "Surely you must see how different things would have been for us, had I only known! Call it hypocritical if you wish, 'tis true enough, but Society allows a duke's daughter far greater latitude than less highly born mortals. As for forcing us to part—''

A sharp pang of disappointment pierced her. Did he truly think her change in *status* would affect her opinion on that? Anger stirred. "Evan, it may make a difference to society, but my own feelings on the subject are unchanged.'' Remembering the unrestrained passion with which she'd just practically begged for his kiss, she colored. "Despite my behavior this morning, you must realize I could no more consider sustaining an adulterous liaison as Lady Auriana than I could as Madame Emilie. Who I was born—''

"Little fool!'' He gave her a shake. "What nonsense are you spouting? I'm saying I love you! Can you really believe, had I known your breeding rendered you even marginally acceptable, I would have asked another woman to be my wife?''

She had opened her lips to argue, but that question shocked her to silence. He had considered making her his bride? She'd known from the beginning he felt a passionate attraction. Sometimes, curled by his side as he slept, she'd dreamed he might express regret that circumstances did not permit turning that attachment into a permanent, legal union. But he had not.

"Never did you say or do anything that led me to think you would consider *marrying* me," she protested.

"How could you have doubted it? Did I not haunt your shop, lavish on you every present I imagined you might accept, even invest in your business so I might share more of your life?"

"Y-yes...yes! But gentlemen often do such things for their paramours while infatuation lasts. You never indicated you would consider me as more than a long-term...friend. Never!"

"Of course I..." His words trailing off, Evan rubbed a hand over his brow. "Perhaps I didn't, not in so many words. But neither did you encourage a declaration of love! On the contrary, the warmest avowal you ever made was to assure me of your 'constant affection.' I hoped you'd come to love me, at least a little, but I never knew for sure. I suppose I didn't wish to look the fool, blurting out love for one who saw me only as a...debt that must be paid."

"Oh, Evan, I—"

"You can't deny 'twas that at first! Had I not wanted you so desperately, I'd have been too insulted to accept. But I did want you." His strident voice gentled. "I never stopped wanting you. And when you insisted we must part—well, you certainly gave a convincing demonstration of a woman ready to move on to a new lover."

"I thought it kinder. For us both. As I could not tolerate being—what I would have become, better to end in a manner that made you angry enough to put me out of mind for good and all.''

He laughed softly. "I concluded as much, once my rage cooled. But I've learned to my misery that nothing will drive you out of my mind for good and all.''

He shook his head, as if bemused. "Had I known your birth outranked my own, I'd never have let you send me away. I would have courted you relentlessly, until you accepted me just to stop the aggravation.''

Despite the rigid hold she maintained over her heart, a rebellion of joy swept through her. He would have wed her? Reason soon damped it down.

"No, my darling Evan, you would not. Duke's daughter or no, I was a portrait painter turned shopkeeper, acknowledged by neither my own family nor my husband's. A man who did not care whether he was received or not might dare marry such a female. An earl who was one of the ton's leaders, who had a sister to present, could not.''

He smiled wryly. "Perhaps. But—to feel such concern for my family's welfare, you must care for me?''

His wistful tone caught at her heart. "Yes. More than I dare admit even now, when it can make no difference.''

"I love you, Emily-Auriana, by whatever name you call yourself. I think I've loved you from that first moment.'' Despite presence of herder and cows, he drew her hand up for a kiss. "If you care a fraction as much for me, it appears we've been working at cross-purposes. However valid our reasons for silence. Now that in Society's eyes you are no longer ineligible to become my wife—'tis too late.''

The bittersweet truth of that struck them both to silence. *No,* Emily told herself fiercely as, horses trailing behind, they continued down the carriageway. *You will not mourn what might have been.*

Finally he halted, stopping her with him. "I've been racking my brain these last few minutes, but I see no way out. I cannot break the engagement—indeed, the wedding date should already have been fixed, had not Andrea gone off in some last-moment dither about the trousseau. She's a dear thing, and her brother was my best friend. I don't think she could survive my jilting her." He took a deep, painful breath. "I can't do it."

"Of course you cannot. No man of honor could." He said nothing she did not already know. Nor did she need to release what had never been hers.

"I should go now." Much as she hated to leave, knowing she dare not risk another meeting, there was nothing to be accomplished by prolonging the sweet torment of being with him. Especially when, herdsman, cows and all, desire still pecked at her will and curled heavy in her belly.

He'd been staring off across the greensward, but then his whole body alerted. He shifted his gaze back to her, his dark blue eyes once more intense. "You do intend to go out in Society?"

"I suppose. I consented to the presentation only because Rob argued that not to do so would seem to confirm the awful rumors about me. And because, as he insisted, Andrew would have wished me to. But..." she paused to flash him a challenging look "...I've every intention of maintaining my business, and you know how unfashionable that will be. Even for a duke's daughter. I daresay I shall not receive all too many invitations.''

"With your talent you should continue. I certainly cannot see you an idle Society matron living on new gowns and gossip. But if you do go out, we are bound to meet.''

She regarded his glowing eyes uneasily. What mischief was he hatching? "I suppose, though, should that occur I think it wiser if we avoid one another.''

"Emily, I can't marry you now. Wishing cannot turn back the clock, but your being accepted in Society does offer us a new possibility. No, hear me out!'' He stopped her automatic protest.

"Just consider this. I admit, before 'twas impossible for us to be seen together without all the world presuming the intimacy of our relationship. But don't you see, we can meet now without arousing comment—we will be meeting in any event. We could arrange a place—out of town if you prefer—where we could be together. Ah, my darling, you must realize when I offered for Andrea I made no promises of love. I pledged friendship and protection only, and she accepted on those terms. There are no vows between us loving you would break. As long as we are discreet, our being together will harm no one. There'll be no rumors, no threats to your son—''

"No honor,'' she interjected. "Evan, you may not have vowed love, but when you marry you must pledge fidelity. Fear of discovery was never the sole reason I sent you away. Our being together would break a holy oath, and that is fact. Neither you nor I can change it just by wishing.''

"I love you, Emily!" he cried, his face once again impassioned. "Can you not compromise your stance even a little? For us and all we can mean to each other? Do you intend to condemn us to no more than chance conversation at some rout or ball or dinner? I shall not be able to live with that, I swear it!"

"I could not live with more."

Evan let out an explosive breath and paced away. After a few moments during which she stood, uncertain whether to ride away or wait, he walked back.

His face was calm and set now. Keeping his eyes averted, he said quietly, "I shall not harangue you further. I cannot see you just socially, Emily—I care too much. 'Twas torture waltzing with you, holding myself to a casual touch when I ached—" His voice broke and he cleared his throat. She felt her own heart turn over.

"Meet me here tomorrow and we will plan a life together that, I swear to you, will hurt no one. If you cannot do that, then tell me goodbye. I must have your love—or see you not at all."

She looked at him, stunned. "That is my choice? A relationship in the shadows, or—nothing?"

"Tomorrow morning, seven of the clock. I pray you will be here. If not—" at last he glanced at her, desperate yearning in his eyes "—then may God keep you safe, my dearest Emily."

Without another word he caught up his reins, threw himself in the saddle and rode off.

For a long while she stood like a statue gazing after him.

*   *   *

At seven the next morning she was still pacing her chamber.

Of course she could not meet him. What would be the point? She'd already refused to continue their relationship on similar terms. The fact that they might be seen in public without everyone immediately assuming her to be his mistress did not alter the essence of argument one whit.

Or did it? She'd ridden for hours in the Park yesterday before coming home, until her heart and mind were exhausted. Despite the foregone conclusion of her refusal, when she tried throughout the day to put aside all thought of his offer, an insidious voice kept whispering at her.

He'd never pledged love to his betrothed. He'd be breaking no vows.

Liaisons based on wealth and family connections were common among men of his rank. Love, if and when one experienced it, was often independent of marriage. As long as obligations were fulfilled, discretion was the only rule.

Was not their love as worthy, as valuable, as his commitment to his friend and family? For though she'd spent months denying it, her ungovernable passion for him in the Park and the staggering difficulty of turning her back on the joy and comfort he offered were finally forcing her to face the truth.

She loved him. Loved him completely, shared with him an immediate, wordless bond that was rare and beautiful. Did not so precious a link deserve to be cherished and preserved as much as a pledge based solely on duty and family obligation?

She'd had one love ripped from her by death. Why should she not now hold fast to the other, if doing so, as he pledged, would hurt no one?

No! She tried to shut out echoes of that seductive rationalization. They would be breaking a vow to God, if not to Andrea. Even though it meant the agony of snuffing out her newborn love, she could not do that.

But as the clock chimed three-quarters past, she went to her wardrobe and threw on her riding habit.

Evan would be gone by the time she reached the park, Emily knew. That was as well; she couldn't bear to meet him. But neither could she envision calmly descending to the breakfast parlor, chatting with Natalie about her work or the visitors her sister-in-law wished her to receive.

Within a few moments she was guiding her mare back through the park entrance. Here, where an hour earlier he had walked and ridden, where the calm air might still hold something of the vital essence of him, she could have the solitude she craved to mourn the love she had only just acknowledged and now must live out her life denying.

If he followed through on his promise, and she had no reason to doubt the sincerity of that vow yesterday, for these few moments in the park she would be closer to him than she was fated to be for the rest of her days.

Tethering her mount to a secluded bench near where they'd walked yesterday, she sat and lifted her face to the pale sunlight. Close her eyes and she could still feel the strength of his hands lifting her from the saddle, taste the touch of him on her tongue.

For how long would the memory be so vivid? Would its inevitable fading bring increase or surcease of pain?

At least to temper the heartache of Andrew's death she could relive their happy days together, fellow adventurers rejoicing in their mutual love. Her time with Evan had always been fettered, her emotions on a checkrein, her head telling her not to acknowledge or trust a joy that must be fleeting. Never had she experienced the delight of watching his eyes brighten as she whispered her love.

Perhaps, given how it must end, that was for the best.

Despite that conclusion, tears welled under her tightly closed eyes and dripped slowly down her cheeks.

A moment later she tensed. Without having to open her eyes, she knew Evan watched her.

Chapter Seventeen

Through a watery haze she looked up to see him standing a few feet away.

Afraid he might misinterpret her presence, she stuttered, "I c-cannot d-do it."

He smiled slightly. "I know, sweeting."

"Then—why are you still here?"

He shrugged. "'Twas the last place we'd been together. I couldn't seem to leave it. Why did you come?"

Her own smile wobbled badly. "'Twas the last place we'd been together."

He sighed. "We are a pair, are we not? I'm glad you're here, if only so I can apologize. Honor could not tolerate a relationship such as that I proposed to you— not even mine. I suspect I only asked because I was so sure you'd refuse. But I should not have, and I'm sorry. You were right."

"Right? About what?"

"Almost everything. That what I wanted has always come too easily. That I arrogantly believed I could arrange people, events, principles to suit my own convenience. Giving up what I want more than life is a sacrifice bitterer than I imagined.'' He laughed shortly. ''You married a hero who answered duty's every call, who didn't quail at any sacrifice, even that of his life. 'Tis small wonder you never really loved me.''

''You're wrong, Evan,'' she said softly. 'Twas little comfort perhaps, but at least she would offer it. ''I did— I do love you.''

He'd been gazing off into the distance, but at that he snapped his head back. ''W-what did you say?''

''You put aside your own desire to honor your commitments and fulfill your duty. Which takes as much courage as facing an enemy's guns. More perhaps, as no one will ever applaud the sacrifice. None but we two will even know of it. So I want to tell you now I don't regret the time we had together—I rejoice in it. I grieve for what cannot be. And I love you.''

He stared at her as if he could not really believe the words. At last he whispered, ''Thank you.''

''I'll not see you after—''

''No. I'll contrive it so we do not encounter one another. But I will carry you forever in my heart.''

Swiftly he untied her horse's reins and held them out. Her eyes blurring once more, she reached for them, and their hands touched. He wrapped his fingers around hers and gripped them hard.

''One more favor before you go,'' he said, his voice uneven.

''W-what?''

''Tell me again you love me. Say the words with my name. I want to store up the sound in my head, be able to listen to it the rest of my days. 'Tis the only thing will keep me sane.''

A hot steel band was tightening around her chest again, cutting into her flesh, constricting her lungs until she could barely draw breath. "I l-love you, Evan.''

He closed his eyes as she spoke, his jaw clenched, his face taut, as if memorizing each syllable. He gave her a short nod.

Then in one swift movement, he pulled her up from the bench and tossed her into the saddle. Face expressionless now, he released the bridle. "Goodbye, my heart.''

Before she could drag a reply from her constricted throat, she felt the slap of his hand on her mare's flank. Felt cold wind on her wet face as the horse set off at a trot. At the turn of the carriageway, when she at last marshaled strength enough to wipe the tears from her eyes and look back, he was gone.

Reaching the wide expanses of Hyde Park, Evan set his stallion to a hard gallop, not slowing until the black's heaving sides and blowing breath signaled the animal was spent.

'Twas not enough, not nearly enough to exhaust his own body or subdue the misery in his heart. Dismounting to walk his winded horse, he thought of what would greet him at home. Clare, Andrea and his mama would be at breakfast, doubtless chattering of wedding details. He owed it to Andrea to enter the discussion with at least some enthusiasm. At this moment he could summon none.

Perhaps he could avoid them and slip into the library. Where the butler would have left a tray of invitations, through which he'd have to thumb, screening out those functions at which Emily was likely to appear. Hardly more appealing a prospect.

By the time his tired horse had rested, he'd decided to go instead to his office. However little he might accomplish there would have to be more satisfying than what awaited him at the town house in Portman Square.

Shortly after his arrival the sleepy orderly surprised him by announcing Lord Blackwell, Chief Officer of the Ministry, into whose august presence Evan was rarely summoned. Never had his superior visited him in his own office.

"Cheverley, good of you to respond quickly. Wasn't sure the messenger would be able to rouse you on such short notice."

Messenger? Instantly he knew it must concern Geoffrey. Skipping an explanation of how he'd happened to arrive so early, he motioned his superior to a chair. "What is it, sir? What have you heard?"

Lord Blackwell, a lean older man with thinning, ash-gray hair, indicated Evan sit as well. "A bad business, I'm afraid. Sorry to bring ill tidings, but Geoffrey Randall was killed over in Spain a day or so ago. We've just gotten the report."

"Killed?" Braced as Evan had been for the worst, hearing it confirmed was still a shock. "How? What happened?"

"We're not completely sure yet. He was found in a back alley in the harbor district, his throat cut."

"Lord in heaven," Evan muttered.

"Indeed. Randall was verifying the discrepancies in supply figures you had both noted for arms and ammunition. He feared someone at the dispersion point was siphoning off arms to sell—did you see his dispatches?"

"Yes. But his instructions were simply to gather information about who had access to or control of disbursements."

"He must have stumbled upon more sensitive information. Information so damning that someone felt it necessary to prevent his ever bringing it home."

First Richard, now Geoff, dutiful meticulous Geoff choking on his own blood in some filthy gutter. Rage at the war and friends it had taken shook Evan.

"Then we must find the bastards who killed him."

"Doing so will likely illumine the supply problem as well," Lord Blackwell agreed. "I wish to move quickly, before the murdering swine figure we've had enough time to determine what to do."

"I've already reviewed all the files—noted quantities requested, who signed for deliveries, who commanded the disbursements. I have a list of names."

"Excellent. We'll turn your information over to our field operatives. Damn, I wish we had someone familiar both with those figures and the supply operation, but I don't." Lord Blackwell sighed. "Of course, 'tis always possible Randall ended up at the wrong place at the wrong time, but my sources say local brigands would have been more likely to have garroted than sliced him, had he stumbled upon a transfer. No, the manner of death suggests the murderer is English, someone who thought

Randall might be able to identify him, someone who knows how slow and bunglingly inept the Army Department can often be. Who trusted any investigation would be so drawn out he'd have his gold and be safely back in England before it got anywhere near him. We shall just have to see that he isn't, eh, Cheverley?''

While his superior detailed headquarters' theory about Randall's murder, Evan swiftly reviewed his list. His list and the plan he'd formulated while waiting to learn Geoffrey's fate, one that would give him a chance to redeem the trust he'd broken by letting Richard go off to the army alone. And as it turned out, by sending Geoff to die.

Lord Blackwell rose, his face grimly determined. ''Again, my regrets about Randall. He was a college mate of yours, was he not?''

''And a friend as well. Another moment, please, my lord.'' Evan halted his superior's departure. ''I already have a plan.''

''Excellent. I'll get it to our field people immediately.''

''That wasn't quite my intention—if you'll allow me?''

''Explain then, if you please.''

''Of the names on that list, the two civilians are acquaintances and the military officer I know slightly. Once your sources check their current financial situations, gaming debts and the like, I propose you let me go there and flush out the traitor.''

''You go? 'Tis unthinkable! You've no more training for this sort of thing than Randall, and I don't need another innocent man's death on my conscience. Absolutely out of the question.''

''Hear me out, sir! If our suppositions are correct, the perpetrator would have even more reason to try to snuff me than he did Geoff. I'm a social equal, so he won't be able to fob me off as he might one of your local operatives. I can claim hospitality, stick to him like a burr on a dog, not just at the depot but for lodging, meals and entertainment. Seeing them off duty, I'll again have a better opportunity than your operatives to observe the activities and spending habits of all the suspects. And we'll let it be known I'm looking into supply irregularities—a few words dropped 'in confidence' at any of the gentlemen's clubs here will quickly make their way abroad. My pushing an investigation much sooner than anticipated and my ability to identify him as readily as Geoff should virtually force the perpetrator to make another move. 'Tis our best hope of a quick resolution.''

Lord Blackwell grunted. ''Perhaps. Also sounds like a prescription for getting your own throat cut before you're much older.''

''Not necessarily. I don't intend to act as more than bait—your experienced field people can bring him in. Have me shadowed constantly. I'm pretty good with my fives in a tight spot, and I'm confident I could hold my own till help arrived if need be.''

''And if he manages to slice you into kidney pie before the professionals can get there?''

''Sir, my friends and college mates with Wellington face danger every day. Someone is selling off the arms they need, either to brigands, or worse yet, to the French.

I may not be able to change the course of battles, but I know I could stop this. How can I stand by and do nothing?''

"Your patriotism is appreciated, Cheverley, but—"

"Please, my lord, just consider. Acquainting a professional with the details will take days at best. And you may not have available someone who can mingle socially with the suspects. My going now gives us the dual advantages of surprise and entrée. If stopping the loss of arms and solving Geoff's murder as quickly as possible are important, isn't that worth my accepting some risk?''

Lord Blackwell regarded him silently for a moment. "You've a glib tongue, I'll give you that much," he said grudgingly. "But you're about to get leg-shackled, aren't you? Cause some speculation, you just up and leaving."

"'Twould add fuel to the plan."

"Perhaps, but don't you think it unfair to expose your intended to the possibility of becoming a widow before she's ever a wife?''

Since, despite his affection for Andrea, he'd found it increasingly difficult to imagine how he was going to go through with this wedding, the idea sounded rather attractive.

"Her brother was one of the friends I mentioned. Died after the battle of Orthes. I think she'd support any action that helped shorten the war that claimed her brother's life." Doubtless a correct assertion.

Again Lord Blackwell considered him in silence. "Perhaps 'tis due to the earliness of the hour that I'd even consider this, but you're correct in assuming at the moment I have no experienced operatives available. Let me think on it and check with some acquaintances more knowledgeable than I about this sort of operation. I'll get back to you.''

''Thank you, my lord.''

''Thank you, Cheverley. Whether the ministry decides to accept your offer or not, I want you to know I feel better about the future of this nation, knowing there are men prepared to risk so much for their country's welfare.''

If he hadn't dreaded what he must face in the safety of London almost as much as what he might risk abroad, he'd feel less guilty about Blackwell's accolade, Evan thought as his superior walked out.

Driven to motion, Emily paced her chamber. She could not remain hiding here, but though she'd changed to a morning gown and brushed out her windblown locks, she could not so easily set to order her disheveled mind.

Natalie would be sorting through the post, cataloging invitations and planning the next sortie in her campaign for Emily's acceptance. As Evan would be sorting through his to make plans to avoid her. 'Twas a blackly amusing parallel, if she'd had the strength for humor.

No, she didn't think she could tolerate sitting through a strategy session just now.

Riding always soothed her—but her stomach clenched at the thought. Two mornings in the Park might just have killed her love of her favorite relaxation for good.

A knock sounded at the door. ''Enter,'' she called, trying to quell her irritation and master a sufficiently calm expression that Natalie wouldn't immediately suspect something was drastically wrong.

'Twas only a footman, and she relaxed a trifle. ''A caller for you, Lady Auriana. A Mr. Blakesly. Said he knew 'twas early, but insisted we ask if you'd receive him.''

When Brent called yesterday with the other post-ball well-wishers she'd been able to avoid speaking privately with him. A respite she'd welcomed, since she was much too agitated to hide her turmoil from his perceptive eyes. For him to be here begging an interview at a time when he knew she'd have no other callers, she must have been less successful at masking that distress than she'd thought.

Being even more distressed this morning, she should probably fob him off. But she didn't think the suffocating ache that inhabited her chest, making it hard to breathe and driving her to restless motion—as if by moving fast enough, long enough she might outdistance the pain— was going to ease anytime soon.

Why should it be worse now? She'd absorbed the blow of losing Evan the first time they'd parted, weathered it hitting harder yet when she'd sent him away after that disastrous midnight visit. She only knew it *was* worse, as if each repeated chorus of his call for her to come back to him strengthened a deeply buried hope that some-how, somewhere she might discover the justification that would allow her to do so.

Or was it because this time she'd been unable to deny she was losing not just a lover, but her love?

She realized the footman was still standing at the doorway awaiting her response.

She was about to deny Brent when a possible solution occurred. Though a drive in any of the parks was anathema, if he'd brought his curricle, perhaps she could ask him to carry her outside the City, to...to Box Hill, perhaps! Yes, the transit there would consume time, provide soothing motion and limit the necessity for conversation.

By the time they reached the site she might have better settled her emotions. She'd seen the look on Brent's face when he'd claimed her after her waltz with Evan, and knew the inevitable inquiries that glare promised. Nor, so faithful a friend had he been, did he deserve for her to avoid him much longer. Better to address the matter honestly, and soon.

After giving herself at least the healing respite of a drive, however.

"Please direct Mr. Blakesly to the small saloon and tell him I'll be down shortly."

When she entered a few minutes later, Brent was standing by the fireplace tapping his riding crop on his boot, his expression troubled.

"Good morning, Brent. You are well, I trust?"

He came to her swiftly and kissed her hands, his eyes inspecting her face. "What is it, Emily?" he demanded, dispensing with a conventional polite reply. "Has Evan—"

"Please, no questions just yet. Did you drive your curricle?"

"My—! Yes, I drove it. Why do you ask?"

"Would you do me a great favor? Would you drive me out to Box Hill?"

"You've a sudden desire to picnic now?"

"Yes. Immediately. I must...get away. I'll answer all your questions when we arrive there, but oh, please, will you take me now?"

"If that is your wish, of course I will."

She sighed with relief. "Thank you. I'll put on a carriage dress and pelisse. 'Twill take but a moment."

He nodded. "While you change, I'll speak with the kitchen and see if they will make up a basket for lunch."

She laughed, the sound a bit hysterical. "Lunch? If you wish—I care not!"

Smiling slightly, he took her chin, rubbed her trembling lip with his thumb. His eyes held a tender sympathy and—something more. "Even in heartbreak, sweet lady, one must eat," he said softly. "But go now. I'll await you here."

Half an hour later, they set out. The day being overcast and the wind chill, they'd likely have the grounds all to themselves.

Once beyond the City's congestion, Brent settled the horses into a steady pace and, evidently ascertaining at a glance she had no desire to converse, kept silent.

As the scenery flashed by, she did find a small measure of calm. The heavy weight at her chest lightened a bit and she could breathe more easily.

And Brent, dear Brent, was all the friend she could wish, handling the horses, handing her down at their destination and then guiding her around puddles and along garden paths that in her abstraction she barely noticed.

He insisted they stop to picnic, and coaxed her to eat a bit of the ham and cheese Cook had prepared, and sip some strong tea.

After, when they both were refreshed, he took her hand and kissed it. "You saw Evan, didn't you? Only that could have upset you so."

She didn't wish to talk of it, but she owed him some explanation. Providing one would likely prove no easier anytime this next decade or so. "Yes."

"Damn him!" he cried, as if unable to help himself. "Did he press you to see him again?"

"No. No, 'twas not that at all."

"Surely he didn't claim he would break with Andrea. He will never do so, I promise you!"

"I know that, nor should he. 'Twas just that I had never confided to him who I am, and he wished to know why. We d-discussed the change in my status that made it possible we might encounter each other at social functions. And agreed 'twas best to avoid meeting if at all possible."

"That at least makes sense. Emily, I hate it that he's come back to torture you yet again."

She essayed a ghost of a smile. "If it's any consolation, I imagine I am torturing him as well."

"Excellent," Brent returned flatly. "He should have broken with you for good after he decided to wed Andrea, having given up then any chance to make you an honorable offer. He's since seduced you into forgetting that on at least one occasion. I fear he may try to do so again."

"He will not."

"I'm not so convinced." He smiled wryly. "This only I will grant him—did I stand in his shoes, I'd find giving you up nearly impossible as well. But I've a simple solution to propose. Marry me, Emily. Marry me now."

Though he'd hinted of his intentions on several occasions, she'd not expected a formal declaration so soon. In her current state she was ill-equipped to deal with it.

"Brent, please—" she murmured.

"Only consider it, Emily. I hadn't meant to push you, but despite your best efforts and Evan's, 'tis likely you will chance to meet. My *wife* he will not dare offer more than the briefest of pleasantries. And should the brilliance of your presence temporarily blind him to that fact, I'll be there to deal with him."

A safe haven beyond temptation's reach. Where the seductive notion of somehow managing to find a way to be with Evan, a hope that even now she still seemed unable to completely kill, would die of slow asphyxiation. Where Brent could protect her from Evan—and herself.

Anger at her selfishness dissipated that chimera.

"Thank you, dearest friend. But if I am to salvage any shred of self-respect, the strength to do what is right must come from me. Besides, you deserve a wife who can match your passion and loyalty with her own. Oh Brent, I don't wish to wound you, but dear as you are to me I cannot promise you that. Nor could I live with myself were I to cheat you of it. In time, you would hate me for it."

"Is it not possible that, in time, you might come to care for me as I do for you?" he countered. "Emily, I know you are distraught now. I don't want you to offer sham vows of love. You did say you care for me, didn't you?''

''Of course, but—''

''Then 'tis enough. I've been delaying going to my farm in Ireland to work this year's crop of yearlings. Marry me now and we can go together, be out of London the whole Season if you wish. By next fall or the following spring, 'twill be easier. You know 'tis so.''

''I suppose, but—''

''And if we're to speak of being selfish...'' He gave her a twisted smile. ''When you were just 'Madame Emilie' of Bond Street I rated my odds of winning your hand pretty high, but Lady Auriana Spenser Waring-Black can look wherever she wishes for a mate. To talk you into marrying me now before you've a chance to entertain the better offers you're bound to attract is, I must admit, the height of selfishness. Given the odds, I'd count it a blessing to settle for affection and the hope of more.''

''And if I never feel more?''

''I expect I love you enough for us both, darling Emily. I could accept that, as long as...'' He hesitated, a slight flush coming to his face. ''That is, you don't find my person—distasteful?''

He looked so like a bashful schoolboy that, despite the discomfort of this whole interview, she felt a flash of humor—and compassion. ''Not at all. I think you quite handsome, actually.''

He grinned. ''That's a blessing. The only inexcusable compromise would be to wed you promising to leave you untouched. I won't pretend I could do that.''

She remembered the touch of his thumb against her lips and similar small gestures. Never blatant enough to make her uneasy, they silently testified to a desire that now seemed more comforting than threatening.

To be starkly honest, she missed the intimacy of the marriage bed. Evan was lost, an inescapable fact. Would not an amicable union with a friend for whom she cared, who cared for her, indeed be a comfort, especially if blessed with the joy of children? Was it not foolish to categorically reject a solution that might, some days or months later when the searing edge of her present pain had dulled, turn out to have been the wisest course?

Offering him friendship, however, was incomparably less than offering love. 'Twould be doing him a grave injustice, despite his brave words now.

Wouldn't it?

Her head was beginning to throb again and her chest tightened.

''Easy, sweeting, you needn't decide now,'' he soothed, sensing her increasing distress. ''The last thing I want is to upset you further. Just promise me, when your mind is easier, you'll consider it. And that if you can't accept me now, you will remember my heart and hand are ever there, yours if you but speak the word.''

With that, tentatively he drew closer. Too drained and confused to resist, she let him embrace her. And in truth, 'twas a great relief to lay her aching head against his shoulder and lean into his steadying arms.

After a few moments he released her. "You will consider it?" he asked softly.

"I'll consider it."

"Good." He smiled and squeezed her hand. She thought he meant to draw her up from the bench, but instead he leaned over and kissed her.

'Twas but a soft, lingering brush of his lips against hers, gentle rather than demanding. And tantalizing enough to leave her more confused than ever.

Chapter Eighteen

He sat in a dark room lit by a single candle, writing notes on a bit of paper he'd taken from its hiding place inside his cuff. ''Portugal heat, dust washed away by fine wine. J: tall, jolly, balding, overhearty laugh—concealing something? R: slim, immaculate, quiet. Competent or devious? Lt: weary, flushed from drink. Am billeted with them now.'' The candle flickered, went out.

Scraps of whispered words in the corridor. Meeting. Midnight. Evan slid noiselessly from his chair, pressed his ear to the rough wooden wall. Muffled footfalls retreating. Ease open the door, peer through shuttered darkness. Was the shadow he saw slim? Portly? Topped with a flash of epaulette? Hands shaking, he slipped the blade into his boot.

Sliver of moon lighting the swirling mist. Footsteps—his own?—echoing on the hard-packed earth of an alleyway. Another set, a ghostly echo following—or lying in wait? A prickling at the back of his neck, every tiny hair a watchman shouting the alarm. Rhythmic pounding—his heart, over the gasp of breath.

Out of the blackness came a point of light, a glitter of pewter that grew longer, leaner, descended in a shining arc like a silver arrow. As it plunged, the light exploded in a hail of red darts that gashed his face, pierced his shoulder, ran down his arm in brilliant crimson rivulets. Then, like the arrow, he was falling, falling through salt-laced air.

He felt the trembling shudder, then the smash of a huge body being struck, heard low groaning. He was in the belly of the beast, on some sort of narrow cot with high sides that kept him from rolling out as the monster writhed from side to side in agony. An agony he shared, erupting in his head and shoulder at every blow dealt the beast, flowing down to the throbbing points of pain that used to be a hand. Until a great heaving higher than all the others slammed him into a wall of oblivion.

He was being lifted out of swirling mist into stark cold light. He fought it, wanting only to fall back into the soothing shroud of gray. Brightness stabbed one eye as he opened it and saw Mama. Her face surprised—no, horrified, crumpling into tears. Andrea behind her, weeping. The engagement, honor—all upheld. Why was she weeping?

But he couldn't think, for the light had awakened the pulsing demon. It stretched, torturing his face into grotesque shapes, and growled, sending pulsating rumbles of torment down his arm into the hand that wasn't a hand. He snarled back, struggled to escape, to break free and recapture ephemeral mist. Caught it.

Ebony blankness swirled, parted to form a lock of dark hair falling over a smooth, sun-browned brow. Bright green eyes mocked him, a thin-lipped mouth twisted in scorn. "Fool," said the red-coated soldier leaning over him, "fool. She's mine, she'll always be mine." Tongues of flame licked from the scarlet coat down to him, singeing his hair, dripping sparks on his face and chest. His body smoldered, ignited, the soldier's derisive laughter a wind whipping the fire to inferno. And then he was burning, burning, his skin crackling with heat, his breath scalding in his lungs.

Emily checked the clock on the mantel once again before pacing to stare out the window. Brent was half an hour late, a most unusual occurrence. The Park would be clogged with vehicles by the time they arrived for the ton's afternoon game of see-and-be-seen.

Which she'd not mind missing, though Brent, with that lazy grin that had charmed her into attending far more social functions than her own inclination would have dictated, would probably insist on their making an appearance. Her "airing" he called the promenade, as if she were linen in need of refreshing.

But with Natalie reinforcing his prodding that she follow up the modest success of her presentation by daily reminding the ton she belonged in their midst, she endured both the Promenade and the fistful of evening invitations to which the more daring or independent host-esses bade her. Though she found the social round even more stultifying than expected, after the risk Nat and Rob had taken to present her she felt she could not refuse what was, after all, the relatively small effort needed to solidify her still-precarious acceptance.

And Natalie did rejoice so in her success. Natalie who, dreamer that she was, still cherished hopes of Almack's, next Season if not this one. Despite Emily's gently worded reminder that her refusal to abandon the unre-deemably vulgar taint of trade would forever damn her as "bad ton" in the minds of the haughtiest in society.

At least, she thought sardonically, the park promenade, either on Brent's arm or seated in his curricle, allowed her to show off her designs, which had resulted in a gratifying rush of additional orders.

Without doubt, her design work and the easy cama-raderie of her outings with Brent were the most pleasant parts of her new life—"pleasant" being the highest su-perlative she could yet manage, with the sting of loss still so sharp in her mind and deep in her bones. Sometimes, making her way through a ball or dinner murmuring the inconsequential chat that passed for social conversation, she felt like a French fashion doll: beautifully gowned in the latest mode, eternally smiling, dead.

Evan had done his work well. In nearly a month she'd not had so much as a glimpse of him. Indeed, so strong was the sense of his absence 'twas almost as if he had vanished from London completely. Though with it now the height of the Season, she knew that to be impossible.

She was nearly tempted to ask Brent if something had happened to him, but Evan was the one subject they both avoided. The only time she'd mentioned him, the name flying from her lips before she could recall it, a hard, shuttered look had replaced the easy friendliness that usually warmed Brent's face, and he'd uttered a terse reply.

On every other subject he was a perceptive and amusing companion. By day he dragged her out of the design office and showed her the London she'd never seen as a girl and that the shopkeeper had had neither time nor money to sample: the equestrian displays at Astley's, the bookshelf-lined pleasures of Hatchard's, the Tower menagerie, ices at Gunter's.

Evening functions he enlivened with outrageous commentary on the life and loves of the attendant personages. If hostesses presented her with dancing partners, he relinquished her with no trace of possessiveness, then watched from the sidelines, seeming as pleased as Natalie at this evidence of her acceptance. Though he often danced himself, sometimes drifted away with friends, Emily could still sense his guarding presence, always close to assist with introductions, to deflect potential snubs or impertinent advances.

And on the evenings he escorted her home, he'd grown bolder. After Natalie and Rob discreetly withdrew, he drew her close, kissing her with barely repressed fire, his clenched fingers on her shoulder a testament to his rigid control. She found his advances—pleasant, their gradually increasing passion drawing from her a spark that might someday be response.

He'd not yet pushed her for an answer to his offer. Reason told her to say no, that to delay was to leave him cruelly suspended in tenuous hope. But the troubled spirit his presence did so much to calm and soothe, the fragile selfish self whose defense against agony was still egg-shell thin, prevented her refusing. Was that not a sign she might someday feel more?

Perhaps, her cynical mind answered. However, was she truly ready to promise her life to a man who made her feel—pleasant?

The clattering rattle of a carriage outside the window recalled her. Brent pulled up his equipage, tossed the reins to a footman and jumped down from his curricle.

His face, when he entered half a minute later, was so grim alarm surged in her breast.

''What is it? What's happened?''

''Nothing...truly serious. Sorry I'm so late. Come, we'll be caught in the crush. I'll tell you as we drive.''

Anxious, she hurried into her pelisse, waited impatiently as he handed her into the curricle. Foreboding curled chill and metallic in her mouth.

The heavy traffic forced her to refrain from demanding an answer as Brent concentrated on the tricky business of keeping two restive, highbred horses moving safely along the crowded streets.

Finally the Park gates beckoned and she could stand it no longer. ''What happened, Brent?''

''You mustn't upset yourself, Emily. Everything will be fine, I'm sure. He's strong and will doubtless recover.''

Fear froze the breath in her chest. 'Twas scarcely necessary, but she gasped out the question anyway. "W-who?"

"Evan. He's been gone over a month on some mission for the ministry. There were rumors circulating White's and Brook's even before he left—something about arms smuggling or embezzlement. He went to check on it. I—I didn't tell you because I feared you'd worry."

That curious, inescapable sense of his absence had been correct, apparently. And she was worried, so worried she pulled at Brent's sleeve, her tone turning sharp. "Recover? From what?"

"Steady now!" He looked up from the reins. "When Lady Cheverley received the news, she sent for me to accompany her to meet him. We've only just made it back to London. Though I expect, as soon as the doctors say he can stand being moved again, we may take him to Highgrove."

"How…how badly injured is he?" Emily managed to ask through trembling lips.

A worried frown deepened the lines at Brent's forehead. Worry, regret—and fear? "I won't dissemble—he looks very ill. Took a knife to the right side of his head and arm. He's…he's not conscious, and the wound's inflamed, I'm afraid. Lady Cheverley's physician is out of town and will not return before morning. For now, he appears to be holding his own, and I'm sure he'll be fine…." His voice trailed off. "But I wish with all my heart," he added so softly she could barely hear, "there were some words I could unsay."

For the rest of the transit in the Park she felt detached from her body, which continued to repose sedately in Brent's curricle, nodding to passing acquaintances or chatting with those who stopped their carriage.

All the while her mind hummed with feverish questions. How severe were his wounds? Were they badly inflamed? What treatment had he been given before or during his transit? If he were "holding his own," why was he unconscious and why did Brent look so worried?

Her mind relived the first harrowing days after Andrew's final injury—the thin trickles of blood that seeped red, turned rust on the bed linens; the ragged gasping breaths. The fever that brightened his sallow cheeks to scarlet as if he'd been riding in the brilliant Peninsular sun. And then the long, slow, agonizing descent into death. Numb terror chased off the dull ache that had inhabited her breast since her break with Evan, and perched there, triumphant.

She scarcely remembered returning home, could not recall what she said to Brent or to Natalie, who awaited them. All she knew was sometime later she was instructing the hackney driver to carry her to Portman Square.

She shouldn't be going. What in heaven was she to say to Lady Cheverley, to his betrothed Miss Marlowe?

Yet she knew no power on earth, not raised eyebrows or shocked faces or the speculation so unprecedented a call would doubtless excite among any who heard of it, could keep her away.

Then she was in the entry addressing the butler, asking for Lady Cheverley. "I imagine she's not receiving, as Mr. Blakesly told me her son has just been brought home wounded. I...I have much experience as a battlefield nurse and wished to offer whatever counsel I might to assist her.''

Would his mama consent to see her? Emily didn't think she could bear it were the lady to refuse. She had to know more of Evan's condition, had to know what had been done and what treatment the physician proposed. Evan would never be hers, would recover to marry another, but recover he must. She could not let him die like Andrew.

To her vast relief, Lady Cheverley, her pale face anxious, her hands clutching a twisted linen handkerchief, joined her soon after.

''Lady Auriana! Billingsly said you—you knew about my son?''

''Yes. I'm sorry to burst in upon you unannounced, but when Mr. Blakesly told me of Lord Cheverley's injuries I knew you must be most distressed. I understand he was brought directly from abroad after his—his injury.''

Lady Cheverley was staring at her, jaw dropped. Emily knew what a looby she must appear, but could not seem to summon any of the usual pleasantries. Instead, she blurted out, ''The care given in the early days is crucial to proper healing. Did a doctor treat him on the packet?''

''I cannot say.'' Recalling her son's injuries apparently wiped out all other thought, for Lady Cheverley replied as if conversing with a caller about the treatment of wounds was a commonplace occurrence. ''He's swathed in dirty linen—I—I wasn't sure whether to have it removed or not, he's th-thrashing about so dreadfully. Of all times, our physician is out of London until morning, and I know no other I really trust. But perhaps I should call someone, anyone…."

A small gasping sob escaped her. "He's so ill, and I don't know what to do! Your message said you had nursing experience. If you have any suggestions, I should be endlessly grateful. He doesn't even…" She pressed her lips together, her voice dying to a whisper. "He doesn't even recognize me."

Feverish. Unconscious. 'Twas torture to be confined to this room when all she wished was to fly to Evan's bedside. Emily forced herself to calm. "Several things you should do at once, beginning with—"

"Visitors?" The angry voice from the entry interrupted her reply. "How dare anyone intrude now? And what possessed you to admit them?"

The words echoed in the marble hallway as Miss Marlowe, her blue eyes flashing fire, limped into the room. "I'm sorry, but I'm afraid you must leave—"

She spied Emily and stopped short. "Lady Auriana?" With an astounded look she turned to Lady Cheverley.

Once more twisting the tortured handkerchief, Lady Cheverley glanced uneasily from Miss Marlowe to Emily and back. "Lady Auriana learned about Evan from Mr. Blakesly, and having nursed her husband through similar injuries, thought to…to offer us the benefit of her experience."

Miss Marlowe's wondering gaze came to settle on Emily. "How…kind of you, Lady Auriana."

"I…I was a frequent visitor to her shop, often in Evan's company, and she knew how…distraught I must be,'' Lady Cheverley continued. ''Was that not so?'' She looked back at Emily, appeal in her eyes.

Miss Marlowe's clear gaze fastened on Emily. What the girl must be thinking, Emily couldn't imagine, but at this moment 'twas unimportant. ''Indeed, ma'am. And you as well, Miss Marlowe. I was about to advise Lady Cheverley on a procedure of treatment that worked well for both my husband and my brother-in-law.''

The blue eyes never flickered. ''Please proceed.''

For the next several moments Emily rattled off recommendations for poultices to draw out fever and recipes for healing infusions and willow-bark tea. Both women listened attentively.

At last she paused for breath. Lady Cheverley came and took her hand. ''Thank you, my dear. I'll jot down the recipes immediately. You'll remind me if I forget anything, won't you, Andrea?''

''Of course. But how rag-mannered we are in our distress. Will you not sit and take some refreshment, Lady Auriana?'' Miss Marlowe asked.

Emily could not help pacing, her hands plucking at her skirts, her eyes continually darting to the door. She could almost crawl out of her skin, so anxious was she to go to him, see for herself the extent of his injuries and begin to administer the medicines that had healed Rob and Andrew and several others.

Not Andrew that last time.

She shut her mind to the thought, trying instead to come up with some acceptable excuse for demanding to be shown to the sickroom of a man to whom she had not a single link of blood or connection that would render such a request reasonable. And dredging up none.

She realized Miss Marlowe still awaited an answer. "Excuse me! No—no, I mustn't stay. You'll be wishing to get back to Ev—Lord Cheverley."

Lady Cheverley smiled wanly. "As soon as I have some willow-bark tea to spoon into him. I shall go to the kitchen straightaway. Thank you again, Lady Auriana. I shall never forget your kindness."

It was a clear dismissal. Emily could manufacture neither a reason to prolong her visit nor a plausible pretext to get near Evan. "You're welcome," she said, tears suddenly threatening. She turned to leave.

His mother followed her out. "Lady Auriana?"

Emily turned to look over her shoulder. "Ma'am?"

In the pallor of her face, fine lines webbed the corners of Lady Cheverley's eyes. For the first time since Emily had known her, Evan's mama looked her age. "I'm sorry," the woman whispered.

If she replied at all she would weep. Emily nodded and walked reluctantly to the entry.

To her surprise, Miss Marlowe ushered her out, apparently intending to walk her to her carriage. She halted upon seeing the empty street.

"Did you not bring a conveyance?"

"No. I took a hackney."

Instead of summoning a footman to find a vehicle, Miss Marlowe turned back to Emily.

"Please, Lady Auriana, I know 'tis most irregular of me to ask, but—would you go to him? Please! I watched

Richard die, and I can't—I don't want—'' Her voice broke.

For an instant Emily wasn't sure she had heard aright. ''I'll come,'' she answered.

Choking back a sob, Miss Marlowe caught her hand and kissed it. ''Thank you. Wait here—I'll return in a moment.''

Her mind fraught with fear, Emily waited with barely suppressed impatience for the girl's return. Later, when she was calmer—when she had tended Evan and assured herself he would recover—she would come up with some explanation to plaster over this naked need to see him. Fortunately, Miss Marlowe seemed too upset herself to notice.

Ten minutes later, finger pressed to her lips to warn Emily to silence, Lord Cheverley's intended guided his former mistress through a maze of service rooms up narrow stairs and into a broad, finely appointed hallway.

The stench of fouled bandages assaulted her before they reached the chamber door. Her face paling, Miss Marlowe put a handkerchief to her nose. Her blue eyes over the linen welled with tears.

''God's blessing upon you if you can help him,'' she whispered as she knocked on the portal.

His valet, Baines, answered. ''You mustn't see him now, miss. He's—he's right feverish.''

''I've brought an experienced battlefield nurse, Baines. You will let her in and follow her directions.''

Emily braced herself for his reaction, prepared to brazen her way through whatever he might reveal. No one and nothing would keep her from Evan now.

Chapter Nineteen

Baines turned toward her and stiffened. Then, before either she or Miss Marlowe could speak, he moved aside.

"Whatever you can do, ma'am, I'd be powerful grateful."

With a nod she swept past him. The sight that greeted her made her want to wail in anguished fury.

Evan lay in his tattered shirt, soiled bandages wound about his right arm and hand, his hair matted with dirt and blood. Even in the dim light she could see the fevered sheen on his face, the dry, parched lips, the twitch as his body fought the contagion raging in it.

"These filthy things must come off—Baines, summon a footman to help you. His head must be bathed, and his arm. Bring me hot water and soap, clean linen for bandages. And send someone to Lord Maxwell for my maid, Francesca. Tell her to bring my medicines. At once!"

A bowl of clear, tepid water stood at the bedside, as if Baines were about to sponge down his master. Emily pulled a chair close, wet a cloth and began gently cleaning blood from the crusted wound over his eye.

She could not tell in the dim light whether the eye was damaged, or just the skin beyond, so swollen and distorted was it. Loosening the matted cloth with water as she worked, she freed the sticky mass of old bandages there and at his puffy, distended arm.

By the time she finished inspecting his wounds and removing all the soiled linen, tears filled her eyes and dripped silently down her cheeks.

Despite the ravages of the knife and lack of care, she was somewhat heartened. His heartbeat was strong, his breathing steady, and her experienced eye said if she could get the wounds cleansed and bring the fever down, his chances for recovery were good.

As she looked up to rinse out the cloth, she saw Miss Marlowe, whose presence she had totally forgotten, still standing by the door, watching.

What her face revealed she could not imagine, being in that moment unable to think of anything beyond the need to reduce his fever.

"A carriage awaits whenever you are ready," Miss Marlowe said softly. "How can I ever thank you?"

Engaged in wringing out the cloth, Emily did not immediately reply. When she glanced up, Miss Marlowe was gone.

Francesca entered soon after with a satchel. "Tea I've brought, and a poultice. Come, he must drink."

Baines helped them raise Evan and dribble liquid into his mouth. Mumbling incoherently, Evan swallowed.

Emily lost track of time as they fell back into a routine they had followed on more than one hellish occasion—Andrew with his side gashed by a saber at Corunna, slashed on the arm by a sword at Talavera; his batman Harrison's leg mangled at Busaco, Rob with his shoulder sliced open almost to the bone after Barrosa.

Soak, wring out, sponge. Put a drawing compress on the puffy hand and arm, a cold one on the injured eye. Soak, wring out, sponge. Lift him to force down more tea or broth. Soak, wring out, sponge. Change the compresses, gently clean out wounds, purify with brandy that, even unconscious, made Evan hiss through his teeth and cry out. Shake in basilicum powder and bandage again. Soak, wring out, sponge.

Once, as she held the cup to his lips, his eyelid flickered open. No spark of recognition dawned in that fever-bright eye, and after a moment he closed it. But when she set down the cup, the fingers of his good hand groped toward hers, seizing them in a surprisingly strong grip. She squeezed back, rubbing his thumb. After a moment, with a little sigh, his hand relaxed and he dozed again.

Finally his skin seemed cooler, his sleep less restless. "You see what to do?" she asked Baines. "Sponge him to bring the fever down and keep offering liquid. When the physician comes, should he call for leeches or gunpowder or such, fetch me at once."

"Yes, ma'am. Thank you, ma'am."

Suddenly bone weary, she turned to Francesca. Without a word the maid helped her up. "God's eye, mistress. He's strong. God's eye is upon him now."

Emily was startled to see pearly pink lighting the eastern sky as a flambeau-carrying footman escorted them to their carriage. Before the footman helped her in, she looked back one last time at the town house.

Whatever speculation her nocturnal visit might arouse, she was fiercely glad she had come. Evan's recovery was by no means assured, but the terrible fear that had haunted her since she learned of his injury had eased. As Francesca said, 'twas in God's hands now. Though, she thought with a gallows grin, when had God ever refused a demand by Evan Mansfield?

Evan opened his unbandaged eye. Thin gray light filtered through the shuttered window and a candle burned low on a table beside the bed.

He was in his chamber in the town house at Portman Square, he realized. He had a hazy idea he'd been here for some time, but most of what had occurred since he left his lodgings to follow the cloak-draped whisperer was an indistinct blur.

Only patches of memory were clear. Watching a knife descend out of the night sky and wondering in that instant if, as his superior had warned, he was about to get his throat cut. A blow to head and shoulder that knocked him to his knees, and then wrestling with the attacker, something warm and sticky blurring his vision and making his hands slick. A grunt when his own blade struck bone. Running feet, numb coldness in his face and shoulder suddenly firing to agony, like a scream in one's ear after silence.

Out of the burning haze of fever, one image hovered: the black-haired, green-eyed soldier of the miniature standing on a sun-splashed balcony beside his brother the Earl, silhouetted against a brilliant peninsular sky, both looking down at him and laughing. *"Fool. You thought to be a hero like me, a man she could love,"* the soldier mocked. *"Just what did you accomplish?"*

What indeed. Who had attacked him—the man he'd followed? One of their suspects—or someone else entirely? Had Lord Blackwell's operative arrived in time to capture the perpetrators?

Evan had no idea.

The right side of his face burned, his shoulder throbbed at a level just below agony, and he couldn't feel his right hand at all. He tried flexing it.

Pain exploded at his thumb, ricocheted up his bones and reverberated into his skull.

When he reached consciousness again, pale sun shone in the windows. Making note to ignore his bandaged hand, with his good fingers he gingerly surveyed his swaddled side.

His eye—would he be able to see from it? The thought that he might have lost his sight terrified him. Until he thought of Geoff and Richard. Partial blindness would be a light price to pay for a successful mission.

But had it succeeded? All he knew for certain was he'd gained an apparently blind eye, a maimed shoulder and one useless hand, plus a burning fever in and out of which he drifted, suspended between bitter dreams and awakening.

Bitter but for one. Filthy, sweating with fever, he'd opened his eyes to see Emily, coolly beautiful Emily beside him. Her fine soft hands had mopped his brow with cold water, her velvet voice murmuring, "I love you, Evan. I love you." He'd clutched at her fingers, not wanting her to slip away, and she squeezed his hand back.

He smiled now, recalling it. *"I love you, Evan."*

"Fool," the soldier sneered.

Angrily, Evan opened his eye. His head ached abominably and desperate thirst coated his tongue. Reaching for a glass, he knocked it over, his one-eyed aim off, and cursed.

"Let me, my lord." From his blind side Baines's hand appeared, holding out the glass. His head throbbing, Evan gulped down the water.

"There's a gentleman come to check on you—a Lord Blackwell. Should I let him in?"

Blackwell! Perhaps the agents who'd found him had learned something. "Yes! Help me sit, then send him in."

A moment later his superior entered. "Cheverley! No, don't give me your hand. I'm mightily relieved to see you're recovering. I must admit, you gave us a fright."

"Sorry, sir. I hope that's not all I've given you."

Lord Blackwell laughed, a sharp barking sound. "Indeed not, thank God! You accomplished more than you know."

"Considering I saw little and remember less, I sincerely hope so."

"The man who attacked you wasn't one from your list, but an accomplice. After we nabbed him, we eventually traced him back to the ringleader—the 'quiet civilian,' I believe you called him in your notes. We're still rounding up the rest of the ring—I suspect we may never trace them all, though we shall certainly give it a go."

With bitterness Evan recalled the slim, silent man with whom he'd supped, been billeted, played cards.

Remembered Geoffrey choked in his own blood, Richard dying in front of his eyes, his own ruined eye and ominously bandaged hand. But for that man, his friends would be living still. Evan would be whole—and free.

''How could a man turn his back on his country, knowingly cause the death of his own soldiers?''

Lord Blackwell shrugged. ''Debts. Greed. Simple venality. But with your help, we've stopped the drain of ammunition—there's not been a single irregular or lost shipment since the attack. Wellington himself sent a message of thanks. I'll bring it to you later, when you're more recovered. Well, I must not tire you.''

Lord Blackwell rose. ''I'll stop by later to see how you get on. Heal quickly now, eh? We need you back at Horse Guards.''

''I will. Thank you, my lord.''

With a nod Lord Blackwell walked out.

Evan leaned back against the pillows, as drained after carrying on a simple conversation as if he'd gone ten rounds with Jackson. At least he'd accomplished what he'd set out to do. A welcome change from recent events, that.

Sometime later, after he'd dozed and breakfasted and dozed, after his mother had paid him a tearful visit, Andrea a soothing one, and the physician with his instruments of torture—clean bandages, cleansing powders, the lance—had gone, Baines announced another visitor. Brent.

His friend—his former friend?—walked in quietly and took the chair by his bed. For a moment neither spoke.

'''od's blood, Evan, you look like hell.''

He laughed shortly, grimacing at the now-familiar discomfort. "Feel like I lingered in its fires, too."

"The sawbones says you're better. You do look better than when we first brought you. I thought..." Brent's voice wavered "...thought for a while we were going to lose you."

"You weren't so lucky."

Brent grinned. "No. Unfortunately, the physician says you're out of danger now, so I guess we're stuck with you."

Out of danger. Physically, perhaps. But his life was still in as great a shambles as when he'd run off to play hero. "I suppose one must be grateful for that." Recalling the news his mother had relayed, he added, "Speaking of grateful, I must thank you for helping Mama drag my carcass back to London. It can't have been easy for her. And for coming so faithfully to check on me. Andrea says you've been by once or twice every day since I arrived."

Brent shrugged. "'Twas nothing. Evan, I wanted to apologize—"

Evan waved his good hand. "No need for that."

"Even so, I said...I said some unforgivable things, and I'm sorry. I know you would never knowingly hurt Emily. I, more than anyone, understand how irresistible she is."

Odd how, despite the fire of his wounds, the mention of her name still sent a bittersweet ache clear to the bone.

He should leave it at that. But he couldn't help asking, "How is she?"

"Good. Worried about you." Brent smiled again, a bit wryly this time. "I suspect she'd have come here to check on you herself if I hadn't promised her daily reports. But otherwise, she's well. The shop prospers, and despite that, she's becoming more and more accepted. Indeed, I'm afraid she'll soon be up to her pretty earlobes in suitors. I'd better get that ring on her finger quickly."

"Ring?" The word struck Evan like a blow to the chest. "You've proposed and she's accepted?"

"Not...quite. Oh, I've made my intentions clear. She's not given me a definite answer—yet. You know, if it were possible for the two of you—"

"It's not." Sorrowful finality colored his words. He'd canceled part of his debt to Richard, but the other was still to be paid.

Brent smiled faintly. "I think I fell in love with her that day in her shop. Though I want her to taste the pleasures of being a beautiful woman in her first Season, I must admit I'm selfish enough to claim her as soon as she'll let me." His gaze left Evan's face and wandered away. "I couldn't bear to lose her now."

A sentiment Evan could well appreciate. Although it caused a physical ache almost as painful as his wounds to think of her wed to another, she deserved a good man like Brent to love and protect her. "I wish you happy, then." He drew in a slow breath. "Take care of her."

Brent studied his face in silence. Finally he gave Evan a brief nod. "I will. Thank you."

All the same, he didn't think he'd be able to bear witnessing the happy courtship. "When do you expect...?"

"I'm not sure. I hope to be able to make the announcement shortly, with the ceremony toward the end
of the Season. I suppose I can wait that long." Brent
laughed, the sound joyous. "How about a double wedding?"

God forbid. Evan shook his head violently and regretted it, the motion seeming to set large rocks crashing
about inside his skull with a force that reverberated to
his toes.

While he was engaged in halting them, Brent rose.
"I'll leave you to rest. Glad to see you so much im-
proved. And thank you. Your...your friendship means a
lot," he finished gruffly.

Still holding his aching head, Evan managed a brief
smile. "You shall ever have it."

Brent patted him on the shoulder and walked out.

Friends, Evan mused as he sank back on his pillows,
once more exhausted, so long as he never had to watch
Brent with Emily. Brent's bride-to-be. Evan's beloved.

He took a deep breath and winced as needles danced
from his shoulder down his arm. Though perhaps his
injuries were worth the suffering for the simple fact that
they relieved him of playing the doting fiancé. Even better, his injury would surely delay the date of his own
nuptials. He tried to suppress a guilty relief.

As for Brent's wedding, only one thing was certain.
Whatever excuse he must generate, Evan meant to retreat
to Highgrove and stay there until that event was safely over.

* * *

Ten days later Evan sat propped on a sofa in the library at Highgrove. The jolting torture of the journey from London sent him retreating into the oblivion of laudanum for most of the first two days after his arrival. Today he'd recovered enough to insist on leaving his bed.

He felt better just being up. Here, in this dearly familiar spot, he could peruse his books and estate ledgers, go through the dispatches from London, and in blessed solitude, glance up at Emily's landscape he'd brought with him to hang above the mantel.

In the garden beyond the window, he'd had the gardeners plant lavender. Despite the coldness of the spring, the herbs seemed to be taking hold. By midsummer, the stiff gray-green stalks should put forth their scented wands.

By then, he should have shed his bandages, be walking without a stick, perhaps seeing out of the eye still swollen shut.

By then she would be married.

From a bowl on his desk he lifted a sprig of the lavender he'd had cut, the evergreen leaves being almost as fragrant as the flowers, his gardener promised. Its odor as he rubbed it between his fingers recalled her image vividly: glossy dark locks in tumbled disarray, violet eyes, mouth with its sensuous full lower lip promising the passion he'd found in her arms, her body wrapped in fluttering tourmaline silk and the scent of lavender....

"Evan?"

As he opened his eye, the tall brunette of his imagining was replaced by a slender blonde in a jade-green pelisse.

"Andrea? What are you doing here? I thought I'd convinced you and Mama not to leave London. There's nothing wrong, is there? Mama's not—"

"Everything is fine. Are you?" She walked over, bent to kiss his cheek and let her hand linger there. "The fever is gone—excellent. May I?" She indicated a chair.

"Please, sit. What brings you to me, then?"

She laughed. She'd always had a pleasing laugh, like the gentle gurgle of a brook over smooth stones. He tried to work up more than tepid appreciation and, with another pang of guilt, failed.

"Something quite important for me to dare breaching your citadel," she teased with a gesture that encompassed the room. Her glance rose briefly to the landscape over the mantel, then returned to Evan's face.

"I suppose I should ring for tea and observe the pleasantries, but I'm much too agitated for that. You'll forgive me omitting them, will you not, my friend? Always, for as long as I can remember, best of my friends."

For calm, serene Andrea she seemed unusually perturbed, he thought with a shaft of foreboding. At the same time, a protective affection arose from its slumber.

"Of course, Andy. What is upsetting you?"

"I hope it will not upset you also. At least, not too much. Oh, bother, I should just spit it out." She took a deep breath. "Evan, I wish to end our engagement."

"End?" Of all the things she might have said, that was perhaps most unexpected. "Why, Andrea?"

"The simple truth is I've fallen in love. Oh, 'tis not a brilliant match, but his family is well respected, his fortune acceptable and, quite frankly, even if none of those things were true, I should still wish to marry him. You see, I love him quite ferociously, and the wonder is, he loves me, too.''

She laughed again, a merry trill that was joy set to music. Her blue eyes sparkling, her whole face glowing, her smile brilliant, she looked—exactly like a woman in love.

His vague fear that she might have suspected something and come to bring him to task for it died a peaceful death.

''Tell me about him—this man who's captured your heart.''

''You've met him, Evan—Giles Winstead, Captain Winstead, and he's wonderful! Oh, he was a bit stiff at first, but we had Richard and the army to talk about, and soon…soon we became the best of friends.''

He had to smile. Her words were tumbling over each other so quickly he needed to attend closely to capture them. Never since the accident that lamed her had he seen her so excited—or so lovely.

'''Twas comfortable speaking with him, as if I'd known him all my life, and yet there was something…oh, exciting, almost frightening about it, too. I thought at first 'twas his lack of an arm—but after a while, I hardly noticed that any longer, and the shuddery feeling just grew stronger. Then, when he kissed me—''

''He kissed you?'' Evan interrupted. ''I should hope he intends to marry you.''

''Oh, that was much later.'' Andrea giggled. ''He most definitely will marry me, as soon as he knows for sure our engagement is over. Which I told him it would be.

Though I also warned him I intend to marry him and no other, whether you release me or not. And I will, even if we must...flee the country, or something.''

Her expression growing serious, she took Evan's good hand. ''I didn't think that would be necessary, though. You will release me, will you not, Evan?''

''I will do whatever you wish, Andy. You know I want you happy.''

She bent and kissed his hand. ''Dear Evan! I've used you abominably, I know. If others call me a heartless jilt, 'tis no less than the truth. I knew from the beginning we shared friendship and nothing more, that you offered for me only out of duty. I should never have accepted. 'Tis humiliating to admit it,'' she continued, a faint blush staining her cheeks, ''but I was afraid. Afraid of going into society on my own—poor Andrea, Richard's crippled little sister. Who would wish to marry such a one? Afraid of ending up old and alone. But if I'd not accepted you, if Giles and I had not both been so sure my future was settled, he would never have let himself befriend me, nor I him. I would never have fallen in love with the one man who means the world to me now.''

''Of course I release you, little one. I wish you both every happiness.''

She seized his neck and hugged him fiercely. ''Thank you, my friend. By the way, I've already written the notice officially announcing the break—it wants only your signature. And I must confess I intended to forge that were you not inclined to sign immediately.''

''What a little hellcat love has made you,'' Evan said with a grin. ''As it happens, you'll get to try out your criminal skills. At the moment I can't even feel the fingers of my right hand, much less hold a pen.''

Andrea's bright eyes dimmed. '''Tis no better, then? I'm sorry. Lord Blackwell told us a little of what you did. I'm so proud of you, Evan. You're just as much a hero as Richard.''

"Stuff and nonsense.'' Despite his denial, her praise warmed a bleak spot somewhere in his heart.

"It's settled, then? I shall stay the night only—I want to get this announcement printed before week's end. Not until he reads the break is official will Giles make a move, he vows. Such a principled darling! Oh—will it make you uncomfortable if he comes to ask for my hand? My cousin's a virtual stranger, so with Richard gone I consider you more my guardian than any other.''

"Not a bit. Send him to Highgrove. I shall look forward to furthering my acquaintance with the man who has put such a sparkle in your eye and such joy in your step.''

"Do you know, I hardly notice my limp now, when before to have to cross a floor in front of strangers put me in agonies! I think you and Giles shall get on famously. However—'' she shook a finger at him ''—mind you agree on the settlements straightaway. I want the banns called the Sunday he returns and the wedding as soon as possible.'' She gave Evan a mischievous grin. ''Kissing is so lovely I can't wait to explore what comes after.''

He laughed, the first time he'd felt genuinely amused in so long he didn't even mind his blasted shoulder screaming protests at the movement. ''Minx. I see we'd better get you wed before we have a scandal on our hands.''

''You will come back to London for the wedding, won't you? I couldn't imagine having anyone else stand with me. Please?'' She raised imploring eyes.

London. Emily. Emily and Brent. An ache shuddered through him. But he couldn't deny her this. ''Of course, Andy. You must tell that soldier he'd best treat you as the princess you are, or he'll answer to me!''

As she rose to leave, her glance went again to the painting over the mantel. After staring a moment, she walked to the hall. Hand on the doorknob, she paused.

''I'll see you at tea. And Evan...''

''Yes?''

''Love is so amazing, so truly wonderful a gift. Should you be fortunate enough to find it, my dearest friend...let nothing and no one keep you from it.''

Chapter Twenty

Emily looked down at the note, her name inscribed upon it in wobbly script as if the writer had had great difficulty forming the letters. Though she'd been warned it was coming, still her hands trembled and her heart beat faster as she unfolded the page and began to read:

"My darling daughter, if you see this it will mean I never had the chance to speak these words myself. I haven't much time now, but still I hope that my agents combing Spain and Portugal will find you and bring you home. Please, God, that I might see your face again and meet my grandson before I die.

If that is not to be, let me tell you now what I should have long ago. I was wrong, Auriana. Wrong to give in to my wrath and threaten to banish you for marrying against my wishes. Wrong not to admit the mistake and beg you to come home after you ran away."

The words blurred and she had to wipe her eyes. She could hardly believe Papa, her stern unyielding Papa, was actually apologizing. Deep within the kernel of her decade-old anger, a child's simple unquestioning love stirred. She raised the parchment again.

"Your dear mama, God rest her gentle soul, tried to tell me so, but in my arrogance I would not heed her. I was so sure you would relent, that the hardships you would experience following the drum would kill your joy in that hasty marriage and bring you back to me.

But we are so alike, are we not, my child? I should have known you would hold fast to your husband with the same tenacity that made you jump my stallion when you were barely big enough to throw a leg on him. The courage that, despite the arm you broke when you tumbled off, made you refuse to be carried back and insist on walking in to tell me about it yourself.

I should have known, after forcing your mama to break off communication and refusing your letters, you would believe my anger fierce enough to send you into hiding after your husband's death.

Your absence now is the penance I pay. I can only hope that someday you will return and read this. Then you will know how much I loved and love you, how much I regret the years of privation my anger caused you. The years together of which I robbed us both.

I can make amends now for the first mistake only. And so I have, as you will discover if you but return.

Ah, my darling child…"

The note continued half a page longer, the characters so distorted she could no longer make them into words, then ended without a signature. Her father, she'd learned, had died a few hours after penning the note, nearly a year ago.

'Twas only then the realization struck her. All that time after Andrew's death as she evaded the agents tracking her—'twas not her father-in-law, intent on wresting away her son. No, it had been Papa, desiring reconciliation. Wishing to bring her back home to wealth and comfort, to acknowledge her before the world as his beloved daughter and her Drew as his grandson.

His beloved and extremely wealthy daughter, as it turned out. The lawyers had contacted her last week, advising her they were in the last stages of confirming she was indeed the missing Lady Auriana Emilie Spenser Weston, daughter of the late Duke of Suffolk and widow of Lieutenant Andrew Waring-Black. Once they were sure, they would forward a letter held in trust for her from her father—as well as an extremely generous inheritance that would make her one of the wealthiest women in England.

She had to smile at that. Emily Spenser, who'd reused tea leaves and agonized whether she could afford the price of a theater ticket, was now to have at her unfettered disposal nearly forty thousand pounds a year. In addition, Papa had insisted the bequest be worded so that the sum was hers and hers alone, beyond the touch of any husband. "My daughter is capable of anything," he'd told the lawyer. "She can manage her own wealth."

Even before the letter in her hand arrived, rumors had begun to circulate. The modest trickle of cards inviting her to dinners and soirées had become a flood, hostesses all over London apparently deciding no entertainment was now complete without the presence of the most un-usual—and now wealthiest—widow in London.

Ladies who had formerly avoided her now stood in line to chat her up—and asked baldly about her shop, a topic of conversation they would have considered anath-ema but a week previous. Just yesterday one such so-cially prominent caller had brought a gift that sent Natalie into raptures—vouchers to Almack's.

The Wednesday night assembly wasn't called the Marriage Mart for naught. Emily wondered, a half smile playing about her lips, which Patroness had a friend or relative with a son or brother, blue of blood but empty of purse, who'd clamored for the opportunity to lead Financial Salvation into a waltz.

How amused Papa would have been by it all. A deep sadness welled up at the thought.

'Twas not Papa's fault alone their break had never been bridged. Stubborn herself as he had always been, she'd not been able to bring herself to come home and beg forgiveness.

Tenderly she folded the letter. Drew was too young for it to mean much now, but when he was older, he, too, would be warmed by knowledge of the love of the tyrannical grandfather he'd never met.

Another bittersweet thought occurred. Papa had died only a year ago, just before she'd secretly returned to London. What difference would it have made had he found her before that? If instead of lurking at the fringes of the ton, she had been acknowledged and presented as the Duke's daughter? If she'd met Evan for the first time as his equal, a woman worthy of his hand?

'Twas far too late to waste time on such speculation. Or was it?

Her newfound wealth and acceptance did not confuse her nearly as much as the unexpected visit she'd received yesterday from Miss Andrea Marlowe.

Emily had been at her design office working on sketches when Francesca ran up to announce the caller. Having not seen Evan's betrothed since the night she'd spent at his bedside, she'd forgotten to construct a plausible story to explain her abnormally intense interest in the wounded son of a mere acquaintance.

However, the young lady followed so directly on the maid's heels that Emily, her head full of line, color and fabric, had no time to fabricate one now.

Wondering uneasily what the young lady wished to discuss that would have brought her to so ungenteel a meeting place, Emily politely offered tea.

"'Tis kind of you, but I don't wish to disturb your work. I, for one, think it marvelous that you have a talent and pursue it. Your designs are so original and clever, and Lady Cheverley thinks so highly of you. In fact, if it would not inconvenience you terribly, I should very much like to see your sketches.''

Though surprised, Emily could not help but feel gratified as well. Miss Marlowe's voice rang of sincerity and she seemed genuinely interested in the designs.

"Certainly. I was about to stop for a dish of tea, and would be happy to have you join me."

"In that case, I should be delighted."

After another ten minutes spent inspecting her sketchbooks, Miss Marlowe both exclaiming with enthusiasm and asking quite intelligent questions, Emily's wariness dissipated a bit.

Even had it not, she told herself as she led Miss Marlowe across the hall to the little parlor where Francesca had set out tea, after the service the young lady had done her in alleviating her anxiety about Evan's injuries, she owed her every courtesy.

They were seated over their cups, Miss Marlowe having petitioned Emily's opinion about the colors that might best become her, when the girl asked, "Would you design a gown for my wedding?"

Emily choked on her tea. It had been all too easy, after their interlude as coconspirators and this animated discussion about design, to forget who this girl was.

Get hold, she told herself brusquely. Miss Marlowe would be just another paying customer. Besides, who more than Evan deserved to find on his wedding day a bride gowned as best enhanced her beauty, aglow with love and eagerness?

As Miss Marlowe was certainly glowing at this moment. And why not, with Evan to be her groom?

Emily took another sip and swallowed slowly, allowing herself time to calm. "I should be honored," she heard herself saying.

If she repeated the phrase often enough, by the time the gown was complete she might believe it.

"I must warn you, I shall need the dress almost immediately. I wish to be married the very day after the second reading of the banns."

The news distracted her. Why the sudden haste? Or perhaps she knew why. Perhaps Miss Marlowe had chosen Madame Emilie not so much for her design skills as to emphasize she would soon make permanent a bond that would place Evan forever out of reach, even for angels of mercy.

"He has recovered, then?" Emily asked, voicing the immediate worry that popped into mind.

"Oh, yes. The arm will always pain him, of course, but he's been back to his usual pursuits for some months now. He even rides beautifully."

"Rides?"

"Um. I was thinking of something in blue. He'll wear his uniform, of course, and I shouldn't wish to compete with the red. Did we not agree that cerulean might suit?"

"U-uniform?" Emily stuttered. Had the mission he'd undertaken for the ministry conveyed some military title upon him?

Miss Marlowe grew very still. "Oh, my dear Lady Auriana. Did you not read the announcement in the *Post?*"

"What announcement?"

To her total bewilderment Miss Marlowe sprang up and hugged her fiercely. "I am so sorry! What a wretch you must think me. Let me tell you straightaway that I ended my engagement with Evan a week ago. I've fallen in love with a young soldier, you see, and we will be married just as soon as can be arranged."

Married. But not to Evan. Emily couldn't seem to summon either coherent thought or polite reply.

Miss Marlowe poured her another dish of tea. "I wish I had something stronger to offer, but you should at least take this. Now, let me tell you what happened."

She settled back on the settee with a sigh. "When Evan asked me to marry him, I knew his affections were not engaged. I accepted him because, with Richard gone, I was too cowardly to face life on my own. That was very bad of me, but it had, I think you will agree, a rather wonderful result. Had I not been an engaged lady when I met my Giles, I would not have had the courage to pursue his friendship. Nor would he have let down his guard. As it was, my betrothal offered the safety that allowed us to be ourselves, and to fall in love."

Andrea glanced over. Apparently noting Emily had not yet managed to reconnect mind with speech, she continued, "I also knew, almost immediately upon returning to London, that something was very wrong with Evan. At first I thought it must have to do with his work, or Richard's death—you must know he always blamed himself, as if had they gone into the army together he might have prevented it. But I soon came to realize 'twas not these things that so troubled him—'twas his heart.

"By then I was glad of his preoccupation, for I had come to know Giles. Later, once I realized I'd fallen in love, I was only waiting for the proper moment to break the engagement. But first he left unexpectedly, then he was wounded.

"Not until I saw your face that night you tended him did I suspect you loved him. How I hoped loving you but feeling honor-bound not to break with me was the cause of his unhappiness! Then, after Lady Cheverley told me you'd painted the landscape he takes everywhere with him, I was sure.''

Emily was still having difficulty framing words. ''I h-hardly know what to say.''

''Dear lady, you need tell me nothing! I'm overjoyed that the woman Evan loves so desperately is a beautiful, talented creature worthy of him, one who, now that our silly engagement has been ended, can end his misery as well by pledging him her heart and love. You do love him, do you not?''

''Yes.'' 'Twas a joy to acknowledge it out loud, however bizarre it might be that the first soul to whom she admitted the truth was the one woman she'd vowed must never discover it. ''Yes, I love Evan.''

With a little shriek, Miss Marlowe hugged her again. ''Wonderful! Then we shall both be happy! Lord willing, you'll make Evan as ecstatic as he has been miserable, for I've known him all my life, and never have I seen him as he's been these last few months, shutting himself alone for hours, avoiding all company. Knowing all will be well, I can at last stop feeling guilty about my own happiness.''

She paused a moment, her smile fading. ''But...if you did not know of our broken engagement, he must not have contacted you yet. He's sent no word?''

''None. I've had no correspondence from him since...since we broke off our relationship months ago.''

Andrea frowned. ''Tis odd, that.''

The seesaw movement of her emotions, which in her dealings with Evan had so often rocked her from cautious affection to elation to grief, dipped again. "Perhaps he...no longer holds me in affection."

Andrea made an impatient gesture. "Nonsense. He loves you still, I'm sure of it. Ah...why did I not suspect it from the first?"

She rounded on Emily and seized her hands. "If Evan does not contact you shortly, you must go to him."

Even in midswing of emotion, Emily had to smile at that. "I assure you, if Evan still cares for me, he will seek *me* out."

Andrea looked thoughtful. "Perhaps. But the Evan sitting in a darkened library at Highgrove is not the same man who left England eight weeks ago. He still has no sight in his right eye, his right arm has little movement and his hand may be permanently crippled. Oh, I know all that would make no difference to you, but I assure you from personal experience, it will to him! When someone who has been whole becomes...damaged, it does something to one's sense of self. It must be even worse for a man who feels he should always be the strong, commanding one, caring for those he loves. If he no longer feels himself capable of that, he may very well not seek you out." She paused, as if to let Emily absorb the truth of that.

"I see how that might be so," Emily admitted.

Andrea laughed. "'Tis that, I'm sure. Gentlemen and their silly scruples! Even my Giles, when I told him I intended to end my engagement to Evan, was horrified that I meant to abandon the protection of a husband in possession of all his limbs and entrust myself to one who was, he said, 'lacking.' Of course,'' she added with a devilish twinkle, ''after I finished kissing him he decided my marrying *him* might be better, after all. So you see, if Evan does not come to you, you shall have to go to him.''

Go to Evan unbidden? The notion both excited and appalled her. ''And if he truly no longer wishes me?''

Andrea shrugged. ''A few moments in his company should suffice to establish that. Prepare some excuse to have ready, if you must—you were visiting friends in the neighborhood and stopped by to see how he was getting on, or some such.''

For a moment Emily stared at her, swayed by the intensity of the girl's conviction. Go to Evan unbidden. Could she summon up that much courage?

''He returns to London in a week for my wedding, which—'' Andrea flashed her a smile ''—if you can finish the dress, will take place in a fortnight. If he's not contacted you before then, I think you should go to him.'' As if reading her thoughts, Andrea added softly, ''If you love him, you can do it. If you truly want him, you may have to.''

Miss Marlowe gathered her gloves and reticule. ''Would you do me one more favor? Would you come to the wedding? Had it not been for the love Evan bears you that made him act so strangely, in my anxiety I might have forced us into a hasty marriage we would have regretted the rest of our lives. Instead, I had the time and confidence to find my Giles. For which incredible gift I can never thank you enough.''

Despite the conflicting emotions battering her, Emily had to smile at life's absurdity: the girl she felt she'd badly wronged seemed to view her as a sort of guardian angel. "If you wish it, I should be honored."

"Excellent! Since Evan is like a brother to me, you and I must be sisters. Mayhap he will have an 'interesting announcement' to make at my wedding!"

Grinning at that romantic thought, the young lady took her leave.

Emily smiled too, then. Nearly two weeks later she was no longer smiling. She'd received no letters. For the first few days after she knew he'd arrived back in London, her ear had continually listened for the sound of his footsteps approaching her office, her workroom, her parlor. Footsteps that never came.

Andrea's wedding was but a few days away. Surely, after all that had passed between them, he would not meet her for the first time since the end of his engagement in front of a roomful of strangers. Even if he no longer wanted her for his wife, they might still be friends— mightn't they? Then why, why had he not contacted her?

Sighing, Emily tapped on her sketch pad, not noticing that evening shadowed the room and the noise of the seamstresses had given way to silence, until Francesca came in.

"Why, mistress, sit you here in the darkness, your tea *frio?* Every day this week I find you thus."

"I've been...sketching and lost track of time."

After a skeptical glance at the mostly blank paper in front of her mistress, Francesca came over and peered down at Emily. "What is it, *querida,* that sets your mind fluttering like a wild bird without a nest?"

"Nothing, Francesca. I'm a bit tired, I suppose."

The maid sighed. "Do not worry, *querida.* By the blessed saints, he *will* come for you."

For two weeks she'd fluctuated between euphoria, hope and doubt. Tears threatened as she replied, "It's been a month since his break with Miss Marlowe. How can you be so certain?"

"His eyes, *querida.* When he was wounded and we tended him, they followed you—yes, even the sound of your voice. Your spirit is in him. He must find you again if he is to be whole."

Emily wanted so badly to believe that. Trying for a lighter tone, she replied, "'Eyes', Francesca? He can only see out of one."

The little maid shook her head and gave her a pitying look. "So...literal, you English. But the master—when he was cut down, his power as dust, he knew better. He was seeing with his heart, *querida.* As you could, if you would but listen and do what it demands."

Telling Emily she would summon the carriage, the maid went out.

As they journeyed home, during dinner, as she sat heedless over her book that evening, the maid's words whispered to her: *listen to your heart.*

One action she had been able to take. With Miss Marlowe's story a powerful reminder that 'twas wrong to marry a man for whom one felt only friendship, she'd turned down Brent's offer. He took the refusal with good grace, saying he hoped she'd change her mind—if someone else didn't declare his.

What did that "someone else" intend? How she wished she knew.

She'd attempted to write to Evan, seizing the excuse of offering condolences on the broken engagement. But every note she began, and she began many, ended shredded and tossed in the fireplace.

Should she go to him as her heart urged? She could hardly imagine the commanding, overbearing man she knew not coming to claim a woman he wanted once he was free to do so. The Evan who'd carried her up to her room that night, who'd begged Lady Auriana to meet him at a country inn, would have come straightaway to London, demanded entry if she tried to turn him away, argued with her to accept his proposal.

He'd said when last they met that he'd never harangue her again. But circumstances were different now. Now they could share together the fullness of intimacy blessed by the legitimacy of marriage.

Unless he no longer wished that.

She recalled the handful of noisy children who, with their mothers, had followed the army's baggage trains. One little lad had begged his papa for a tin soldier like those the other boys had. Finally, when they chanced near a city large enough to have such trifles, his father had bought him one.

At first the child was ecstatic, playing with his new toy all the day and forbidding the other lads to touch it. After a few days he played with it less and less. One afternoon she came upon it at the stream near their encampment. When she returned it, he thanked her politely, then handed it to his mama without so much as a glance, having apparently little interest in his prize now that it was available whenever he wished.

Had the intensity of the emotion Evan felt for her been based in part on the impossibility of achieving the union he'd sworn he desired? And now that he might at any time claim the prize, he no longer wanted it?

Or was it as Andrea said: wounded, half-blind, he felt himself unworthy, that in honor he could not ask her to bind herself to a man less than he used to be?

Perhaps being wounded *had* changed him. If she'd heard anything at all from him, even a laconic note saying he'd returned to town and would call when his health permitted, she'd feel more confident going to him.

Go—or stay away? Wait—or try to put him out of mind entirely?

With a groan she paced to her bed. How many nights these last two weeks had she sat sleepless by the window, shunning the society affairs she now found stifling, avoiding Natalie's and Francesca's concerned glances, even her design work losing its power to distract?

She must do something soon or go mad.

Chapter Twenty-One

Evan sat on a bench in his London garden letting the soft sun play on his ravaged face. Such light was beneficial to knitting skin, the doctor said. The bandages were off all but his eye, and the doctor was hopeful, once the scarred skin around it fully healed, the eye might realign and clear enough to restore his sight.

In any event, for the rest of his days he'd carry a scar from cheekbone to brow that gave him the appearance of a West Indies pirate. If only the eye resumed functioning, he'd happily settle for that.

With the fingers of his good arm he laid a letter on the bench beside him, grimacing slightly. Though he was regaining limited use of his weak shoulder, any movement still pained. His right hand was completely useless.

He looked at the letter again and sighed. Ever since the implications of his broken engagement had registered, he'd been battling between action and silence. His first response had been rapture. Emily could now be his with all the solemn legality and permanence she'd always desired. He could make the woman of his dreams his wife in truth.

With his second breath he remembered Brent. *"I couldn't bear to lose her now,"* his friend had said. Having given them his blessing, what kind of selfish cad would press his own claims at the cost of his friend's heartache?

Still, with every breath Evan had to fight the seductive whisper that said go to her he must. He loved her, had loved her first and longest, and she loved him still.

Or did she? Could not even a pure love eventually collapse under the weight of hopelessness? Perhaps, knowing his union with Andrea was but weeks away, hers had. And when her love fell apart, standing by with a strong shoulder and a sympathetic ear had been Brent. Brent, who had always stood her friend, who'd never forced her to yield to his passion or harangued her to act against her conscience.

"I used to be an honest woman," she'd whispered, her cheeks wet with tears of shame that first night. Why would she wish to pledge herself to a man who had caused her such pain and humiliation? How could Evan be presumptuous, arrogant enough to think she might?

Only by speaking with her could he know for sure.

"Let nothing stand in your way," Andrea had said.

Good advice, his heart urged. Or was it?

With a sigh he reread the letter. Mr. Manners disclosed that Emily had been reclaimed by her father's family, declared the Duke's heir and awarded a sizable bequest. She had done him the honor of asking him to manage it for her. As a very rich woman, one of the first steps she desired him to take was to pay off the remaining mortgage on the house Evan had given her. Since she now had available sums greater than Evan's own, he saw no reason, the lawyer wrote with a touch of dry wit, to dissuade her from that course.

At first Evan had laughed at the irony, but his humor had swiftly faded. First he'd discovered she outranked him. It now appeared she would be wealthier as well. Why should she want him, a cripple, when every unattached male of good birth in London would be clamoring for her?

Still, he loved her. Should he not at least affirm that and let Emily make her choice?

But he wanted her so badly, he wasn't sure he could present his case without pressuring her. Besides, he'd looked in a mirror. The last thing he wanted was for her to marry him out of pity.

Perhaps if he were to write her...

With scorn he looked down at his still-useless hand. What effrontery possessed him to think he might try to win her back when he couldn't even pen the note?

He'd combed the papers every day and as yet there'd been no announcement of her engagement. He'd see her at Andrea's wedding. Perhaps he should wait, observe her behavior toward Brent and himself, take that as his guide. Besides, being surrounded by a crowd would prevent his succumbing to the temptation to press his suit. But how could he see her at last after so long and be unable to speak his heart?

Damnation, what a miserable, dithering idiot he'd become, he thought, slapping the letter down in disgust.

*　　*　　*

Emily followed Billingsly down the hallway, her heart thudding against her ribs. All during the ride to Portland Square she'd reminded herself of Miss Marlowe who, once she'd met the man she wanted, had not hesitated to do whatever it took to make him hers.

Yet Emily, who prided herself on her independence, had always waited for the men in her life to act—Andrew to approach her father and his, to bid her flee with him; Evan to dictate the course of their relationship. She'd hidden behind memories of her dead husband to deny her growing love for Evan, let shame over mistakes of the past dissuade her from reaching out to correct the future.

Did she have the courage to boldly admit her love and risk the humiliation of a refusal?

"Listen to your heart," Francesca urged.

Listening had brought her here, still unsure what she would say to him. If he turned her away, she hadn't even devised some polite excuse for her visit that might cover the embarrassment of rejection.

They halted outside the library door. "He's in the garden just outside, Lady Auriana," the butler said. "As you requested, I'll not announce you."

She wiped nervous hands on her skirts. The butler bowed, and she spied the edge of a smile before he walked away. Heavens, did everyone suspect why she was here?

A few steps into the room, she stopped short, attention caught by her landscape hanging over the fireplace. Her anxiety eased a little. Evan must still care something for her to so prominently display the painting in what Billingsly said was his favorite room.

Her pulse accelerated as she spied him. Gathering her courage, she seized the door handles and walked out.

"Put the tea on the bench if you please, Billingsly."

He'd obviously heard footfalls, but as she advanced from his blind side, hadn't seen who approached.

"Hello, Evan," she said softly.

His whole body tensed. "Emily?" he breathed, still staring straight ahead.

"Yes." As she drew closer, her thoughts scattered like leaves in a high wind. She could think of nothing else to say.

Ah, but there was so much to regard. The nasty scar beside his eye, fiery pink but healing. The right shoulder he seemed to keep hunched, his right hand motionless on his lap. His color was good, if pale; his hair luxuriant with the sheen of recovering health and his body as commanding and powerful as she remembered.

The almost overwhelming desire to run to him dissipated a bit as he continued to sit silently, not even glancing at her. She halted uncertainly.

"A-are you well?"

"Yes. Much recovered. Thank you. Please, be seated."

Andrea had warned he might appear distant, but this was beyond anything worse than she'd expected. Not knowing what else to do, she took a chair beside his bench.

"Andrea tells me you designed her wedding gown."

"Yes."

"She's in raptures over it—Mama, too. Something in blue, I believe? A good color for her."

"Yes, cerulean shows her hair and skin to advantage. I'm glad it pleases her."

If they uttered any more polite banalities, she'd scream. Every nerve cringed in embarrassment and she felt ready to bolt.

He seemed totally indifferent. Whatever love he'd once felt had apparently fled as swiftly as the descending blade that slashed his face.

The prize no longer sought, now that it was within grasp.

She should gather the tatters of her dignity and go.

If you truly love him, you will do whatever it takes. Andrea's advice played in her ears.

She'd come this far—she should brazen it out to the end. Baldly tell him why she'd come, be definitively accepted or rejected.

But how to begin? Somehow, after that exchange insipid enough to feature as conversation at morning call, she couldn't just blurt out, "Evan, do you still love me?"

"Did Brent come with you?" Out of the silence, Evan's question startled her.

"N-no. He…he's left London for a time. To tend his horses in Ireland, he said."

"He generally does this time of year. I expect he'll be back soon. He'll not want to be away from you long."

"We…we don't see each other very much now."

He turned slightly toward her. "Don't see—Emily, have you quarreled? I half expected to hear you were engaged."

"Engaged?"

"Yes. Brent gave me to understand he expected you would soon accept his suit."

"Brent told you we were about to become betrothed?"

"He certainly hoped so."

Could that be the reason for this cold, impersonal response? An upsurge of hope coursed through her.

"Evan, I'm not betrothed to Brent. 'Tis true he made me an offer, which to my shame I didn't refuse out of hand."

"Perhaps you should reconsider. He's a fine man and would make a superior husband. I know he loves you deeply."

As a reaction, that was hardly encouraging. "I...I had another fine man in mind."

"I must wish you well, then."

Her strained nerves frayed to breaking. "Damn and blast, Evan, I meant you!"

He seemed almost to...recoil. Was the thought that distasteful to him? Her confidence, never high, wavered further.

"Why would you wish to marry me?" he asked quietly. "You are beautiful, wealthy, and could have your pick of any unmarried gentleman in London. By the way, congratulations on your inheritance. Manners wrote me you'd paid the mortgage on our—your house in full." He lifted his chin and stared once more determinedly away from her. "I expect you didn't want even that link remaining to remind you of a past...you'd rather forget."

"'Tis not that at all! Actually, I had hoped my paying off the debt would at least generate a note from you."

He smiled, more of a grimace. "As you can doubtless see, my writing skills have deteriorated of late. Emily, I know you once held me in...affection, but I'm not the man I once was."

In body...or spirit? She had to know. "In what way?" she whispered.

"I should think that was rather obvious."

"If you are speaking of your scars, those are badges of honor of which any man should be proud. Andrea told me what you've done. You're a hero, Evan."

He made a scornful noise. "Hardly. I had some small part in bringing down a smuggling operation. Not the stuff of which legends are made."

"What, then, is a hero? Do you think soldiers in uniform do more? My husband took part in eight battles, was wounded four times and twice mentioned in the dispatches, but never could he boast a battle won by his efforts. He persevered, fought valiantly and perhaps inspired others to fight better, no more."

"Honoring his commitments and fulfilling his duty," he paraphrased quietly.

"Exactly. When you left England, you did not think of safety or convenience or self, only of doing what must be done, regardless of risk. That's a hero in my eyes. As for your wounds...I much prefer a live hero to a dead one."

His face twisted and he turned his head even further from her. His voice, when he finally spoke, was ragged and so low she could barely hear him. "I don't want your pity."

Pity? Is that what he feared? At last he'd shown some spark of emotion, said something that recalled Andrea's predictions. Emily would soon put that fear to rest.

Assuming she could bring herself to the sticking point before she lost what little nerve she still possessed.

As it had so many months before when she'd steeled herself to invite his illicit offer, her heart started to pound and she felt dizzy.

"Did you not wonder why I'd come to visit? I've something special for you."

"Indeed," he replied, falling back into that cool, maddeningly disinterested voice.

"Do you not wish to see it?" Why was he making this so hard? Exasperation pushing her to greater boldness, she leaned over and held out a paper. With her other hand she seized his injured one. "Here, read this."

For a moment she thought he might use his good hand to snatch the useless one back from her grasp. Instead, slowly, grudgingly, he took the paper, keeping his eyes averted as he flipped it open.

Then he let the paper fall and for the first time looked straight at her, astonishment on his face.

"It...it's a special license. Emily, what in the world..."

"Will you marry me, Evan Mansfield? Be my hero now and forever, for the rest of my days? And I warn you, if you refuse I'm likely to buy the house next door—I'm a wealthy woman now, you know—build a willow cottage by your gate and pine away until you relent."

The barest wisp of a smile touched his lips. "Emily, that's ridiculous."

"No more ridiculous than the two of us loving each other and remaining apart. Oh, Evan, we truly worked at cross-purposes once, both of us keeping silent when we should have spoken out. Let us commit no more sins of omission! I love you and I shall not go away unless you convince me you no longer care at all for me."

"Ah, Emily." Now that he'd turned to her, she could see the yearning in his gaze. For the first time in this interview she felt a renewal of the euphoria that had gripped her when Andrea first conveyed the news of their engagement's end. *No, he was not indifferent.*

"You may think you do the right thing coming here, Emily, and it's so like you—bold, brave and beautiful woman that you are. Which is precisely why you deserve better than a crippled—"

She put a finger to his lips, effectively stopping his sentence.

"Tell me you don't want this," she murmured, finally beginning to enjoy herself. She slid her arms around his neck, brought her face close to his. "Tell me you want me to go away."

He closed his eyes. "I want you to—"

She kissed him. For perhaps half a second he resisted. Then his good arm came up to pull her roughly against him. He kissed her with the desperate intensity of a man finding faith again after believing all hope was lost.

She returned the favor. After some marvelously breathless moments that set her heart pounding and excited promising reactions all over her body, she made herself pull back slightly.

"A gentleman," she whispered, kissing his ear, "would make me—" she kissed his chin "—an honest woman—" she ran her tongue down to the base of his throat "—at long last."

"Are you," he groaned, "trying to seduce me?"

"Am I succeeding?"

"Not until after we see the vicar. That is—" he tipped up her chin, his one-eyed gaze searching hers intently "—if you're sure this is what you really want?"

"Do you love me Evan?"

"I've always loved you."

"Say the words. Say them with my name."

He smiled, a world of tenderness in his gaze. "I love you, Auriana Emilie, my heart, my life."

"Then this is what I really want," she replied, and proceeded to demonstrate that conviction beyond possibility of doubt.

* * * * *

HISTORICAL ROMANCE™

LARGE PRINT

THE DISGRACED MARCHIONESS
Anne O'Brien

Henry Faringdon, Marquis of Burford, returns home to make a shocking discovery – his late brother married Miss Eleanor Stamford, the woman who stole Henry's heart! Eleanor is now in mourning, with a babe in arms, and is as dismayed to see Henry as he is to see her. Soon they are embroiled in a scandal that could lead to Eleanor's disgrace. It is up to the Faringdons to uncover the truth…

HER KNIGHT PROTECTOR
Anne Herries

Alain de Banewulf has triumphed in the Crusades, but he needs to prove his skills as a knight lie beyond the battlefield. His life is set to change when he rescues Katherine of Grunwald from brigands. For Katherine carries a treasure desired by all in Christendom – one that men will kill for – and Alain has sworn to protect her.

LADY LYTE'S LITTLE SECRET
Deborah Hale

Lady Felicity Lyte is in a quandary. How can she tell her lover that she has conceived his child? Even though Hawthorn Greenwood will surely make an honourable offer of marriage, she means to marry for love! Her solution is to end her liaison with Thorn, despite the deep hurt. But has she made a huge error of judgement?

MILLS & BOON®

Live the emotion

HIST1205 LP

HISTORICAL ROMANCE™

LARGE PRINT

BETRAYED AND BETROTHED
Anne Ashley

Poor Miss Abbie Graham had never felt so betrayed!
She had found her betrothed in a compromising position
with another woman! Refusing to marry Mr
Bartholomew Cavanagh has resulted in six years of
family quarrel, and now Abbie's been packed off to Bath.
Can things get any worse? They can, and they do –
when Bart joins their party…

MARRYING MISS HEMINGFORD
Mary Nichols

Miss Anne Hemingford acts upon her grandfather's final
wish that she should go out into Society and make a life
for herself. In Brighton, Anne is frustrated by the lack of
purpose in those around her. The exception is Dr Justin
Tremayne – he is a man she can truly admire. But then
his sister-in-law arrives. There is some mystery
surrounding her – and it intimately involves Justin…

THE ABDUCTED HEIRESS
Claire Thornton

Lady Desire Godwin's gentle existence is shattered when a
handsome brigand crosses the parapet into her rooftop
garden. She watches, dismayed, as the impudent stranger is
carried off to gaol. But as fire rages across London Jakob
Balston uses the confusion to escape. He expects that
Desire will have fled town – only she's still there, alone…

MILLS & BOON®

Live the emotion

HIST0106 LP